The Tenor Wore Tapshoes

a Liturgical Mystery

by Mark Schweizer

Liturgical Mysteries
by Mark Schweizer

Why do people keep dying in the little town of St. Germaine, North Carolina? It's hard to say. Maybe there's something in the water. Whatever the reason, it certainly has *nothing* to do with St. Barnabas Episcopal Church!

Murder in the choirloft. A choir-director detective.
It's not what you expect...it's even funnier!

The Alto Wore Tweed
The Baritone Wore Chiffon
The Tenor Wore Tapshoes
The Soprano Wore Falsettos
The Bass Wore Scales
The Mezzo Wore Mink

ALL SIX now available at
your favorite mystery bookseller or sjmpbooks.com.

"It's like Mitford meets Jurassic Park, only without the wisteria and the dinosaurs..."

Advance Praise for *The Tenor Wore Tapshoes*

"One of those beautiful rare books that churns in a reader's stomach long after you put it down...It should do wonders for our Purple Pill® sales."
David Cavanah, pharmacist

"A beautiful fugue of ideas evoking a real and genuine sense of place...a scrupulous observer and a wonderfully intent writer... oh, who am I trying to kid?"
Kristen Linduff, sister

"Don't ever call here again. And don't call me at the office either."
John Rutter, orthodontist, Great Falls, Montana

"I believe it was Steinbeck who said, 'Writers are a little below clowns and a little above trained seals.' This is high praise for Schweizer."
His Grace, Lord Horatio "Wiggles" Biggerstaff, retired bishop

"Good writing...finely developed plot...wonderful collision of suspense and characters...all words that describe some other book."
Richard Shephard, composer

"How did you find my house? Didn't you see the NO TRESPASSING sign?"
John Rutter, orthodontist, Great Falls, Montana

"It's like Mitford with dyspepsia."
Dr. Karen Dougherty, physician

"From the moment I picked this book up until I put it down, I was breathless with laughter. Some day I intend to read it."
Ron Buck, minister

"You want a quote? I'll give you a quote! Get that *!@*%^$#!* goat off of my lawn!"
John Rutter, orthodontist, Great Falls, Montana

"Can I use this book for my book report? Um, never mind. The covers are too far apart."
Tami, eleventh grade honor student

The Tenor Wore Tapshoes
A Liturgical Mystery

Illustrations by Jim Hunt
www.jimhuntillustration.com

Published by
St. James Music Press
www.sjmp.com
P.O. Box 1009
Hopkinsville, KY 42241-1009

ISBN 0-9721211-4-5

Printed in the United States of America

3rd Printing December, 2007

Acknowledgements

Donis Schweizer
Matthew Schweizer
Rebecca Watts
Sandy Cavanah
Kristen Linduff
Allison Brannon
Richard Shephard

And all the many anonymous writers of bad similes that never failed to inspire and of which I borrowed more than a few.

The Tenor Wore Tapshoes

a Liturgical Mystery

by Mark Schweizer
Illustrations by Jim Hunt

For Chris and Liz

Prelude

"I think you're finally famous."

I looked across the top of my old typewriter and saw Meg coming out of the kitchen, a newspaper held open in both hands and her face buried behind page two.

"Famous, you say?"

"There's an interesting article in the *Charlotte Sun Herald,*" she said, lowering the paper and giving me her hundred-watt smile. "Want to know what it's about?"

"Yes, please," I said, removing my visor and clicking off the green-shaded banker's lamp. The black typewriter, a moment ago bathed in pale yellow light, now vanished into the shadows of the old roll-top I used as my writing desk. "I need to get a beer anyway."

"I'll bring you one. What would you like?"

"I've been waiting to try a Malheur Black Chocolate. I got some yesterday. It's been at the top of the beer charts for a couple of months now. Look in the door of the fridge."

"Top of the beer charts? There are beer charts?"

"Absolutely."

"Any other 'charts' I should know about? For when your birthday comes around?"

"Well," I said, "there's the cigar charts, the wine charts, the stereo equipment charts, classical recording charts, gun charts, new church music charts...that's all I can think of at the moment."

"In other words, every magazine you subscribe to has a chart."

"Yep."

"I'll get your beer."

Meg put down her paper and disappeared into the kitchen, followed closely by Baxter who was obviously hoping for a doggy treat. Baxter, being almost a year old and a Burmese Mountain

Dog, was always on the lookout for a handout.

I clicked the stereo remote and the sounds of Englebert Humperdinck filled the room—the composer, not the lounge singer.

"This looks like champagne," said Meg, returning with a couple of elegant bottles. "Is that *Hansel and Gretel* I hear?

"It is," I replied, taking the Belgian draft from her outstretched hand and settling into my worn leather club chair. "I love this opera. As far as Romantic opera is concerned, it's brilliant."

"I thought it was a Christmas opera. Doesn't the Met always do it on Christmas Eve? It's only October."

"I've never understood that really. Maybe it's the gingerbread house. There's really nothing Christmassy about it unless you count the witch, the attempted homicide and resultant cannibalism and, of course, the hallucinogenic mushrooms."

"Yes, hallucinogenic mushrooms always say 'Merry Christmas' to me. Anyway I recognized the tune," said Meg, sitting on the sofa. "My grandmother used to sing it to me."

"Yep. Humperdinck was one of the first composers to use his tunes in his overtures. Quite an innovation. And did you know that the first example of *sprechstimme* has been traced to one of his early operas? The amazing thing is that..."

"Yes, I know," she said, cutting me off. "I read your thesis. Now stop changing the subject and listen to this." She snapped open a newspaper and started reading:

> AP, Charlotte, North Carolina.
>
> What do Rosemary Brown, J.Z. Knight and Hayden Konig have in common? They are all famous "channelers." But unlike Ms. Knight (one of Shirley MacLaine's favorite channelers and the 20th century vessel for the 35,000-year-old Cro-Magnon warrior called Ramtha) Rosemary Brown and Hayden Konig are channelers for creative personalities and have actually produced new works through their dead benefactors' influence.

Although born to poverty and working part-time at a school cafeteria, Rosemary Brown was a personal friend of Beethoven, Mozart, Stravinsky, Rachmaninoff, Debussy, Bach, Brahms, Liszt, Chopin, Schumann, Handel and a host of others. She took dictation of hundreds of works from a veritable Who's Who of great composers, compositions that were performed and recorded during a brief psychic craze in the early 1970s. Rosemary, whose amazing talent became recognized during a spiritual healing session, was not at all remarkable according to the *Psychic News*. "It is comparable to what hundreds of other mediums have done—the only difference is that you have some famous composers involved."

As her notoriety flourished, Rosemary rose to the task. She would chat cordially with seemingly empty chairs. "Mr. Bruckner is standing next to you now," she'd tell a visitor, or "Oh, I do like his lovely violin concerto," even though the composer had seemingly failed to write one. Her conversations with the dead always took place in English, even with composers who spoke no English during their lifetimes, but who may have since had time for sessions with Mr. Berlitz—also deceased. All, according to Rosemary, are still busy composing—except Debussy, who has switched to painting.

"I don't like where this is going," I muttered.

"Oh, it gets better," said Meg.

Hayden Konig, of St. Germaine, North Carolina, is the proud owner of Raymond Chandler's 1939 Underwood Number 5 typewriter. Raymond Chandler, one of the creators of the "hard-boiled" detective genre of the 30s and 40s died in 1959. Many of his books translated to the silver screen and made Humphrey Bogart and the character of Philip Marlowe a household name.

Now Hayden Konig, a police chief by trade, is fashioning the same imagistic prose and crackling dialogue as Mr. Chandler, albeit, with a twist. Where

> Raymond Chandler's writing is inventive, witty, and carries the crime story to levels of artistry that have rarely been matched, Konig-Chandler's efforts are simply awful. So awful, in fact, as to garner an honorable mention in the Bulwer-Lytton competition, a national literary competition to come up with the worst opening line of a novel since "It was a dark and stormy night."

"Really? I got an honorable mention? That's great!"

"Hush. Let me finish."

> Hayden sits in his cabin in the woods. He places his fingers over the keys of the old typewriter, puts himself into a trance and begins channeling the spirit of the famous author. His eyes glaze over, his mouth drops open, and his fingers fly over the keys. "I can feel his ghost take hold of me," says the mountain detective. "I ain't even myself. It's almost like my own mind just gives over to him." Yet much like Rosemary Brown, the effort is hackneyed, rough and a poor substitute for the real thing.

"I sent in a few entries, but I hadn't heard anything. An honorable mention? Wow."

> If Chief Konig really is channeling for Raymond Chandler, the least he could do is to give us another *Killer in the Rain*. And Rosemary might well oblige us with *Beethoven's 10th*.

"Do you think that there's an awards ceremony or something? I wouldn't mind going. Even just for an honorable mention."

"Hayden, you're not paying attention. This is an Associated Press story. It's just strange enough to get picked up in any number of papers."

"Who wrote it?"

"Some woman named Rachel Coolidge."

"Well, she didn't get the quote from me. I hardly ever say 'ain't.' At least not to a reporter."

"You're not worried?"

"About what?" I asked.

"The fact that most of the people in St. Germaine, as well as in the county, will think that you're a psychic detective who's channeling for a dead author. In other words, a crazy man with a badge and a gun."

"I don't carry a gun."

"Nevertheless," said Megan, putting down the paper, "I think you should sue for slander. At least get a retraction. This story makes you look like a nut case."

"Well, the thing is..." I started.

"What?" asked Meg, suddenly sounding concerned.

"Well," I said, "sometimes late at night, when I'm typing, I sort of feel like there's someone else in the room with me."

"You mean you think you *are* channeling for Raymond Chandler?"

"No, of course not. But it's a bit spooky."

"Maybe it's the ghost of Daniel Boone's granddaughter. She used to live in this cabin, didn't she?"

"Yep," I answered, finishing off my beer and putting the empty bottle on the side table with a dull clink. "But I don't think it's her. If I had to guess, I'd say it was Ray, sure enough."

"You're serious?"

"Not too. But if you hear me talking to someone in here, don't be surprised."

"Has he said anything about your writing style? Has he begged you to stop defiling his typewriter?"

Meg was always criticizing my literary efforts. Granted, they might be less than stellar, but I give it my best shot. And I'd been rewarded with an honorable mention in one of the most famous writing competitions in the country. My Liturgical Detective stories had made the rounds at St. Barnabas Episcopal Church where I am employed as the part-time organist and choir director. They were now finding their way, slowly but surely, through the small mountain town of St. Germaine. Ever since I had bought the famous typewriter at an auction, I'd had an insatiable urge to put my own prose to paper. Computers were fine, as far as they went, but there was something intensely gratifying about clicking on the banker's lamp, putting a fresh piece of bond into the antique contraption and then seeing the words appear slowly behind the clattering hammers.

"You're starting a new story, I suppose," said Meg with resignation.

"I was just warming up when you came in."

"What's this one called?"

"I'm not saying. But I'll let you read it when I have a few chapters finished."

Meg sniffed, picked up my empty bottle and headed back to the kitchen. "Supper will be ready in about an hour, if you can wait that long."

"That'll be just about right," I called after her, as I pulled myself out of my too-comfortable chair and made my way back to my writing desk.

I clicked the light on and sat down at the typewriter. The paper slid easily around the roller. I got the typewriter re-fitted when I purchased it and it worked just like new. Looking at the blank piece of paper, I placed my fingers on the keys and typed

`The Tenor Wore Tapshoes`

I could sense it. Another masterpiece was on the way.

Chapter 1

I walked noiselessly into the dining room and saw her lying motionless, face up, on the table; her hair--white in the moonlight--swirled about her head like a shimmering sea of mashed potatoes highlighted by streams of melted butter; her cranberry lips parted slightly in a perpetual pout; her apple-cheeks still red with the glow of unsullied youth; her eyes--small black currants surrounded by glistening pools of dark-brown gravy, a garland of pearl onions around her swan-like neck--and as I noticed the knife jutting from her chest like one of those plastic pop-up timers in a frozen turkey, I thought to myself, "this bird is done."

"Kit!" I called to my Girl-Friday. "You'd better get in here and get a couple of snaps."

Kit scuttled in like a crab on hind legs. She'd been with me for a while and I could trust her--at least as far as I could trust any dame.

I'm an L.D. That's Liturgy Detective. Duly licensed by the Diocese of North Carolina and accountable only to the Bishop. At least that's what it said on my card. I flipped on the light switch.

"Wow!" said Kit, fumbling with the oversized camera hanging around her neck. "Is she dead?"

"As dead as Fishstick Friday," I said. "And make sure you pick up your flash-bulbs this time. We don't need any extra trouble from the coppers."

The entrée's name was Candy. Candy Blather. I had first met her at a hymnology conference where she was presenting a paper on the Pietic hymns of the late 19th century. I didn't care for the lecture--one verse of "I Come To The Garden Alone" gave me the shaking jakes--but she was a dame with a come-hither Madonna look and gams till Advent, and when she was finished, I made my way to the front of the autograph line, throwing more elbows than a Japanese tour group on Dollar Day at Gatorland.

"How 'bout those Calvinists?" I said, using my tried-and-true conversation starter. "Think they'll win the pennant?"

She smiled demurely and reached for the copy of her latest book that I was pushing across the table.

"Whom should I make it out to?" she asked.

"Make it out to me, Doll-face. Just write 'To my dinner date. I'll see you at seven.'"

"October is a rare month for boys." So began one of my favorite books, and it was as true for me when I first read it at age twelve as it was now, some thirty-five years later. The drive from my house into town took about twenty minutes—thirty if I wanted to stretch it, and in October I usually did.

The Appalachians in western North Carolina are a continuous sunset during October, each day the colors spreading further across the mountain-scape. It's these colors that fueled the economy of St. Germaine. October and November comprised the peak tourist season. We have quite a few summer visitors and a number of seasonal residents, but most of the businesses in town relied heavily on the autumn months for the bulk of their annual income. As a result, on most days the traffic was heavy. On weekends, it was ghastly. The town council had decided that the weekends during these two months required a full staff on duty at the police department. It was my idea, actually, but the council had to come up with the money to pay the overtime.

A "full staff" at the St. Germaine police department consists of myself, Nancy Parsky and Dave Vance. Nancy is an excellent officer and could easily run the department if I ever decide to hang up my spurs. It was Nancy who showed up at my house last Easter just in time to foil what could have been a very nasty murder and save a rich and handsome gentleman, namely me, from an untimely end. To show my gratitude—I am, after all, very rich as well as handsome—Meg suggested I get Nancy a nice present for her birthday. I did. A silver Harley-Davidson Dyna Super Glide. Now she's a motorcycle cop.

Dave works part-time at the station. He answers the phones and generally puts in more hours than show up on his time card. He enjoys the work, and Nancy and I think that he has some sort of trust fund set up. He doesn't ever seem to be hurting for money. Dave has an obvious crush on Nancy, but she ignores his mooning and they get along fine.

I am the Chief of Police. Criminology was the third stop on my collegiate path. A couple of degrees in music followed by an even less practical one. And finally, after all of that education, I ended up inventing a little contraption that the phone company thought was worth a couple of million bucks. So, as it turns out, I don't have to work at all. I do it because I enjoy the job, and that's a nice position to be in.

My part-time position as choir director and organist at the Episcopal church on the square is a reasonable use of my music degrees and, although I rarely find any practical use for my degree in criminology, the fact that I had one landed me nicely in the Police Chief's chair. I was recruited and then hired by the mayor of St. Germaine—coincidentally my old college roommate—Peter Moss, who moved back to his hometown after finishing at UNC-Chapel Hill with a degree in philosophy. Pete put his education to good use by opening a diner.

I pulled onto Main Street and drove my '62 Chevy pick-up past Pete's establishment, the Slab Café. I didn't bother to stop at the Police Station when I saw that, once again, some nitwit had parked in the spot that had a sign clearly stating "NO PARKING—Reserved for the Chief of Police." It was the same thing every day. The traffic was so bad downtown that the out-of-towners decided it was worth the price of a ten-dollar parking ticket to park wherever they could find a spot. It was easy enough to park if you lived here and knew the layout. There were plenty of places for those in the know, my favorite being in the rhododendrons behind the parish hall at St. Barnabas. From the church, it was only a few short blocks back to The Slab Café where, I fervently hoped, Nancy had gotten us a table for our "staff meeting." Tables, this time of year, were as hard to get as parking places.

I was walking up to the front door of the Slab when I heard, rather than saw, Nancy pulling up. The Harley had a very distinctive rumble. Nancy had no problem parking. She just drove right up onto the sidewalk.

"Sorry I'm late, but I called and told Dave to get us a table," she said, taking off her helmet and pulling her hair back into a quick ponytail.

"It's going to get too cold for that bike pretty soon."

"It's pretty cold now. I'll switch back to the Nissan, I guess, but it'll kill me. I love this bike."

I had to laugh out loud. She was still, after five months of riding the big bike, like a little kid at Christmas. I held the door open for her as she wrestled off her leather jacket, walked in and looked around the room for the table we hoped Dave had reserved for us. He was there all right. Table for four, biscuits on hand, the coffee already poured.

"I went ahead and ordered for you," said Dave as we walked up, ignoring the line of twenty or so glaring customers waiting for a table. "It'll be up shortly."

"Excellent police work, Dave," I said.

Nancy draped her jacket over the chair and settled into it, managing to pick up a biscuit in the same move.

"Is Meg joining us?" she asked, pointing to the fourth place setting.

"Nope. She's working this morning. In Boone, I think."

"When are you going to get married, Boss?" Dave asked with a smirk.

"When someone asks me."

"That's a pretty smug answer," said Nancy between bites. "You'd better be careful though. It could happen."

"Hmmm," I said, in what I hoped was a non-committal fashion.

"You've been going with her for what? Four years? Five?" Pete, always an ex-officio member of our staff meetings, at least as long as breakfast was on-the-house, pulled up a chair and jumped into the conversation. "I think you should go ahead and pop the question."

"This advice from a three-time divorcé?"

"I love getting married. What can I say?" Pete waved to his new waitress-in-charge, Noylene Fabergé, who was still buoyant with last week's unexpected promotion. She scurried over with a full coffee pot and began to refill the half empty mugs.

"What do you think, Noylene?" asked Pete.

"'Bout what?" said Noylene, her eyes glued to the task at hand.

"'Bout the Chief here getting married."

"You're getting married?" Noylene looked up suddenly and the stream of coffee, originally intended for Dave's cup, went straight into his lap.

"YOW!" yelled Dave, leaping to his feet. "SON OF A ..." He stopped short and looked around at the startled customers. "Well...son of a gun."

"Nice save, Dave," said Nancy, not even cracking a smile.

"Dadgumit," he muttered, looking down and blotting at the stain on the front of his Dockers with his quickly disintegrating paper napkin. "Dadgumit, dagnabit, and crud! This is my only pair of clean pants." We all pushed our napkins dutifully across the table.

Noylene was around the table before Dave had hit his feet, having put the coffee pot down, readying her cleaning rag for the task at hand. "I'm so sorry," she said to Dave, squatting in front of him. "Here, let me help."

"As much as Dave might enjoy that, Noylene," said Pete, "you'd better let him take care of it himself. People are starting to stare."

Noylene took the hint.

"That's quite a blue streak, Dave," I said, grateful for the interruption that had changed the direction of the conversation. "We don't want to offend any of Pete's customers though. Can you tone it down a little?"

Dave looked sheepish and continued blotting.

"Let's get back to your upcoming marriage proposal," said Nancy.

Noylene was suddenly back on track, her serving gaffe momentarily forgotten.

"Are you gettin' married? You know, I'm thinkin' about getting into the wedding business myself. I could do the hair, the flowers, the bridesmaid dresses...everything! And I'll prob'ly be openin' a salon..."

"Stop gushing, Noylene. I'm not getting married."

"I think you should reconsider," said Pete. "Meg is the best thing that ever happened to you, that's for sure. You don't want her getting away. And Noylene would be more than happy to help."

"She's not getting away, and I don't want Noylene's help. Now let's change the subject please. Here's breakfast."

Megan Farthing and I had been together for the last four years. We had met just after she'd moved to town to take care of her mother, and we'd been something of an item ever since. She was a savvy investment counselor and had taken charge of my small fortune quite handily. She is divorced, a few years younger than me, well-versed in music and the arts, a pretty darn good soprano and the town beauty. But I didn't think that marriage was in my future. Like most men comfortable in their current situation, I get extremely nervous when talk turns to nuptials—anyone's nuptials. It gets certain people thinking.

Collette, another of Pete's serving minions, came up to the table with a tray full of food including pancakes, scrambled eggs and country ham, grits, cinnamon buns, another basket of biscuits, toast and gravy, all served "family style." I noticed that all talk of marriage was curtailed as the entire group attacked the food and turned its attention to more important matters: that is, who was going to get the last pancake? My money was on Nancy.

"We can get more," I said, as Nancy fixed Dave with a murderous eye.

"It's the principle of the thing," growled Nancy. "I'm a girl. He should give it to me. It's the polite thing to do." She aimed her fork in his direction.

"Fine," said Dave. "Just take it."

"I'll get some more," said Collette. "Just give me a minute. I don't even have the tray unloaded yet."

Pete sighed. "You guys are like piranhas. These free breakfasts are costing me a fortune."

"Send the bill to the department," I said. "We can afford it thanks to the parking tickets we're handing out."

"Hey, look at this," said Dave, holding up a cinnamon bun he had placed on a saucer. "This roll looks just like the Virgin Mary."

"Let me see that," said Noylene, her coffee and hostess rounds bringing her back to our table.

"You stay away from me with that coffee pot."

"Relax, honey. I just want to see the bun."

Dave tilted it up so we all could see it, the sticky glaze holding it firmly to the plate.

"My God. It does look like someone," said Pete. "I don't know who exactly. It could be just an old woman with a head scarf."

"Be serious," I said. "Why would just any old woman show up in a cinnamon bun? It *has* to be the Virgin Mary."

"I think it looks more like Jimmy Durante in drag," said Nancy.

"Maybe it's a sign," said Noylene.

"A sign of what?" asked Nancy.

"I dunno," said Noylene with a puzzled look. "But whatever you do, don't eat it."

Chapter 2

It was a Friday--not a T.G.I.F. Friday where you don't get anything done because you're too excited about the opening of fishing season and you've got a new rod from Orvis sitting on the davenport, three fresh-tied flies, and a tub of night crawlers wriggly enough to be deacons at a discernment weekend--but rather that kind of Friday that you dread to see come to an end, knowing that your sister-in-law has four tickets to the Junior Ballet (that gawd-awful Giselle) and one of them has your name written all over it.

"Kit," I barked, "you have those pictures yet?"

"Not yet, boss. They probably won't show anything you didn't already see."

"I was thinking we could sell one or two to the daily rag and make this month's nut. Our bank account is emptier than a housefly's bladder."

"That ain't ethical, Boss."

Ethics don't buy the stogies, I thought as I lit one up and picked up the phone.

"Marilyn? The bishop call yet?"

"Nope."

"How about the hymns? Did I pick them out already?" I knew the answer.

Marilyn snickered. "Not unless you did it in your sleep --as usual."

"Very funny." I chomped on my cigar. The fifteenth Sunday of Pentecost. Ordinary time. Usually I could come up with hymns faster than Granny Pearl on You-Pick-'Em Sunday, but today I was as stumped as the three-legged pig whose owner loved him so much, he vowed "I just can't eat a pig that cute all at once."

I flipped through the hymnal. It was tough being

in the doghouse every week and this hymnal had some real hounds. Sure, they were all nice and singable when you were sitting in a music conference with a bunch of professionals, but try some of these mutts at home and they'd be barking like the cheerleader squad at St. Mary Margaret's.

"Shall I just use the ones from last week?" asked Marilyn amiably. "And the week before that? And the week before..."

"Yeah, whatever," I interrupted. "It's the fifteenth Sunday after Pentecost. I doubt anyone will notice."

"The bishop will notice. He's standing right here."

If I had been paying attention, I might have noticed Marilyn's intonation change from her no-nonsense secretarial clatter to her sickly sweet stick-a-communion-fork-in-your-neck voix de pudding, but I wasn't and I didn't.

"You misunderstood," I chirped. "The hymns are 435, 623, 15 and 238. In that order." I thought at least a couple of the numbers sounded recognizable. "Type it up." I hung up the phone.

"Still want that cup of joe?"

It was a voice that was familiar, but not too. I looked up and measured her like an undertaker at a nursing home. Her hair was short, her legs were long and the rest of her fell somewhere in between. It was the "in-between" I was interested in.

"I'm Starrbuck. Starrbuck Espresso. But you can call me Starr. I brought you some coffee."

"Of course you did, Kitten."

"May I read it yet?" asked Meg.

"Not yet. You're too critical. Your negativity will stem the tide that is my creative impetus."

"No, it won't. I promise. Just let me see the first chapter."

I gave no indication I was giving in.

She shrugged. "I'll see it Sunday, anyway."

I was in the habit, for better or worse, of putting the finished chapters into the choir members' folders before the Sunday morning service. I had found out later that these chapters had been making the rounds of the locals in St. Germaine. Not that I minded. I thought some of the prose was pretty darn good. Well, if not good, then not extremely bad. Or, if extremely bad, at least bad on purpose.

"Fine," I said, knowing I'd get no peace until the unjust criticism was leveled. I handed Meg the top page of the story. Although my missives were very short—less than a page—I thought they were clever beyond words. My entire novelette would be under thirty pages. Yes, it was short and sweet, but I wasn't making a career out of this. It was just my way of relaxing. I braced myself for the onslaught.

"Not too bad," said Meg. "In fact, you're getting better."

"You think so?"

"Absolutely. So good, in fact, that you should start your real novel. I'm sure it'll be splendid."

"I don't know. It might take me a couple of years to finish it."

"Really?" she asked, pseudo-innocence dripping from her treasonous lips. "That long?"

"Aha! I see right through your tricks." I snatched my paper back from her hand. "I am, after all, a trained detective. Nope. No way. This shall be my masterpiece."

"Ah well. No one can say I didn't try."

She swayed delightfully up to my desk like a Polynesian palm tree on a couple of good-looking stumps, her Miss-Middle-America walk defined by her high-heels, a little grace, a lot of practice, and the taffeta clinging to her curves like plastic wrap and rustling like a cockroach in a sugar-bowl.

"The girl you found. She was my sister."

"I see the resemblance," I said, lighting another cigar and thinking of last Thanksgiving.

"I'll pay you to find out who did it."

That sounded like a deal to me. The bishop would pay me. Starr Espresso would pay me. If I could get a couple more people to pay me, I could take the rest of the week off. Suddenly the phone rang. I picked it up. It was another dame.

"Yeah?"

"Vee vant you to find out who killed her."

I recognized the accent right away. She worked for the feds--undercover, of course--and I'd had that pleasure more than a few times. It was Alice. Alice Uberdeutchland.

"How're you doin' Alice?"

"Cut zee small talk. Vee vill give you two hundred a day plus expenses."

I took a long drag, put my feet up on my desk and blew a smoke ring that hung above Starr's head like a smoggy halo. Then I smiled.

"What's the scoop on the new guy?" I asked.

The staff meetings at St. Barnabas were different from our staff meetings for the police department in that we didn't have a full breakfast—just coffee and donuts. The "new guy" I was referring to had come into the congregation like a whirlwind and was hard to miss. He'd been attending services for a couple of weeks and had met almost everyone in the congregation, shaking hands and kissing babies like a seasoned politician.

"His name is Rob Brannon," said Georgia. Georgia Wester was one of the Lay Eucharistic Ministers and on the Worship Committee. The other people at the table were Marilyn, Father George and Carol Sterling. Our Christian Ed director, Brenda Marshall, was absent from the conclave. Brenda was a very emotional and hug-oriented woman. I had thought she might resign after our interim priest left, but she'd decided to stay on—at least for the time being.

In some Episcopal parishes, it's traditional for the entire staff to write letters of resignation as soon as a new priest is hired. Usually, but not always, the letters are refused. Sometimes, they're kept on file for a couple of months to see how all the personalities work out. Father George had decided to keep them all on file. The scuttlebutt around St. Barnabas was that Princess Foo-Foo (as Megan had nicknamed Brenda) was on a short leash and currently absent because she was attending a conference on Puppet Ministry that she had scheduled prior to Father George's arrival.

"Rob's been a visitor here since he was born," said Carol. "His grandparents have passed away, but his family's from St. Germaine."

"The name's familiar," I said. "Ahh. Robert Brannon, as in the Robert Brannon whose name is on at least three of the stained glass window memorials?"

"That's the family. I think Rob is Robert Brannon the fourth. His great-grandfather was one of the founding members of St. Barnabas."

"And is he back to stay?" Father George asked.

"It seems so," said Georgia, holding her now empty cup out to me for a refill. I obliged.

"Well, he's on my list for a visit. I'll try to see him sometime this week."

Father George Eastman had come to St. Barnabas in the early summer. He had interviewed just after Easter and had been well received by almost everyone. His wife, Suzanne, was a good alto and had joined the choir the first week they'd arrived. During the five months George had been at St. Barnabas, things had run smoothly. Compared to the last two priests, he was literally a godsend. The atmosphere of St. Barnabas felt as if a huge cloud had been lifted. The whole congregation could feel it. He had his quirks, but I liked him. We got along just fine.

"You'd *better* visit him," smiled Marilyn Forbis, the church secretary. "He's already joined. I received his letter this morning. He also turned in his pledge card."

I was impressed. His pledge card? In the Episcopal church, pledge cards were as rare as hen's teeth—at least before Thanksgiving when the screws were tightened.

"We have a vestry election in a couple of weeks," Father George said. "I've read the procedures. Is the nominating committee in place?"

We all looked at Marilyn. She nodded and flipped a couple of pages before settling on the correct document.

"There are four retiring members, so they'll make up the committee. Meg Farthing, Katherine Barr, Carol..." She nodded toward Carol. "And Malcolm Walker."

"How long has Malcolm been Senior Warden?" asked Father George.

"Four years," said Marilyn. "He should have left last year, but we were in transition, and we thought it would be wise to keep the leadership in place. We didn't have an election last year."

"Will Billy Hixon remain as Junior Warden?"

"He has another year, but I've heard rumblings that he might like the job of Senior Warden instead."

"Could he do it?" asked Father George, turning toward me.

"Sure," I said with a shrug. "I don't know why not."

Father George looked at Georgia, then to Carol.

"Yeah," said Georgia.

Carol nodded. "I guess so."

After the meeting, I made my way up to the choir loft to look at some music. St. Barnabas was an old church—old for this part of the country anyway. It was built in the traditional shape of the cross, the choir loft and the organ being in the back balcony. I had just settled in for an hour of practice on the Reger *Ein feste Burg Fantasie* when JJ Southerland came up the stairs and stuck her head though the doorway.

"I have some vittles for you in the kitchen if you want some lunch."

I grinned at her. "Are you here cooking every day?"

"Almost." JJ pulled the errant strap of her white painter's overalls back onto her shoulder, adjusted her baseball cap and gave me a smile. "I'm working on tonight's church supper anyway. You coming?"

"What are you making?" I was always wary of JJ's cooking. Sometimes it was a delicious pâté de foie gras. Sometimes it was pâté de possum. And you never knew which it would be.

"I don't know yet, but it could be good. Billy and John are grilling."

"I don't want to miss that. Give me about an hour, and I'll come down and give it a taste."

"Well, the real reason that I came up is that there's a huge rat in the pantry, and we can't get it out. Would you bring your gun down and teach it some manners?"

I reached under the organ bench and pulled out my 9mm Glock. "Let's go then."

The rat in the pantry was pretty big, and it had been living on the largesse of the kitchen committee for so long that it was too fat to move very quickly. There were three choices as I saw it. Shoot it, trap it or poison it. Shooting it was the fastest. Once the deed was done, I got it out the door and into the dumpster as quickly as I could. I didn't want to leave it for JJ because I wasn't altogether sure where it would end up.

"Thanks," said JJ, standing at the stove and pushing her current concoction around the blackened frying pan with a fork. "Grab a plate."

I looked over her shoulder. She had some sausages, onions, garlic and green peppers sizzling dangerously close to culinary perfection.

"It smells great. No wonder the rat didn't want to leave."

"Well, I've known about him for quite some time. But, live and let live I always say. That is, until he got into my potatoes."

I filled my plate and took it back with me to the choir loft. I didn't even care what kind of sausage this was and, by all accounts, it was probably best not to know. I'd heard that JJ stuffed her own.

An hour later, I was satisfied with the prelude for Sunday, had locked up and was walking back toward the police station when I heard a man's voice.

"Hayden! Hayden Konig!"

I looked across the street and saw Rob Brannon coming out of the Ginger Cat, obviously his choice for lunch judging from the napkin with which he was still busy wiping his mouth. It looked to me as if he'd seen me from the window and jumped up to catch me before I'd passed by.

"Do you have a minute?" he hollered from across the street.

I waved and gave him a smile, then crossed Main Street, ducking through the line of cars that was creeping down the busy thoroughfare.

"Hello, Hayden. I'm Rob Brannon."

"Glad to meet you," I said, taking his outstretched hand.

"Want to come in and have a bite?"

"No thanks. I just ate."

"How 'bout a coffee then? They have great coffee here."

"Sure. That'd be fine."

The Ginger Cat was an upscale coffee shop that did very well during tourist season. Cynthia Johnsson was behind the counter, as usual. She wasn't the owner—that was Annie Cooke—but Cynthia worked the lunch crowd during the peak months. She'd also started giving belly-dancing lessons at the rec center. I'd been after Meg to enroll. I thought she'd be a natural.

"Hi, Cynthia. Just a coffee for me, please."

"A double-shot half-decaf skinny mochachino crème de mint?"

"No. Just coffee."

She giggled. "How about our Ethiopian Yergacheffe?"

"Is that coffee?"

"Why, yes. Yes it is," said Cynthia.

"Fine. I'll have that then."

"I'll bring it in a sec."

I walked over to Rob's table, and I saw that I'd been right. The seat he had chosen was at a table facing the picture window where he could eat and watch the town go by. His meal was almost finished, and he resumed eating as soon as I sat down.

"I've been wanting to meet you," he said between bites.

"I've heard about you as well."

"Nothing bad, I hope."

"No particulars. Just that you're new to the church."

"Well," he said, swallowing the last bite of his sandwich.

"I'm not exactly new to the church. I spent every summer in St. Germaine from the time I can remember until about fifteen years ago. My grandparents lived here and since my folks both worked, I came to the mountains as soon as school was out. We were in church every time the doors opened."

"So your home is...?"

"I grew up in Charlotte. But I'm opening a law office here in St. Germaine."

His complimentary dill pickle wedge disappeared with a muffled crunch, and he ran a finger over the last vestiges of his potato chips, popping the crumb-covered digit into his mouth with a debonair kiss. "Mom always taught me to clean my plate," he said, offering a mock apology, "and these are good chips."

My Ethiopian Yergacheffe arrived and, to my surprise, actually tasted like coffee.

"Have you been practicing in Charlotte?" I asked him as Cynthia whisked away his empty plate.

"Yep. I'm a medical malpractice litigator. I just settled a big case so I don't really need the work, but I'd like to keep my hand in. Maybe get into politics a little."

"That sounds like a good plan. Although there's not too much happening on the political front in St. Germaine.

"Well, you have to start somewhere," he said with a grin. "And there's a congressional seat opening up here in a couple of years."

"Ahhh. Now it becomes clear."

"Well, you must admit that Watauga County has its advantages. A less dense population for one. And no minority vote to speak of."

"Not to mention a retiring twelve-term congressman," I added.

"Exactly. But, as I say, it's a couple of years down the road."

"It doesn't hurt to start early."

"Too true. Anyway, I just wanted to say that I really enjoy

your organ playing at St. B's. The trio sonata last week—Bach, right?"

"Buxtehude."

"Yeah. It was great. We're lucky to have you."

I noticed his use of the word "we" and smiled. "I tell them that often."

"Somehow, I doubt that," he said with a good-natured laugh and another outstretched hand. "But it's good to finally meet you and, by the way, I'd appreciate your vote."

"Hey," I said as I stood up, "why don't you get your political feet wet and run for the vestry at St. Barnabas. They can always use some new blood."

"I was on the vestry at St. Paul's in Charlotte. That's something I'll *never* do again! Anyway, it's good to finally meet you."

"Good to meet you, too," I said, mentally checking him off my vestry list. I shook his hand and walked out, purposefully sticking him with the tab. I knew he was getting the bill as soon as he uttered the words "I'm a medical malpractice litigator." In my view, he was one of the reasons medical insurance was through the roof. Not the only one, of course—and there is certainly a case to be made that these lawsuits keep doctors on their toes—but certainly enough of one that he could buy the coffee. Rob was a politician from his two hundred-dollar haircut to his six hundred-dollar Ferragamos. But, in spite of his chosen vocation, he was one of those folks who most people took to immediately, and I didn't doubt that he'd go far in his new career.

As I walked out of the Ginger Cat, crossed the road again and headed back to the police station, I couldn't help but notice that in the scant two hours I had been absent from my constabulary duties, there had been a tent partially erected in the vacant lot that had been the site of last year's Kiwanis Christmas Nativity.

A festival-sized tent in downtown St. Germaine is not an uncommon sight. We had our share of craft shows, outdoor church bazaars and Bar-B-Que fundraisers for the high school. However, this tent was more noticeable than most due to its enclosed sides, its faux-stained-glass windows and what appeared to be an inflatable steeple. The assembly was drawing a bit of a crowd. A round little man scurried around the site, alternating between glad-handing the onlookers, handing out flyers, and pointing out flaws in the locally hired crew's tent-raising techniques. I knew what was coming.

Pete had alerted me the week before, and now I saw it emblazoned across a trailer hooked to a small Ford pick-up truck. The trailer proclaimed—in bright orange letters on a yellow background—Hogmanay McTavish's Gospel Tent Revival. Brother McTavish had received his permit and would be in St. Germaine for a month—one service every Friday and Saturday night with special music provided by local churches and soloists. I'd seen the advertisements plastered around the town. The ads also mentioned that the good reverend had an assistant who would be choosing the Gospel passages on which Hogmanay McTavish would preach each and every evening. This assistant was what many politically correct folks might call "Poultry-American." Other folks might call her "dinner." Her name was Binny Hen. Binny Hen the Scripture Chicken.

Chapter 3

The sounds of Respighi's *Ancient Airs and Dances* filled the cabin. Actually, I had two stereo systems. One for when Meg was around—that was my Bose Wave system; good sound, nice balance, compact and easy to use—and one for when she wasn't and I wanted the true audiophile experience. This system included Marantz components and four Panasonic SB-Moa1 surround speakers pushing two hundred sixty-five watts per channel. I used it when I wanted to actually *feel* the music as well as hear it. This was one of those times. The twelve orchestrated dances were a favorite of mine when the cold weather hit. They were vaguely holidayesque in a Renaissance Festival sort of way and never failed to lift my spirits. I admit it. This was movie music written before there was movie music. I'd always thought that if Respighi had lived another ten years, he might have moved to Hollywood and become as famous as Erich Korngold. Nah. Who was I kidding? As famous as Korngold? Well...maybe...

So Candy Blather was Starr Espresso's sister. Candy was her stage name, of course. Her real name was Latte. Latte Espresso. Together, Starr and Latte made up the famous Espresso twins--social gad-abouts and heirs to their grandfather's coffee fortune. No wonder I was feeling like caffeine-free day at the Maison d'Beatnik.

I walked down the street, my hat pulled low, my collar pulled high, my hands stuffed into the pockets of my trench, and headed to my favorite bar. I had to think. Something was gnawing at my brain; gnawing like one of those tiny carpet beetles that crawls inside your ear when you're asleep and lays a hundred thousand eggs and when they hatch, you decide to become a TV Evangelist--it was like that, but with less bad singing.

I walked in, sat down and ordered a beer and a bump. Then another. By the time I was on my third bump, I was hitting on all eight. The bishop wanted the hinky on the dead babe. Starr had her own reasons for finding the dink that iced her sister. Then there was the feds. Did they just want to talk? I didn't think so. It was like the old song said. "Hinky dinky parlez vous."

I made my way down to The Slab the next morning and to my surprise, the usual crowd waiting for a table had thronged to about three times its normal size. I snuck past the line and found Pete at our customary table. Nancy and Dave were absent. Paperwork had taken priority over breakfast. I'd pointed to the mound of unfinished reports when I stopped by the office on my way to the diner, and their conscientiousness won out as I suspected it would. Dave would have come with me, but Nancy wouldn't let the reports rest until they were finished. I also figured Dave's guilt would kick in, and he'd stay and help. I, myself, felt no such remorse.

"Why the huge crowd?" I asked as I sat down. "Is there a special on waffles?"

"Nope. I had this great idea," said Pete. "I put an ad in the paper. It came out this morning." He handed me a copy of the *Watauga Democrat*. There, on page three, was a full-page ad for The Slab Café. In the middle of the ad was a picture of the Virgin Mary Cinnamon Roll with the caption, "Come See The Immaculate Confection!" The ad went on to relate the history, such as it was, of the sugary miracle—complete with several quotes from Noylene Fabergé and others.

"A full page ad?" I asked. "That's got to be expensive."

"It isn't really. If they have space and they're about to go to press, you can get a full page pretty cheap. And as you can see,"

Pete said, gesturing around his packed café, "I've more than made the price of the ad."

"I guess," I said, catching Noylene's eye and signaling for my usual breakfast. "Where is the holy artifact?"

"In the pie display case on the counter. I took the rest of the pie slices out. I don't want anyone confused. There's only one Immaculate Confection."

"I'm not going to have to provide police security am I?"

"I don't think so. But I'm having some t-shirts and coffee mugs made up. It's all about merchandising. Once the word gets out, I'm thinking national exposure. I've also got a guy working on a website."

"Does Dave get a cut? After all, he discovered it."

"He may have discovered it, but he didn't pay for it, so it's legally mine."

"Pete, listen to yourself."

"You're right. Sheesh. I sound like one of those lottery winners that has to share his loot. I'll make sure Dave gets a cut."

"Well, he might not want one, but it doesn't hurt to ask."

Nancy and Dave were still hard at work in the office. The end-of-the-month reports were usually filed by the second or third of the next month, but we had let it go for almost a week. By we, I mean that I forgot to tell Nancy and Dave to do it earlier. It wouldn't take more than a few hours. They should be finished by lunchtime. With the two deputies actually doing some police work, I figured it was my job to answer the phone—which I did on the second ring.

"Police Department."

"Hayden, it's Marilyn."

"What's wrong?" I asked. I could recognize tension when I heard it.

"You'd better come over to the church. And bring Nancy with you."

"I'm on my way."

"What's going on?" asked Nancy as we walked briskly down the sidewalk.

"I don't know. Marilyn just said to come down to the church."

"And you didn't ask?"

"Nancy," I explained patiently as we walked. "It will take us three minutes to get there. Nothing will change in the meantime. We couldn't have gotten to the church any faster, and I would have wasted even more time trying to get her to tell me over the phone."

"But aren't you curious?"

"Of course I am. But we'll find out soon enough."

Marilyn met us at the bright red doors in the front of the church. Doors of Episcopal churches are traditionally red. In earlier times, it was understood that anyone passing through the doors would find literal sanctuary. Over time, however, this meaning had changed, and it was behind these doors that people were now offered spiritual rather than physical refuge.

"What's going on?" asked Nancy again, this time directing her question to Marilyn.

"You aren't going to believe this," said Marilyn, ushering us in and closing the door behind us. "You've got to see this for yourself." She hurried in ahead of us and pointed to the ceiling. "Billy was going to change the light bulbs in the nave—the ones at the top."

"It's a lousy job. I'm glad it's not in my job description," I said, as we followed her down the center aisle and up to the altar.

Sitting next to it was a scissor lift with a basket on top. Billy was waiting for us, shifting from one foot to the other in an obvious display of agitation.

"Okay. We've got something to show you," said Billy as we walked up. I could tell he was rattled. "I put everything back just the way we found it."

"Calm down, Billy," I said. "Take a deep breath."

"What's this thing?" asked Nancy, pointing to the large piece of equipment. I knew what she was doing. It was a pretty common technique: changing the subject briefly to put a witness at ease.

"It's called a 'man-lift,'" said Billy with a stiff shrug. "I borrowed it to put some lights on the big fir tree in my front yard. You know, for Christmas. While I had it, I thought it'd be a good idea to go ahead and change out all the light bulbs in the nave."

"It's pretty neat," I said, following Nancy's lead. "How did you get it in here?"

Billy relaxed a bit. "Right in the front doors. You just sit in the bucket and drive it. Then when you've got it where you want, you lock it down and use the joystick to go as high as you want. Well, up to thirty-five feet anyway."

"Billy!" yelped Marilyn. "Show them!"

"Okay, okay." Billy's anxiety returned immediately. "We got in here and we realized that we had to move the altar a couple of feet to the right to get the lift where it needed to be. I called three of my boys who were working down at the cemetery to come and help me move it. It's pretty heavy."

Billy Hixon was the Junior Warden of St. Barnabas and as such, he was in charge of the maintenance of the church. He also ran a very profitable lawn-care service.

"They came in about a half hour ago. I told them to be real careful, but Steve dropped his corner. Said it slipped out of his hands, but I think he was just being lazy. Anyway, that made Joe lose his grip and the whole end of the altar dropped."

"Where are the boys?"

"I sent 'em back to work."

"Did it break when it dropped?"

Billy shook his head. "Didn't break, but look here." He jiggled the back panel of the altar. "This come loose." I looked up at Marilyn. She was standing stock still, chewing on her lower lip with her arms crossed in front of her.

The altar of St. Barnabas had been at the church since it was founded in 1846. This was the second building, the first having burned, and was built by the congregation in 1904. The altar was one of the two things left from the fire; the other was the church bell. Local legend holds that when the town arrived on that cold Sunday morning in January of 1899 to find their church in smoldering ruins, the altar had somehow been carried outside the wooden structure and was sitting on the snow-covered ground with all the communion elements in place. The people of St. Barnabas gave thanks for the angelic intervention and had the morning service right there in the snow. The legend had become gospel in St. Germaine. I found it a good story. The altar had to weigh close to four or five hundred pounds including the marble top which, as far as I knew, was not removable. The only way it *could* have been carried out was by angels. Either that, or a company of very strong men with a heavy-duty piano dolly. In addition to the marble top and the thickly carved woodwork beneath it, the altar was enclosed on all four sides with dark panels. The wood was probably mahogany, although no one I knew ever bothered to find out for sure. I had been working at St. Barnabas for about ten years, and I had never seen the altar moved. It was simply too heavy.

I tested the long panel in the back. "So, it came loose. We can put it back on. It's not a big deal."

"Just a second," said Billy. He bent down and lifted the rear panel of the altar off of a couple of old wooden pegs. I could see where one of them had broken off.

"It doesn't look too bad," I said.

"O my God," said Nancy in a whisper.

"No, look," I said, still looking at the peg. "We can replace that without too much trouble. No one will even be able to ..."

Nancy lifted my chin up and directed my gaze. The light in the church wasn't the best and was particularly dim on the floor behind the altar. My eyes focused down the length of the enclosed communion table. At the other end—the end I hadn't been looking at—was a man. He was wearing a gray suit and tie, and had a mop of brownish hair. A pair of glasses hung off one ear and sat crookedly on his nose. He was sitting up, his hands and arms clasped around his knees, his head bowed as if he was asleep. But he wasn't asleep. He was dead. And, by the look of him, he hadn't been there long.

Chapter 4

We stared at the body for a long moment.

"Well, what're we gonna do?" asked Billy.

"Let's get him out," I said, motioning for Nancy to lend a hand.

"How long has he been in there?" asked Marilyn, as Nancy and I maneuvered ourselves to lift the body out of its hiding place.

"Not too long," said Nancy. "There's not even any rigor present."

"This doesn't make any sense," I said, more to myself than anyone else. I had my hands under the arms of the dead man. Nancy had his feet. He was a slight man and didn't weigh much—maybe one hundred thirty pounds—and although the angle was awkward, we lifted him easily out of the altar. His limbs were loose, his cheeks still pink. He looked for all the world as though he were asleep.

"Rigor generally lasts about seventy-two hours," Nancy said. "Then the muscles relax. But look at the dust on this guy's suit."

I had already pulled a wallet from the inside coat pocket. The style of the suit was all wrong—the material was too heavy and the cut seemed clumsy and outdated. It was made of wool, but of a coarser quality than I had ever seen. Maybe this guy, I thought to myself, was from an Eastern block country. I rifled through the wallet and found a black and white photograph of a man and a woman who, I presumed from their affectionate pose, were married. Then, a moment later, I came up with a driver's license. There wasn't a picture on it because the license was dated 1936.

"According to this," I said to the group, now looking at me for answers to questions that I'd only begun to ask myself, "the deceased's name is Lester Gifford. He lived in Boone at 423 Councill Street. His birthday is June 12..."

I paused for effect—a habit I had that Nancy found continually irritating.

"June 12...1892. That would make Mr. Gifford 112 years old."

No one said anything.

Billy broke the silence. "He don't look that old."

"Maybe that's not his license," said Nancy in a quiet voice. "Is there a picture on it?"

"Not on the license. But look at this." I handed her the license and the photograph I'd taken from the billfold. On the back of the photo, obviously taken and printed by a professional, was the inscription in a fine cursive hand: "To my darling Lester on our anniversary" and dated "27 May, 1934."

"It's him all right," said Nancy, comparing the photo with the body stretched out on the carpet behind the altar. "But look at his condition." She sniffed the air and then, with a puzzled look, stuck her head inside the makeshift crypt and took a deep breath through her nose.

"Nothing," she said. "There's no smell. In fact..." She sniffed again. "Roses. The whole inside of the altar smells like roses."

"Maybe he was embalmed," offered Marilyn.

"Maybe, but that wouldn't explain this kind of preservation," I adjusted his glasses and touched my fingers to his cheek. "He's cold, but his flesh is soft. And look at his hair. It's perfect. Not dry at all. Go ahead," I said to Billy, who was now bending over the body. "Touch it."

"I ain't touchin' nothin'. This is just spooky. We've been usin' that altar for a hundred years. Now you're telling me that there's been a dead body inside of it since the 30's?"

"Anything else in the wallet?" asked Nancy.

I opened it back up and looked again. "A couple of dollar bills circa 1932 and 28. The 1928 is a silver certificate. A library card and a voter registration, both with Lester's name on them. And here's a business card. Watauga County Bank in Boone. No name on it though. And here's a dime."

"Is that silver certificate worth anything?" asked Billy.

"A couple of bucks. They're not that rare." I turned to Nancy. "Let's get an ambulance up here and get Lester down to the coroner as quick as we can. Preferably, before word of this gets out."

"Too late," said Nancy, looking toward the front door. "Here they come."

"How'd they find out so fast?" I asked.

"Billy's crew, I'll bet," said Nancy.

Billy was not amused. "Those stinkers stopped for coffee. I'm gonna kick their butts!"

"Didn't you lock the door?" I asked Marilyn.

She shrugged. "Sorry."

"Well, let's lock it now."

Rob Brannon and Pete Moss were already coming up the aisle with several more folks coming in the door. I gestured toward Nancy. "Let Pete and Rob in. Then go with Marilyn to lock the door and invite the rest of the onlookers to wait outside."

Nancy nodded and followed Marilyn out. Pete and Rob came around the altar and stared at the scene in front of them.

"We just heard the news," said Pete. "Billy's crew came in and they all started talking at once. Never seen them so excited. Everyone in the Slab will be coming over as soon as they finish their lunch."

"I swear..." mumbled Billy under his breath. "I told them to go right back to the cemetery."

"Well, I'll be," said Rob, bending over the body. "How long has he been dead? A couple of hours?"

"As near as we can figure, about seventy years."

"That can't be right."

"Let me see," said Pete, maneuvering his way past the scissor lift and closer to the body. "He looks like he's asleep."

"The ambulance is on the way," said Nancy as she walked back up the aisle and clicked her cell phone closed. They were in town anyway on a false alarm. Mrs. McCarty thought she was having another heart attack. Mike and Joe should be here in a couple of minutes."

"Look here," said Rob, reaching into the back of the altar.

I looked. Against the wooden panel, behind where Lester Gifford had been resting, was a brown accordion folder that was stuffed full of papers. It was almost the same color as the wood and, being covered with dust, was almost indistinguishable from the wood—especially in the darkened corner of the altar. At least, that was my story, and I was sticking to it. Still, I was more than a little embarrassed that this lawyer spotted the folder before I did. Me! A highly trained detective! Rob lifted the folder out.

"We haven't completed processing the crime scene yet," I grumbled. "Don't touch anything."

Rob grinned and handed me the file. "Sorry. Here you go."

"Yeah, yeah," I said. "I would have found it, you know."

Pete laughed. "Just open it up, will you. And maybe Rob can find a few other clues while you're going through it."

The elastic band had rotted and it snapped as soon as I tried to remove it. I opened the cardboard folder, pulled out a sheaf of papers and thumbed through them quickly.

"Looks like a few loan documents. Here's some correspondence." I flipped through a couple more. "Here's a letter of farm foreclosure signed by Lester to a Wilmer Griggs. He hadn't mailed it yet. It looks to me like a bunch of take-home office work. I guess things haven't changed much in seventy years. We'll go through it when we get back to the office."

"Maybe Wilmer Griggs killed him to save his farm," offered Billy.

I ignored him and pointed to the altar. "Anything else in there?" I asked Nancy.

After Rob had found the folder, Nancy, as chagrined as I, had flipped out her flashlight and begun scouring Lester's tomb for any other clues.

"Nothing, boss."

"Not even a last message scratched into the wood with his fingernails?" asked Rob.

Nancy almost started looking again before realizing that Rob was joking. Then she looked anyway.

"Anyone tell Father George?" I asked.

"He's not here," said Marilyn. "But I left him a voice mail."

"No last messages," said Nancy, finishing her inspection.

There was a banging at the front door.

"That'll be the ambulance guys," I said. "Go let them in and let's try to keep the commotion to a minimum."

Nancy and Marilyn headed back up the aisle for what seemed like the umpteenth time. We fitted the back panel onto the altar and waited in silence as we stared down at what was probably the strangest case I'd ever come across. It didn't take Mike and Joe long to load Mr. Gifford onto the gurney, cover him with a sheet and wheel him out the front door. I'd be seeing him again soon. He was headed into Boone and straight to Kent Murphee's office.

"If you'd like a legal eye to look at those papers, I'd be happy to help," said Rob. "Pro bono, of course."

"Sounds like a deal," said Pete who, as mayor, was always on the lookout for a budgetary bargain.

"That'd be fine," I said. "Why don't you stop by tomorrow and give the papers the once-over."

"I'll be there," said Rob. "Am I also invited to join you in one of those fancy 'free breakfasts' at the Slab I've been hearing about?"

"No," I said.

"Nope," said Nancy, shaking her head.

"Definitely not," said Pete.

Chapter 5

"So who did it? You solve the case yet?" asked Kit, as curious as that cat that got itself killed for exactly the same reason that I told Kit to shut up for.

I looked out the window. It was a dark and stormy night--not so dark that I couldn't see the feminine form lurking in the shadows of the building across the street, the business end of her lit cigarette glowing in the haze like a lone Christmas bulb on some lurking Christmas thingy, nor stormy enough that a "Severe Weather Watch" had been issued by the National Weather Service, and to tell the truth, it was more like late afternoon rather than night because I think that Jerry Springer was still on, but a dark and stormy night nevertheless.

"I know two things," I said. "One. Candy Blather was in over her head and she got herself iced. The word on the street is that she was into Piggy Wilson for fifty thou."

"Fifty thou? That's a lot of bim--even for Piggy."

"It sure is," I said, lighting up a stogy.

"What's her dodge?"

"Hymn fixing," I said, puffing away like a three hundred pound woman with a beat-up ThighMaster and an upcoming high-school cheerleader's reunion. "There's a new hymnal coming out. The pressure is on from all sides. As the expert on pietic hymnody of the early 20th century, she was on the hot-seat to justify some of the committee's idiotic choices."

"So why was she killed?"

"Don't know yet."

"And who's that skulking across the street?" Kit asked.

"That's Alice. Alice Uberdeutchland. I'd recognize that silhouette anywhere."

"How 'bout if I get us some dinner?"

I flipped her a fin. She snatched it from the air like a walleye hitting a Crab Wiggler.

"Get out of here and get yourself some grub. I've got work to do," I said.

"What's the other thing you know?"

I smiled. "I know Alice."

"You know," said Megan, after I had filled her in on the happenings at the church, "it seems to me that ever since you got this typewriter, there are more bodies piling up in St. Germaine than in Cabot Cove."

"Cabot Cove?"

"You know. *Murder, She Wrote*. Angela Lansbury as Jessica Fletcher, the mystery writer. Cabot Cove, Maine—the murder capital of the world."

"Really?"

"Oh yes. Jessica solved over two hundred fifty murders in Cabot Cove."

"How many residents?"

"About a thousand I think."

"So St. Germaine doesn't seem so bad," I offered.

"Well, that was a TV show. Not real life."

"Ahhh. But here's the thing. That first body was a legit murder. We can count that one. But the clown's demise was an accident—not a homicide. The chorister was killed in England—not here. Jelly Barna didn't die—even though she was shot. And this guy would have been dead by now anyway. He's one hundred and twelve years old."

"Even so," said Meg. "You will admit that it's getting rather peculiar."

"Just coincidence."

"Has your ghost come back?"

"We've chatted a couple of times," I said.

"You should ask him then."

Choir rehearsal started on time for once. Or seemed to. All the new music had been passed out. The choir was punctual, in their seats and apparently ready to begin as I launched into the introduction of *Behold the Tabernacle of God.* All indications were for a productive rehearsal, and I played all the way to the choir entrance before things came apart.

"Hang on," said Rebecca Watts from the alto section. "You can't just start choir practice. What about the dead body?"

"What about the anthem?" I countered, now that the rehearsal had ground to a halt.

"Well," said Meg, happy to tell all she knew. "It seems that Billy was changing some light bulbs and discovered a body in the altar."

"He was changing a light bulb in the altar?" asked Marjorie.

"He was changing bulbs in the nave," I explained, now realizing that rehearsal was a lost cause, at least until everyone's curiosity was satisfied. "They were moving the altar—the back fell off and there he was. His name is...was...Lester Gifford. He's probably been in there since the 1930s. We don't know how he was killed although we suspect it was foul play—mainly because if it weren't, there wouldn't be any need to hide him in the altar. That's all we know at this point."

"Was he a member of St. Barnabas?" asked Rebecca.

"Not that we know of. He's not on any of the membership rolls."

"What about the miracle?" asked McKenna, another alto. I began to suspect that the alto section was trying to forestall the rehearsal of the Harris piece. The alto line had been giving them fits for the last two rehearsals. The soprano section, on the other hand, was sitting quietly and smiling demurely, having already mastered most of the notes in the upcoming anthem. Basses and tenors were, by all indications, asleep.

"I don't know about a miracle," I said, "but I will say that the body was remarkably preserved. Lester is down at the coroner's office. We'll get a report tomorrow. Now then...altos alone ...measure fourteen. "

"Wait," said Rebecca, now close to panic as she watched me adjust my music and prepare to begin again. "What about your new literary masterpiece? When do we get to read about the tenor? And what is he wearing?"

"No," hissed Meg to Rebecca. "Don't ask him. It's not worth it. Not even to escape this anthem."

"You'll see soon enough," I sniffed. "Measure fourteen, altos. And sing it like you mean it."

I skipped breakfast the next morning. It was an easy decision. The line for a table at the Slab was, if possible, even longer than it was the day before. I could probably sneak in and get a seat, but I wasn't anxious to brave the crowd and the plethora of malicious stares that would be leveled in my direction if I tried it. I didn't even slow down as I looked in the window of the diner, but as I walked by, I did notice that the Immaculate Confection had moved to the center of the counter and was now displayed under a very fancy cake cover along with an "artist's representation" of how the Mother of Our Lord might look if she were to make a surprise appearance in a pastry. In fact, I was trying to dance my way through the queue outside the café while looking at the picture through the window when I ran smack into Skeeter Donalson. Skeeter was just coming out the door of the Slab and pulling a new sweatshirt over his overalls. His new purchase was a light coffee color and proclaimed in large black letters beneath a copy of the same picture I had been studying: "The Immaculate Confection, The Slab Café, St. Germaine, NC." The picture of the bun bore more resemblance to the Madonna than the actual artifact, but that was to be expected. It was artistic license.

"Careful, Hayden," said Skeeter, good-naturedly.

"Sorry, Skeeter" I said, "I didn't see you. That a new shirt?"

"Pretty nice, eh? It was only $29.95."

"Only?"

"Well, the t-shirts are $14.95, but I figured that with winter coming and all, I'd go ahead and get the sweatshirt. I got this coffee mug, too," Skeeter said, holding up a mug, roughly the same color as his new shirt. "It came with a certificate. And," he said with pride, "it's notarized."

"No kidding. Notarized?"

"By a bishop and an archbishop. You should get one while they're still available. There's a limited number, you know."

"I'd heard that," I said, fighting a smile.

"You going in to see the Holy Virgin?"

"Not today."

"Don't wait too long," said Skeeter, moving down the sidewalk and waving his notarized certificate in my direction. "There's a limited number. You take care now," he called. I waved back and headed across the street toward the police station.

Dave met me at the door of the police station, coming from the opposite direction and carrying a box of donuts.

"No breakfasts for a while, I guess," said Dave, "so I went down to Dizzy Donuts and got us a dozen."

"You're a good man, Dave," I said, holding the door for him and following him into the station. "Your police work is getting better all the time."

"I should have eaten that stupid thing while I had the chance."

"I'm inclined to agree. But it may all work out for the best. We'll miss a few breakfasts, but Pete will make a whole bunch of money and he may share some with you."

Dave shrugged and put the donuts on the counter. "I guess."

"Is Nancy here?"

"She's patrolling."

I nodded, took two donuts, walked over to the sink and found my still unwashed coffee cup. I gave it a quick rinse, filled it with fresh coffee and went into my office to check my messages.

"Hayden," said the machine. "This is Kent. It's nine o'clock in the morning. You sure don't keep regular hours, do you? Give me a call."

I made a note and punched the erase button.

"Detective Konig," said the machine, working backwards through the list, "this is Rob Brannon. I can come over and look at those papers in the morning if you'd like. Give me a call. I'm free pretty much...well...whenever."

Erase.

"This message is for the Police Captain. This is the Reverend Hogmanay McTavish. Our first tent service is scheduled for tomorrow evening and I wonder if it would be possible to have a policeman on hand to help with parking and traffic control. Mayor Moss said to tell you it shouldn't be any trouble and that the Slab Café will be open after the revival for those who'd like to get a bite to eat. Thank you very much."

Erase and slump.

My first stop was at the tent now filling the vacant lot on Main Street. The blinking yellow arrow on the portable marquis pointed the way to the faithful and the lost alike, proclaiming in large, clip-on letters, "Rev. Hogmanay McTavish's Gospel Tent Revival."

The tent was empty. Empty of people anyway. I walked up the center aisle, past what looked like plenty of chairs, and up to the white plywood pulpit. In front of the pulpit was a table with a raised lip, the edging a good three inches higher than the top.

The entire surface was covered with about an inch of sawdust, restrained by the rails, and in the center of the four by four foot table was perhaps the largest Bible I had ever seen. I opened the cover. It was the Biblical equivalent of the Humvee, a red-letter, annotated King James with a concordance, a sixteen-page family tree, thirty color prints by the Renaissance masters and finished off with thick brown cordovan embossed-leather upholstery. In other words—loaded. It was at least eight inches thick and as large as a small coffee table. I'll bet it weighed close to forty pounds.

"It's a nice one, ain't it?" said a voice behind me.

"Sure is," I replied, closing the Bible carefully and turning around. There, in front of me, was the man I had seen a couple of days before, hustling to get the tent raised.

"Dr. Hogmanay McTavish at your service, sir."

The man in front of me was short and plump, but what struck me immediately about his appearance was that he possessed one of the finest comb-overs in the Western Hemisphere. His hair—perhaps the only hair he had, began on the left side of his head, slightly below his ear. It was salt and pepper in color and had a wiry texture to it. From behind his ear, the thatch of hair came forward, made a north-easterly swing across his brow, circled the top of his head twice like a wreath, the second revolution nesting inside the first, with the final strands of his long tresses glued to the center of his dome. Unwound, I suspected his hair was probably a couple of feet long. I took his outstretched hand, and despite his small stature and rounded physique, his grip was enough to give me a twinge.

"Glad to meet you. I'm Hayden Konig."

"Ah, Chief Konig. The pleasure is all mine. I was hoping you'd stop by."

"First stop on my list," I said with a smile. "Now, Doctor, what can I do for you?"

"First off, call me Brother Hog. Or just plain Hog." He

laughed. "I know I introduced myself as 'Doctor,' but I don't hold with all that snooty stuff. Puts folks off."

"What can I do for you Brother Hog?"

"I was thinkin' that we might be able to get one of your officers to help with some parkin' and directin' traffic on Friday and Saturday nights for the next few weeks. It'd sure be a help."

"We're a small department—there are two other officers besides myself. I'll be happy to ask them, but it'd have to be on their own time. And you'd have to pay them yourself."

"Wouldn't have it any other way," he said happily. "How about yourself? You need any overtime?"

"No, thanks."

"Well, you're welcome to come and worship with us anytime. I'd introduce you to my assistant, but she's resting up for this evening." He paused and looked at me as if sizing me up. "Well," he said, "I hope you can make it out to the revival once or twice."

I shrugged in my most noncommittal fashion. "I'm pretty busy."

He smiled again. "You never know what might happen."

I pulled up at the coroner's office in Boone about an hour later just as my new recording of *Pictures at an Exhibition* was heading toward the *Great Gate of Kiev*. The CD player in my truck was quite a marvel of electronic engineering. My truck was not. The '66 sky-blue Chevy pick-up had at least 480,000 miles on it that I knew of, but it might have more. The odometer rolled over every 100,000 miles and may have rolled once before I bought the truck. I kept track of the hundred-thousand milestones with a small notch in the steering wheel. In the twenty-five years I'd owned the vehicle, I had replaced the radio/tape player/CD player and speakers six times, the engine once, the transmission twice, and the clutch more times than I bothered to count. I sat in the parking lot for a couple of minutes and let the orchestra finish Mussorgsky's masterpiece before reaching behind the seat and pulling out a bottle of Maker's Mark for Kent. When I had called Kent on my cell phone earlier, he suggested that I'd better come in and see him. And I always came bearing gifts.

"Morning, Kent," I said, as I walked into his office.

"Morning, Hayden. Coffee?"

"Don't mind if I do."

I opened the Maker's Mark and poured a shot into both coffee mugs sitting on Kent's desk. Kent leaned across his desk with the coffee pot and filled the mugs the rest of the way.

"Coffee and bourbon," said Kent with a smack. "Can't beat it to get your day going."

"I don't usually imbibe this early," I said. "But it is coffee, after all."

"Darn tootin'."

Kent was in his usual attire consisting of an old tweed jacket with its obligatory elbow patches and leather buttons, a vest, corduroys and a bow tie. He leaned back in his chair and took a sip.

"Ever heard of Incorruptibles?" he said over the top of his cup.

"Yeah, I guess. Dead bodies that don't decompose. There are a couple of famous saints, aren't there?"

"More than a couple. They're found in Europe mostly."

"And they don't decompose?"

"They have an interesting history."

"I'm all ears," I said, settling back.

"There are basically three ways bodies have of being preserved after death," Kent began. "The first is accidental preservation. This can happen when a body is buried in hot, dry sand or lava, or has been placed in an area with little or no moisture, or in a frigid climate. As long as air or moisture doesn't reach these bodies, often, they can be preserved from significant decay. However, when accidentally preserved bodies are discovered, they are typically discolored, wrinkled, distorted, are skeletal looking and have no elasticity. In addition, they always have a bad odor and always decay rapidly once they're exposed to the air."

"Like the mummies found in the Andes? Or the peat-bog man?"

"Exactly," said Kent. "Secondly, there are those corpses that were purposely embalmed or otherwise treated before burial with the intention of trying to prevent decomposition. In most older cases of deliberately preserved human bodies, the body cavities were emptied and filled with specific materials like resin or resin-soaked sawdust, or the entire body was submerged in preservatives such as honey, rum, or sand. In the past few hundred years, there have been other methods used to prevent corpse decomposition. The body was typically submerged or filled with resin, tar, salt, alcohol, or a combination of these. Now, of course, we use chemicals, and embalming is primarily done to disinfect and preserve the remains for viewing by the family. We use a formaldehyde-based solution. Again, when older deliberately preserved bodies are discovered, like accidentally preserved bodies, they are typically discolored, wrinkled, etc. You get the point."

"Egyptian mummies. Got it."

"There is another way that bodies can be preserved. And, as a Catholic, I'd be remiss if I didn't tell you about it."

"The Incorruptibles," I said. I poured another cup of coffee—this time a double. Kent picked up his pipe, stuck it in his mouth and began the ritual of relighting.

"These types of preserved bodies," he said from between clenched teeth, holding his match above the bowl and giving the pipe a couple of good puffs, "started being discovered back in the early centuries after Christ, though surprisingly, they do not fall into either the accidental or deliberate preservation categories. Incorruptibles are discovered in many different environments, including environments that would typically cause an accidental or deliberately preserved corpse to decompose rapidly. They remain free of decay regardless of manner of burial, delay in burial, temperature, moisture, rough handling, frequent transference, having been covered in quicklime, or proximity to other decaying corpses."

"And the scientific explanation?"

"There isn't one, really," Kent said. "Science can mimic the phenomenon, but a true Incorruptible is...well...unexplainable."

"And is there such a thing as a true Incorruptible?" I asked. "It seems like a probable stage for a religious scam. Let's just say that it's 1580 and you're a Bishop of a cathedral that's having some franchise problems. The Protestants are pretty much undefeated going into the series. Your counter-reformation isn't going too well. Then one of your young nuns dies so you secretly embalm her, put her in a locked glass case, make up a story about how she's incorrupt and died in ecstasy during her first communion, get her canonized on the fast track and kazow!—you're in clover again. Pilgrimages, offerings, the world-wide tour... everything you need to put your cathedral back on the map."

"Yes. St. Imelda. A good point. She was earlier than 1580, but it did happen exactly as you say. In fact, up until recently, one of the two miracles that could be attributed for sainthood could be incorruptibility. And the other miracle had to be posthumous. Somebody healed of something dreadful by leaning over and touching the glass of the coffin or even simply praying to the pre-saint in question."

"Sounds like a racket."

"It was. But still taking all that into account, there are still more than a few actual examples around. St. Bernadette Soubirous in France is the most famous. She died in the 1870s.

There are more." He shrugged.

"And these Incorruptibles are always Catholics?"

"Well, yes and no."

I waited for the explanation.

"The holy people that were already devout Catholics and were found incorrupt became canonized."

"Were there others?"

"Oh yes. The other people that were dug up for whatever reason and found to be incorrupt—the non-Catholics, the heretics, or even practicing Catholics that weren't up to snuff—were viewed quite differently."

"And they were...?"

"Witches mainly, demons..." Kent paused, thinking. "In Eastern Europe, they were vampires. Sometimes werewolves."

"They weren't, of course."

"No, no," Kent said. "Of course not. But you can see how such legends could easily get started. When anyone found an incorrupt body, the thing to do was to cut the head off, burn it, scatter the ashes, kill everyone the deceased knew and consider themselves lucky to be rid of the abomination. So although there were probably many more examples of this type of thing happening, there aren't any bodies left to study. And, of course, the church isn't about to let science take a swipe at the ones they have."

"What about in North America?"

"Totally different cultures. The natives of North and South America didn't bury their dead in stone mausoleums and crypts. And they certainly didn't bother to dig them up once they were buried. Even if a body is incorruptible, worms and insects still have their job to do.

"What about in the 20th century then?" I asked. "Surely, there are some examples you guys can study."

"Not really. It's a very rare phenomenon anyway and once we started embalming..."

"What about that pope?" I asked as something jogged my memory.

"Pope John XXIII" said Kent sarcastically. "Not a good example. He died in '63. His body was moved in 2001 and was well preserved. The Vatican claimed a miracle and used it to validate Vatican II, but it's a dubious claim at best. First, the Vatican admits that the ex-Pope was sprayed heavily with anti-bacterial spray and sealed inside three airtight coffins. Hardly a case for incorruptibility. Not to mention that later there was quite a scandal concerning the pope's physician and a scientist in Rome who had perfected a formula for keeping cadavers incorrupt. A mixture of formaldehyde and methyl alcohol if I remember correctly. The scientist says the pope was pickled."

"So he isn't an Incorruptible?"

"The official Vatican position is that he is."

"But no tests have been done."

"No."

"So," I said. "Do you believe in all this stuff?"

"Yesterday I would have said no."

"Something change your mind?"

"He's lying on the table."

Chapter 6

"How ya doin', Alice?" I said, lighting a cigar. "Glad you could come up."

Alice Uberdeutchland entered the office pelvis first if that could have been anatomically possible which apparently, thanks to yoga, double jointed knees and Arian fortitude, it was. Her flaxen hair hung across one eye like a blonde pirate-patch and the scar that I'd given her during our last encounter was fading but still visible on her porcelainic cheek. Her cigarette holder jutted from between two lovely fingers like another long wooden finger painted black with a glowing cigarette stuck in the end and her red sequined dress hung on her like a Hollywood actor hangs onto his Valium prescription.

"Vat have you found out?" she demanded. "Vee need to know, schnell!"

"Schnell, eh?" I said, narrowing my eyes and giving her a half-smile like one of those cats who looks as though it knows something, but in reality is just a dumb animal with a brain the size of a large walnut--the smile, most probably a little gas from eating some dead lizard--the knowing look, a product of an over-anthropomorphizing culture. "How schnell?"

"Sehr schnell!"

"Sprechen sie English, Alice? I seem to remember that you do."

"Ja." She sank into a chair. "Vee need to find out who killed Candy. She vas taking money from different special interest groups to include zere hymns in zee new hymnal."

"How does Piggy Wilson figure into it?"

"He vants the graft, but he doesn't have zee connections. We don't sink he killed her. It vould be like killing zee golden moose."

"You mean 'the golden goose,' Alice. Or maybe just a special goose that lays golden eggs. Any way you spread it, it's still pâté."

Kent and I bent over the body of Lester Gifford.

"He smells like roses," I said. "Nancy smelled the same thing in the church."

"It's sometimes called the *odor of sanctity*."

"This is amazing," I said. "Did you do an autopsy? I don't see any incisions."

"I haven't started yet. Actually, I was sort of afraid to, you know."

"Yeah."

"I know I have to do it, but once I start, I have to finish. The organs have to come out. Everything. Then, according to North Carolina law, he has to be embalmed. Couldn't we wait until we can study him for a while? After all, he's already been dead for sixty years." I could tell that Kent was really torn.

"Here's the thing, Kent. There was obviously foul play—probably a murder—and I have to have an autopsy. If we put this guy on public display, we will, in all probability, never get one. You agree?"

"I do."

"Once you begin the autopsy, the point is moot. Correct? I mean, the church wouldn't want him if you remove his organs and, by law, you have to embalm him anyway."

"That is correct."

"So," I said, thinking out loud. "Although he wouldn't technically be an Incorruptible when you were finished, you could possibly have adequate time to do some research while he was here. That is, before he was embalmed."

Kent brightened considerably. "Yes. Yes I could. What about burial?"

"No rush."

"Next of kin?"

"Haven't found anyone."

"I'll get started then. It'll probably be Monday before I have anything."

"That's fine. I've got Nancy digging around in the public library and the newspaper archives. Maybe she'll come up with something."

I met Megan in the downtown park at exactly twelve o'clock. Sterling Park was in the middle of the square. It wasn't a large park—just a full city block square—but, in my opinion, it had everything a park should have. A lot of old trees—chestnut and poplar, a few benches, flower gardens, grass, and a white wooden gazebo placed right in the center. St. Barnabas faced east on the west side of the park; City Hall faced west across the way. There were shops and law offices surrounding the square. Main Street came in from the north, ran around the square and exited south. Addresses were therefore divided into North Main and South Main with all the addresses on the square simply designated as "On The Square." For example, the address for St. Barnabas was simply On The Square, St. Germaine, NC. This used to drive the UPS drivers crazy, but they'd gotten used to it. All the buildings had numbers, of course—they were required by law to have them for 911 calls—but no one ever used them. Most of them weren't even displayed.

"Right on time," I said as Meg walked up.

"I'm always on time."

"I meant me."

Meg smiled one of those dazzling smiles that made me glad I was the one at whom it was aimed. "Yes, you are on time. I'm very pleased. You may kiss my hand."

"Yes, mum," I said, gallantly taking her outstretched hand and brushing her fingers with my lips. "Now then. What's for lunch?"

We sat down on a bench, Meg's basket placed between us. She took the red-checked napkin off the basket and began to unpack. Two bottles of cold Harpoon Ale, turkey sandwiches on thick whole-grain bread, hot German Potato salad and a block of aged Jarlzburg.

"Wow," I said. "This is great. I don't know why I don't marry you."

"Why indeed?" asked Meg, looking at me quizzically. I gulped and tried to change the subject as quickly as etiquette would allow.

"Yes, well...ahem..."

"Never mind," said Meg with a laugh. "You looked positively panic stricken."

"Whew."

"What did Kent have to say?"

I filled her in on Kent's narrative over lunch. I told her about meeting Hogmanay McTavish. We discussed the weather (which was perfect) and some church business. You know, I really *didn't* know why I didn't marry her. Other than the fact that I was terrified.

"You know that I'm off the vestry this election," Meg said, cutting a sizeable piece of the Jarlsburg and handing it to me.

"I'd heard that."

"And I'm on the nominating committee."

I nodded, my mouth too full of cheese to answer.

"What do you think of that new lawyer? Rob Brannon."

I swallowed. "He seems to be a good guy. Rich. Smart. Plenty of time on his hands. He'd be a good choice I guess, but I don't think he'll do it."

"Really. I think he might be interested if I asked him in the right way."

"Nah. You forget that I'm a professional," I said, remembering my recent conversation with Rob. "I can read people. There's no way he's going to be on the vestry. He's not the type."

"You certainly are sure of yourself," Meg said.

"I'm almost always right."

"Would you care to make a wager?"

"I certainly would. What are the stakes?"

"Well," she said, biting her lower lip. "If you win—which we both know you will because you are, after all, a professional—then I will go with you to Seattle next summer and sit through the entire Wagner Ring Cycle."

I could feel my eyes growing wide.

"Really? What's the flip side?"

"If I win—which we both know I won't because I'm only a woman and couldn't possibly convince a single, good-looking lawyer to be on the vestry—then you have to do whatever I ask you to do. No complaining."

"Is this a ploy to get me to marry you?"

"Nothing to do with marriage," Megan said. "Cross my heart. I just don't know what I want you to do yet."

"I don't know. A wager with unidentified stakes? Sounds fishy to me."

"What about this then? If I have to go to Seattle for a week, then you have to go wherever I say. Not to exceed five days."

"Still a bit vague. Will you be coming with me?"

"Maybe. Maybe not. But, if you're chicken, I understand."

"It's a bet," I said. "Seattle, here we come."

"You can't tell him I'm going to ask. That wouldn't be fair."

"Oh, shoot!" I said, suddenly remembering my other quasi-appointment. "I knew there was something else I was supposed to do this morning! The lawyer in question is coming by to look through those papers we found with the body. I'd better run."

"Don't you tell him! I mean it!"

"I won't say a word. Thanks for lunch."

I found Rob back at the station. He was sitting at my desk with a stack of papers in front of him and an empty accordion folder off to the side.

"Find anything interesting?" I asked, my irritation just under the surface, but certainly palpable.

"Oh, hello, Chief," said Rob with a disarming smile, then, seeing my expression, added, "Nancy just stepped out for a moment. She was in here with me till about three minutes ago."

As if on cue, Nancy walked up behind me.

"Sorry, boss," she whispered. "I had to go to the bathroom. Pete came in with Mr. Brannon here and made it clear that he wanted this guy,"—she nodded toward Rob—"to go through the Gifford file."

I nodded and smiled at Nancy who was obviously as irked as I at the intrusion.

"Thanks, Nancy. I'll take it from here."

I turned back to Rob who was busy putting the sheaf of papers back into the folder.

"Find anything interesting?" I repeated.

"Well," Rob said looking down at his notes, "there are two sets of mortgage papers. Unsigned. I don't know if they were refiled, but I suspect they were. Once Lester disappeared, these folks would have started again with his replacement. In the old days, you knew your banker. He knew you and your family and his assessment of your ability to pay back the loan carried a lot of weight. There's the letter to Wilmer Griggs detailing his delinquency and noting the foreclosure date on his farm. There is a ledger with about thirty short-term loan accounts including payments and interest. Nothing over five hundred dollars though. And nothing in arrears. Except for Mr. Griggs, Lester seemed to have quite a good record of making and collecting his loans."

"Wouldn't foreclosing on the farm be advantageous to the bank?"

"Not in the 30's. Coming out of the Great Depression, the last thing a bank wanted was a farm that wasn't making any money."

"Good point."

Rob closed the folder and secured it with a large elastic band. He laid it on the desk.

"Maybe you can find something that I missed."

"I doubt it. I can't imagine that the murderer left any kind of a clue in the folder. Still, we have to go through it."

"Well, call me if I can help," he said, shouldering past me, giving Nancy a nod and disappearing out the front door.

"Harumph," I grunted under my breath.

Chapter 7

"Get me Toby on the phone," I called to Marilyn, Ace Secretary, as I breezed into the office the next morning. My evening with Alice had left me feeling as chipper as the deluxe floor model at Mr. Mulch.

"Toby who?" asked Marilyn, not looking up from the clattering keys of her typewriter.

"Toby Taps. That's who."

Marilyn stopped clattering and peered at me over her half-glasses, her eyes appearing to be half-full, or maybe half-empty, depending on your perspective.

"Toby Taps?" she said through pursed lips. "I thought he was retired."

"He's retired," I said. "But not that retired."

"I don't have his number," said Marilyn as offhandedly as Captain Hook and just as seemingly uninterested as he would have been had he--Captain Hook--been sitting where Marilyn now sat; although typing would be much more difficult, seeing that he couldn't use standard touch-typing technique, having only five fingers and one hook.

"Sure you do, Cupcake. I know you're still seeing him."

Marilyn shrugged and adjusted her glasses, raising and lowering the lenses like the opaque third eyelid of a very pretty crocodile.

"Off and on."

"Well, pretend you're on, and get him for me, will ya?"

"He doesn't like you, you know."

"No one does, Doll-face."

The house was dark. It was six in the evening and this being mid-October, the sun was already an hour gone. I had turned out the lights, fixed myself a sandwich and gotten one of the two remaining Malheur Black Chocolate beers out of the fridge, vowing to myself to save the last for a special occasion.

I shared my house with two pets. There was Baxter, of course. I had gotten him for Meg as a Christmas present, but he had moved in with me as soon as he outgrew Meg's house. My other pet, or rather, part-time lodger, was an owl we had named Archimedes. He had shown up on my windowsill last year and I had begun feeding him the mice that had been foolish enough to try for the cheese in my traps. Eventually he became accustomed to the house. Now came and went at will by way of the automatic window I had installed.

Baxter was in his usual place—asleep in front of the fire. Archimedes had already left for the evening. He tended to leave the house at dusk or just after. Owls are, by nature, creatures of the night and although I still supplemented Archimedes' diet with frozen rodents, he still covered the mountains from dusk till dawn. Occasionally, he'd be gone for a few days or even a week. Then one morning I'd find him sitting on top of the stuffed buffalo in the den, preening his feathers.

The den of my house was actually a log cabin first built in 1842 by, if the authentication certificate was correct, Daniel Boone's granddaughter. In fact, Daniel may have actually stayed in this very cabin. At least, that's what I liked to imagine. It wasn't the only reason I bought the cabin, but it was a good story—and I always liked a good story. I found the cabin in eastern Kentucky and had the logs taken down, numbered, trucked down to my two hundred acres, and reassembled before building the rest of my house around the old structure. The den was two stories with a loft. Twenty feet by twenty feet was about average for a cabin in those days. A census report from 1880 shows eight people were living in it.

I settled into my writing chair and flipped on the banker's light, the only illumination save for the fire. I had the evening to myself—Megan was home with her mother in St. Germaine—and as I lit one of my *Romeo y Julietta* Cubans, I pondered briefly whether I'd want to give all this up and tie the knot. It was something I'd have to approach carefully.

I sat back, punched the button on the Wave remote and heard the first strains of Gorecki's *Symphony Number 3*. Gorecki's symphony had become immensely popular when it was first recorded in 1993, selling well over a million copies. In the classical world that's almost unheard of, especially for a contemporary composer. I had the recording—it was one of the "features-of-the-month" from the record company I subscribe to—but I was enough of a musical snob not to listen to it. Even though Meg recommended it highly, I certainly was not going to be drawn into listening to something so trendy. I had filed it away, unopened and forgotten, until this evening. I had been flipping through the CDs, looking for something mystical and Catholic, both to suit my mood and recent events. A recording of Gregorian Chant just would not do. It was too early in the year for Christmas music. A requiem was out of the question. So I settled on Gorecki—*The Symphony of Sorrowful Songs,* for soprano and orchestra . This evening seemed a good time to hear it. It was dark and cold outside. I would be listening to it simply out of professional curiosity. And besides, I thought, it would be a good time to knock out a couple of exceedingly bad chapters of my latest opus.

I heard the tap, tap, tap coming down the hall toward my office, tiny rhythmic clicks synchronized to elephantine footfalls like the castanets of a Sumo Flamenco dancer. Then I saw him. He filled the doorway like banana pudding forced into a crème-filled donut, all the way to the edges and oozing though the keyhole. He was bigger than the last time I had seen him, but then I remembered that Toby Taps had a lifetime pass to the Hungry Hippo All-You-Can-Eat Buffet courtesy of a little problem he had taken care of for the owner. A little problem called an ex-wife. Not that she had been "ex" when Toby had been hired. But she certainly was "ex" now. Ex-tinguished, that is.

"Ise hoid youse was lookin' for me."

"Youse hoid correctly," I said.

Three things about Toby. First, he was always dressed in a black sharkskin suit, black shirt, black silk tie, a red carnation in the lapel and a black top hat sitting on his head. He was stylish. Second, he always wore tapshoes. It was his trademark. When you heard the tapshoes, you knew you were in trouble. Toby never wanted to sneak up on anyone. He wanted you to know he was coming. And third--Toby Taps had a beautiful tenor voice, small and crystalline. I had heard him sing "Dies Bildniss ist bezaubernd schoen" from The Magic Flute on more than one occasion. It was his favorite aria--the only one he knew--and he sang it at the funeral of every one of his assignments. Toby thought it was a grand gesture and although neither he nor anyone else knew what the words meant, no one said "no" to Toby Taps.

I clicked the return lever on the old typewriter and re-read what I had just written. Genius! I swung my chair around and picked up my sandwich. Then, in spite of myself, I started paying attention to the music. It's an occupational hazard. Usually I can put on some Leon Redbone or Elvis Costello or even Lyle Lovett and type away to my heart's content. It's music to type by. You can hum along to the songs—even sing them if you know the words. This recording was different. I didn't know yet if I liked it or not, but it was one of those works that commanded my attention.

I finished my sandwich and turned off the desk light. Then I took my beer over to my leather chair, put another log on the fire and settled in, cigar in hand, to listen to the recording. And, to be fair, I started it over.

The symphony begins very softly with the basses, then cellos, and then slowly progresses through the orchestra in what one critic called a "canon of despair." It is of the genre labeled "mystic minimalism." Not my cup of tea, but I could see why Meg liked it. The beginning was quite beautiful. I closed my eyes. I might have dozed off.

"So how's my old typewriter holding up?"

I opened my eyes and there he was...again...sitting in my desk chair, his pipe smoking vaguely—although I didn't notice the smell of pipe tobacco—his eyes bright behind his horn-rimmed glasses.

"The typewriter's good," I said, staring.

"You know, sometimes I used a blue ribbon. Just for fun."

"I didn't know."

"So how's the story coming?"

"Okay, I guess. I've got some really first-rate prose ready for the Bulwer-Lytton Contest. I'd really like to win it this year."

He clicked on the desk light. "You know this is pretty good bad writing," he said, flipping through the pages on the desk next to the typewriter.

"Well," I said with a modest shrug. "Thanks."

"But your plot creaks like a broken shutter in an October wind."

"Hey, that's good. Can I use that?"

"I'm sure you will."

I woke up with a start. The Gorecki CD seemed to be stuck and my cigar had fallen into my lap, burning a hole in my sweater. As I patted out the smoldering ash, the symphony reached its final chord and I realized that the CD hadn't been stuck at all and that I had been hearing the same three-chord progression for the past five minutes. I vowed then and there to never again listen to minimalistic music with a lit cigar in my mouth. Then I looked at Baxter. He was standing up, the hair on his back bristling, his gaze firmly directed at my desk, and a low, almost inaudible growl in his throat. I walked over to the desk. It was different than I had left it. The papers beside the typewriter were ruffled and out of order.

And the light was on.

Chapter 8

"You should have seen it! It was so cool," said Moosey.

I had driven up to Ardine McCollough's place on Saturday morning to pick up a couple of apple pies that she had made for me.

Ardine McCollough lived with her three kids in a mobile home up near the Pine Valley Christmas Tree Farm where she worked. She was a single mother and struggled to make ends meet. I helped her out occasionally with groceries and clothes for the children, but she was a proud woman and had informed me early on in no uncertain terms that she didn't take charity. Every time I took the McCollough family anything, the gift was reciprocated. I had taken Bud, the oldest, a couple of my old—but still good—sweaters. I was getting a couple of pies in exchange.

Ardine's husband was abusive when he lived with them. No one had seen him for several years and no one asked where he was. He was one of those people that were never missed once they disappeared. In fact, the entire town breathed a sigh of relief when he stopped frequenting the local establishments. The only interest he ever took in the three children, other than knocking them around, was to name them—which he did—after his only friends. Beer. Bud was fifteen. His sister, Pauli Girl, was twelve. The almost-seven year old was a gregarious little boy named Moose-head. Moosey for short.

Moosey met me at the truck, and, as soon as I stepped out of the cab, he started frisking me with practiced ease, looking for the candy bar I always brought with me on my visits.

"You should have seen it," he repeated.

"Seen what?" I asked. Moosey had found the Mars bar in my coat pocket and was already unwrapping it.

"The Scripture Chicken!" said Moosey, jamming about half of the candy bar into his mouth.

"Did you go to the tent service last night?"

"Mmou mnbeb weeb mmoomd," said Moosey, his mouth now full of chocolate.

"I'll wait," I said. "Why don't you swallow first?"

Moosey chewed as fast as he could and gulped down the first half of his candy bar.

"You bet we went," he said with a gulp. "We was on the front row. You shoulda seen that chicken."

I looked up and noticed that Ardine had come out onto the front stoop of her trailer. She looked like a woman who had lived a hard life. Looking at her, anyone might guess her age at fifty or so judging from the premature lines etched into her face. She was probably about twenty years younger than that. Ardine was thin, kept her hair pulled back, rarely wore makeup and had a habit of crossing her arms in front of her that gave her a look of perpetual distrust.

"Brother Hog," said Moosey, "...that was his name, swear to God...put this chicken on top of this giant Bible and the chicken started scratching around and then started peckin' at one of the pages and Brother Hog had a man read where the chicken was peckin' and then said he was going to preach on what the Holy Spirit had told the chicken to pick." I was impressed. Moosey got the whole sentence out in one breath.

"He let us pet the chicken afterwards," said Moosey. "He said that she was a holy chicken and that we shouldn't pull her feathers. Her name is Binny Hen." Moosey started on the other half of the Mars bar.

"That sounds like great fun," I said as I walked up to Ardine.

"It was pretty good," said Ardine in her flat voice. "I liked the sermon better than the chicken, but I guess that if that's how the Lord chooses to speak through Brother Hog, I don't guess I can fault the Almighty for it."

"The chicken really picked out the scripture?"

"Far as I could tell. And I was sittin' right up there. That chicken started scratchin' at them pages, and then, after some pages had been turned, she started peckin'. That's when Brother Hog says 'The Holy Spirit has shown Binny Hen our scripture for this evening. Brother Gene shall now read it, and then I shall preach on it.' And he did."

"What scripture was it?"

"It was Second Corinthians. The Love Chapter."

"That was a good choice by the chicken."

"It was the Holy Spirit," said Ardine with finality. "And there were five people saved and three rededications."

"I'm glad it was a success. Are you going back tonight?"

"Yep. And takin' the kids, too. Brother Hog's gonna let 'em take up the offering tonight."

"Sounds like a fun evening."

"Nothin' fun about it," said Ardine, opening the door and holding it for me to enter. "This is God's work."

"You saw *who*?" asked Meg. We were sitting in a booth at the Slab having a late lunch. The crowd of bun-lookers had slimmed for the time being.

"You know, I hesitate to even bring this up," I said. "I may have been dreaming. I'm pretty sure I dozed off during that Gorecki piece you've been after me to listen to."

"Did you like it?"

"The symphony or the ghost?"

"Well, the symphony. We're both pretty sure you were dreaming about the ghost."

"Why are we pretty sure?"

"Because," said Meg, "if you actually did see Raymond Chandler's ghost and talked with him, he would have begged you to stop defiling his typewriter."

"He said I was pretty good."

"Which simply proves my point. You had to be dreaming."

"It seemed pretty real. He left the light on."

"No kidding," said Pete pulling up a chair to the end of the booth. "He left the light on?" I hadn't known Pete was listening in. But I should realize by now that there are no secrets at the Slab.

"Hmmm. What about the symphony then?" Meg was persistent.

"It was OK. I liked the first movement."

"But then you fell asleep?"

"And burnt a hole in my sweater," I added in disgust. "I could have burned the house down. All thanks to minimalism."

"Well, at least you listened to it."

"Yep. Now I have to listen to *Belshazzar's Feast*. Or maybe *Falstaff*. Just to cleanse my palate."

"Back to the ghost," said Pete. "What did he look like? Could you see through him? Did you feel a cold wind?"

"Nope. It looked just like the pictures I've seen of him. He was smoking a pipe."

"You saw a ghost?" asked Noylene, walking up behind Pete with the coffee pot. "I never saw a ghost, but I talked to one once. Through Madam Cleo. You know, that woman on TV. I talked to my old beautician. She told me to go back to my original hair color and to switch from red nail polish to 'passion pink'. It made all the difference."

"He was just dreaming," said Meg through clenched teeth. "See what you've done," she hissed at me.

"I was probably dreaming," I agreed.

"He was dreaming," agreed Pete.

"I don't know," said Noylene, doubtfully.

"Thanks for coming in, Hayden," said Father George, making a rare Saturday appearance at the church. "I need to talk to you about something."

"No problem," I said, sitting down in the chair that the priest had offered. "I was coming in to practice a bit anyway." Father George took his seat behind his desk.

"We're going to have a new position at St. Barnabas. A Parish Administrator."

I shrugged. "I've heard of them. What would he do exactly?"

"Well, mainly he...or she," he added thoughtfully, "would be in charge of all the business affairs of the church. Budgets, writing the checks, scheduling the sextons, hiring and firing non-salaried workers. That sort of thing."

"Who does all that now?"

"Well, the duties are spread around. I do some of it. Marilyn does some scheduling, but she really doesn't have time. Carol comes in and writes the checks once a month, but she doesn't keep track of budgets. I just think it's time to get it all consolidated."

"Fine by me. You have anyone in mind yet?"

"Not yet. We'll probably advertise for the position." Father George stood up indicating that he'd said what he had to say—a quality I admired about him. I nodded and got to my feet as well.

"By the way, I read that article about you in the Charlotte paper."

"I had nothing to do with that. I don't even know where that stuff came from."

"Hmmm," said Father George with a small nod. Then he changed the subject. "Is there any word on the man found in the altar?"

"He's at the morgue. There'll be an autopsy, but I probably won't hear anything until next week."

"If they need money to bury him properly, I have some in my discretionary fund."

"I appreciate that. I'll let the coroner know."

"Do you want to go over to the revival?" asked Meg. "Apparently, it's the best show in town."

"I think I'll skip it. Thanks for asking though."

"You know, he didn't have any music lined up, but then, after folks heard about last night, every service is booked with a choir. It was the chicken that did it."

"I'll consider it. I would like to see that chicken in action."

"Well, I think you should. Mamma wants to go so I'm going to take her next week, I think."

"I have these two apple pies," I said. "We could rent a movie, have some dinner and finish with some dessert.

"Then we could have some pie," Meg said with a smile.

Chapter 9

Chapter 9

"What's the grift?" asked Toby, still out of breath from tapping up the stairs. His voice was wheezing like a broken accordion in a Lutheran nursing home dance band. His tapshoes were beginning a rhythm on the linoleum.

"I've got a dead girl. I need to know who iced her."

"How would I know?" said Toby Taps, getting his wind and moving into a step-ball-change-flap-ball-change beside the desk.

"You know everything, Toby. If there is a murder in this neighborhood, you know who did it."

"What's in it for me?" Toby executed a very nice paddle and roll.

"I'll teach you another aria."

I had his attention now. Another thing about Toby Taps. He didn't want to be thought of as a one-trick pony. That was four things about Toby--he was stylish, he always wore taps, he had a good tenor voice, and the one-trick pony thing.

"Yeah? Which one?"

"Well, you've got a nice leggiero tenor with a good range. I've heard a high B, haven't I?"

"High C."

One more thing about Toby Taps. It didn't pay to disparage his range. That was five things then: style, tapshoes, good tenor, the pony thing and his high notes.

"I must have been thinking about Cleamon 'Codfish' Downs," I said, backpedaling as fast as Lance Armstrong on rewind.

"Yeah, Codfish had a high B. It's a shame someone dropped a piano on him." Toby implemented a single outward pirouette followed by a slap-riffle-scuff-scuff-repeat.

"How about 'Deposuit' from the Bach <u>Magnificat</u>?"

"I don't want nothin' in Latin."

I had forgotten that little fact about Toby Taps. He didn't want anything to do with Catholics. He went to a parochial school when he was a kid, but was tossed out after an incident involving the Mother Superior, a lit cigarette, a live ferret, and a can of potted meat. That was six, I thought, still trying to keep track--fashionable, tapshoes, good tenor, the pony thing, high notes and a bad case of cathlo-phobia.

"How about 'The Holy City?'"

Toby stopped dead in the middle of a shim-sham-shimmy and put a hand to his chin in thought.

"Yeah. I kinda like 'The Holy City.'"

"What do you say?" I asked.

"Let's dance," said Toby.

That's one thing about Toby, I thought. Nah. Never mind.

"I hear you've been chatting up a ghost," said Rob Brannon on Sunday morning. As a substitute usher, he'd come up to the choir loft to leave the bulletins for the choir. I was putting the hymn descants along with the first chapters of *The Tenor Wore Tapshoes* in the back of the choir's music folders.

"Well," I said sheepishly, "I was probably dreaming."

"That's probably it. Any word on our dead body?" I noticed that Rob had taken ownership pretty quickly.

"Maybe tomorrow."

"I talked with Meg this morning during Sunday School. She seems pretty keen on me being on the vestry."

"She mentioned it to me. I told her that I thought you'd be a good choice."

"Well, I guess if they really need me, I'll be happy to serve."

"That's great, Rob. Just great."

"I guess Rob told you the news," said Meg with what might have been just a hint of triumph in her voice.

"Yes, I guess he did," I said sullenly. "What a schmuck. What a turncoat. What a weasel. What a ..."

"Oh, stop. You don't have to be so grumpy. Why don't you just admit that I have some charms that you may have been taking for granted?"

"Yes, well, I admit it," I said sullenly. "But now we don't get to go to Seattle."

"Oh, we're *going* to Seattle. I already have the tickets."

I'm sure I looked confused.

"But you have to go somewhere for me," Meg added.

This was ominous and I didn't like the sound of it one bit. "And where would that be?"

"You have to go to the Iron Mike Men's Retreat."

My worst fears were realized. The Iron Mike Men's Retreat was sponsored by the Council of Churches in Boone every year at about this time—cold enough for campfires but not too cold to stay in tents under the stars at the Baptist Conference Center. I had been making fun of it for years.

"Absolutely not!" I said.

"Well, I never figured you for a welsher. And I did get the tickets for Seattle."

"Opera tickets, too?"

"Fourth row orchestra."

"Aww, sheesh. Not the Men's Retreat," I whined.

"You need to get in touch with your inner-man."

"Who says? My inner-man is just fine. He doesn't like to be touched."

"It's only overnight. And a bet's a bet."

Monday morning, bright and early, Nancy, Dave and I decided to make the trek across the street and brave the throng of now ever-present pilgrims to the shrine of the Immaculate Confection. It wasn't nearly as crowded as it had been last week when Pete took out his ad, but there was still a line.

Nancy had called ahead and reserved our table, so we snuck in the back door, through the kitchen, around the counter and sat down before the other patrons noticed their position had been usurped. It probably didn't matter that much, but we didn't want Pete's customers to be irked at our preferential treatment. Nancy, at least, was dressed in her uniform. That gave us a little credibility. Everyone knows that the police force always gets a table.

"The bun is looking a little peaked," I remarked as Pete came over and sat down, completing our foursome.

"I should have gotten it glazed."

"I thought it *was* glazed," said Dave.

"No. I mean shellacked. Covered in polyurethane. Sealed for all eternity."

"But then we couldn't eat it," said Dave.

Nancy rolled her eyes. "We're not going to eat it anyway, Dave. It's already a week old. If we wanted a cinnamon roll, we could just get a fresh one."

Dave shrugged. "I would have eaten it, I guess."

"No one's going to eat it. It's a national treasure," said Pete. "I'll go down to the hardware store and get some polyurethane this afternoon. It'll be as good as new tomorrow morning."

"It looks like the Virgin Mary is getting wrinkles," I said.

"Now she *really* looks like Jimmy Durante," Nancy chimed in. "Look at her nose."

"Shhh," Pete said. "The other customers are looking at us. You guys want a t-shirt? Twenty percent off."

"No, thanks," said Nancy.

"No, thanks," I agreed.

"I should get a free one," muttered Dave. "I discovered her."

Our breakfast came family style as per Pete's order—plates of pancakes, scrambled eggs, sausage, a basket of biscuits, a big bowl of grits, and a pitcher of gravy. We dug in as Noylene came around and refilled our coffee cups.

"Any news on the body?" asked Pete, happily polishing off his scrambled eggs.

"Nothing yet," I said. "Maybe Kent will have something today. You have anything, Nance?"

"Matter of fact, I do."

I didn't expect Nancy to have any information. Not this early. But Nancy frequently surprised me. I looked over at her in expectation. She finished the last bite of her pancakes, put down her fork, took a gulp of coffee and pulled out her notepad.

"Lester Gifford—our victim—was born on June 12th, 1892, in Watauga County. He was married to Mavis O'Quinn on May 27th, 1924. He was thirty-two years old. She was twenty when they married. I checked the birth records in Watauga County for the years 1924 to 1937. No record of any children that I could find. The last known documentation of Mr. Gifford's presence is a mention of him in the newspaper on January 15th, 1937, in conjunction with a bank merger.

"Mr. Gifford worked for the Watauga County Bank. He was an assistant manager. A loan officer and in charge of the tellers. In 1937, Watauga County Bank was taken over by Northwestern Bank. The merger article was the piece in which Mr. Gifford was mentioned."

"Was there a missing persons report?" asked Dave.

"No police records from that far back."

"How about the wife? Do we know what happened to her?" I asked.

"No clue. She may have left the area. She might have remarried. I didn't check the marriage records."

"I don't think it matters," I said, "unless she killed him. Does either Lester or his wife have any connection to St. Barnabas?"

"I asked Marilyn for the membership roles. They've got all the information on computer now. It's a lot easier than looking through a bunch of old birth records in the county courthouse."

"And?"

"No connection. But here's the strange thing. There was a fire at St. Barnabas in 1937."

"Really? I didn't know anything about that."

"February 8th. The fire began in the records room. According to a small blurb in the *Watauga Democrat,* although arson was suspected, the fire went out pretty quickly. Some stuff was destroyed. Mostly financial records from what I can gather. A few years of baptismal records. But most of the records were recovered and recopied. Marilyn didn't know anything about it either."

"Well, it was almost seventy years ago. I doubt that there's anyone around that *would* remember. Especially if it wasn't a major fire."

"It wasn't."

"So," I said, "Lester Gifford is murdered sometime after January, 1937. There's a bank merger where he works, and a fire in the records room of St. Barnabas in February. Do you know when the merger took place?"

"Of course. February 25th was the official date." Nancy looked extremely smug.

"And?"

"And there's no record of Lester Gifford ever being on the payroll of Northwestern Bank."

"So he was either canned or he quit," Pete said.

"Or was murdered," Dave added. "Maybe it's all coincidence."

" Is that all?" I asked Nancy.

"Nope."

"There's more?" asked Pete.

"I don't know how she finds all this stuff out in two days," said Dave.

"Because, Dave, I work at it," said Nancy.

"Yeah, well I have to answer the phones."

"And get the donuts," I added, turning back to Nancy. "What's the rest?"

"The president of Watauga County Bank at the time of the merger—a Mr. Harold Lynn—was the Senior Warden at St. Barnabas."

"That's no coincidence," Dave said.

"And a Sunday School teacher named Jacob Winston—also a bank teller at Watauga County Bank—was arrested, but never tried, for murder."

I was in the office later that morning when I answered the call from Kent Murphee.

"Hayden. This is Kent."

"What's the news?"

"Well, two things."

I waited.

"First," Kent began, "the cause of death was as you expected. Your boy was killed by a blow to the back of the head. Easy to see once you and Nancy got him out of the altar. It was a pretty good shot—broke the skull causing hemorrhaging in the brain. An amazing autopsy, quite frankly. I videoed the whole thing."

"Amazing in what way?"

"The body was perfect. Except, of course, that he was dead and his head was smashed in. His tissue was in perfect condition—even the part of his brain where the trauma occurred. It was like Lester had just died yesterday."

"So you were right about the incorruptible thing. What else?"

"It's very strange. I did most of the autopsy on Friday afternoon, then put him back in the cooler. This morning, when I pulled him back out, there was severe rigor. The body had started decomposing at a normal rate. Starting—and I'm only guessing here from the rigor in the muscles—on Saturday evening."

"So he's not an incorruptible?"

"Well, not any more. I keep trying to think if it had anything to do with the autopsy, but I don't think it did. Scientifically, anyway."

"Scientifically?"

"Well, the other explanation would be sort of...well... miraculous."

"And that would be?"

"That an Incorruptible only remains incorrupt as long as we believe in the miracle. As soon as I did the autopsy, the miracle came to an end and the body returned to its earthly condition. Right where it left off."

"You believe that?"

"Hell, Hayden. I'm a Catholic. I don't know what to believe."

I laughed over the phone.

"You know what I mean. Anyway, I'll do some more tests and let you know. So for now, he was definitely murdered. Blunt trauma to the back of the head. Nothing in the wound."

"I don't know how far we'll go with this thing. There's no statute of limitations on murder, but unless he was killed by a young teenager, whoever did it is most probably already dead."

"Maybe Nancy wants to work on it."

"Yeah, maybe she does. If she solves it, she can at least get some regional recognition—maybe write up a paper and present it to a couple law-enforcement conferences. It's an interesting case." I nodded to myself as I thought about it. "It's a great idea, Kent. I'll see if she wants to give it a go. Thanks."

"No problem. I'll keep you informed."

Chapter 10

"Who youse got?" asked Toby Taps.

"I've got the dead girl, Candy Blather, alias Latte Espresso. She was killed on the dining room table."

"Knife in the heart, head in the mashed potatoes?"

"That's her. You know who did it?"

"Maybe," said Toby. "Who else youse got?"

"I've got her sister, Starrbuck. I've got the feds, too."

"Alice Uberdeutchland?"

"Yep."

"Anyone else?" asked Toby T, tapping a tantalizing tarantella on the terrazzo.

"I've got Piggy Wilson. Candy was into him for about fifty large."

"Yeah, Piggy. Youse knows about the hymnal scam?"

"I've heard. But you could fill in the gaps."

"Piggy didn't do it," said Toby Taps. "It's not his style and besides, he still needed her to woik the fiddle."

"You got another name for me?"

"Jimmy Leggs."

"Jimmy Leggs!?" said Megan in obvious disgust. "That's the stupidest name I've ever heard."

"It's a tap-dancing motif."

"Jimmy Leggs? Alice Uberdeutchland? With names like these, you'll never get an agent. You'll never make millions of dollars and become the John Grisham of your generation, whiling away your time on your Mississippi riverboat, fighting off hoards of beautiful, money-grubbing, half-naked law clerks."

"John Grisham *is* my generation."

"It's too late then. You should give up now and maybe start a new career selling Bell-Tone hearing aids door to door."

"Did someone come a-knocking at your door?" I asked with a chuckle.

"Yes, and he was deliberately talking too softly."

"I have a career, my dear. I'm a highly paid law enforcement professional."

"Really? Highly paid? You forget that I do your taxes."

"Well, I have a lot of money."

"Yes. Mostly thanks to me."

"OK, then. Do you have a better name for the hit-man than Jimmy Leggs?" I asked.

"Hmmm. Let me ponder a moment," Meg said, putting a finger to her lips in mock-thought. "Instead of Jimmy, how about his brother, Harry? Yes! That's it! Harry Leggs!"

Meg was almost fast enough to make it out of the room ahead of the sofa cushion. Almost.

"I've been robbed!"

Pete was frantic. I hadn't heard him this frantic since his walk-in went out on a Friday afternoon and the repairman couldn't get parts for a week and a half.

"We'll be right over," I said, hanging up the phone and motioning to Nancy.

"We'll be back in a bit, Dave."

"What's up?"

"Pete's been robbed."

"Should I come?"

"Nope. Someone has to stay in the office."

"Bring me a sandwich then."

Pete met us at the door of the Slab Café.

"How much did they get?" asked Nancy. "Did you leave the money in the register?"

"They didn't take any money," said Pete, holding the door open for us. Noylene was cleaning the fancy glass cake plate in the middle of the counter. The empty cake plate.

"The bun?" I asked.

"Stolen," said Pete. "I'm ruined."

"You're hardly ruined. But all good things must come to an end."

"That's easy for you to say. I took out another newspaper ad. It's going to run tomorrow. There's only one thing to do," Pete said. "I've got to make another roll that looks just like the last one."

"You can't do that," said Noylene. "It was a miracle. If the Virgin Mary chooses to appear in a cinnamon roll, and it gets stolen, you can't just make another one. She doesn't work like that."

"Well, I've got to do something."

"What about fingerprints?" asked Nancy, pulling out her pad. "Was there a break-in? Was the lock forced? A window broken? How did the thief get in?"

"All good questions," I said. "Why don't we all sit down and get the whole story. Noylene, quit cleaning up. You're destroying evidence. Now, how 'bout some coffee?"

Pete, Noylene, Nancy and I chose a table in the back of the café. Collette brought over a coffee pot and four cups.

"I came in at five-thirty as usual to get breakfast ready," Pete said. "Through the back door. I didn't even go into the restaurant—just into the kitchen."

"Was it jimmied?" asked Nancy.

"Not that I noticed."

"Any windows broken?"

"I don't think so. Collette can go check," said Pete, indicating his suggestion to Collette who scurried into the kitchen.

"I came in at six," said Noylene. "Through the back. I said hello to Pete and came into the restaurant to make some coffee and do the prep for the breakfast shift."

"Did you notice the roll missing?" I asked.

"Not at first. But after about a half hour or so, I was wiping down the counter and I noticed that she was gone. I remember it was 6:30 because I was just going to open the doors. Collette was waiting for me to let her in."

"The bun was just gone? Did you tell Pete?"

"Yep. Gone. The glass lid was on the plate just like it is now, but the plate was empty. I thought that Pete took it out. You know, to shellac it like he was talkin' about yesterday. I didn't even go ask him about it till JJ asked where it was. She was in here for breakfast."

"I bought the poly yesterday, but I hadn't dipped it yet," said Pete. "It should have been on the plate."

"Then you called us?" asked Nancy.

"Well, we had to wait until you showed up for work," said Pete. "Lucky you're early this morning."

I looked at my watch. It showed 8:10. It *was* early for us. The door opened and Dave walked in.

"You're supposed to be answering the phones," said Nancy with just a little annoyance in her voice.

"Got it covered," said Dave, pointing to the cell-phone dangling from his belt. "All calls forwarded to my cell." He pulled up a chair.

"The windows are all okay," said Collette, coming back into the dining room. "Hi, Dave," she said, her cheeks coloring nicely. Nancy noticed it as well and bristled visibly. Although she had never shown any interest in Dave that I had seen, he was, after all, her own private lap dog.

"Did you have any customers this morning?" I asked, turning my attention back to the crime at hand.

"The usual morning crew plus a few newcomers. The bulk of

the customers have been coming in around 9:15. I don't know what I'll tell them," said Pete.

"Tell them that the Vatican has asked for the bun to be loaned to the Catholic Diocese of North Carolina for a few days, to confirm its validity and to have it certified by the Pope," said Dave.

"Hey, that's really good, Dave," said Pete, nodding in agreement. "It just might work. At least until I can cook up another Virgin Mary roll. It may take a few tries."

"Thanks," said Dave. "I discovered her, you know."

"Why don't I give my son a call?" said Noylene. "He could come up and help find her."

"I didn't know you had a son," said Nancy.

"Yep. Livin' in Hickory. He's getting' his license to be a private detective. I'm sure he'll come up if there's a reward offered."

"A reward?" asked Pete. "What kind of reward?"

"I dunno," said Noylene with a shrug. "Maybe fifty bucks."

"What if there's a ransom demand?" chimed in Collette. "They'll probably ask for more than fifty dollars."

"I don't think there will be a ransom demand," I said. "It's probably just a prank. Let's give it a day or two. How about some breakfast?"

"You guys go ahead," said Pete. "I'm going to print up a sign saying that pope-y stuff that Dave was talking about. Tell me again, will you Dave?"

"How about this?" said Dave. "The Virgin Mary Cinnamon Roll, also known as the Immaculate Confection, is temporarily unavailable for viewing. It has been sent to the Vatican for authentication and blessing by the Pope and will be returned in a few days.'" Dave was obviously inspired. Collette gave him a suspicious look.

"That'll work," said Pete, writing furiously on a napkin. "I'll put 'Thank you...The Management' underneath and give a thirty percent discount on all the shirts and mugs. That should make the customers happy and buy us a couple of days."

"But it's a lie," said Noylene.

"It *may* not be a total lie," I said with all the seriousness I could muster. "Maybe it was the Vatican that stole it. If it really *is* the Virgin Mary, that would make sense. The Pope would want to see her first-hand. He might have sent some of those Swiss Guards in here to purloin the holy pastry."

"Although I haven't seen anyone suspicious wearing yellow pantaloons," added Nancy.

"I think you're making the miracle too commercial," said Collette quietly. "I don't think she'd like it if you said the Pope was going to bless her and he wasn't."

"I was just kidding, Collette," I said hastily, seeing the seriousness in her face. "I don't think that the Vatican is behind the theft."

"Oh please, " Pete said, maybe a little too sarcastically. "It's just a cinnamon roll. Have you guys ever been to the Vatican? You can buy most anything—all blessed by the Pope. You can get holy water, rosaries, crosses, Bibles...even pizza. If the Pope actually waved his hand over everything that was sold as 'pope-blessed,' he'd never have time to do anything else. Besides," he said, raising his hands in a gesture of innocence, "I'm just saying that we sent it to the Pope for a blessing. I never said that he actually would bless it."

"That's a pretty thin hair to split," I said. "Especially since you didn't send it at all. Don't forget that you're colluding with the police here. I'd think twice about this if I were you."

"I'm just trying to soften the disappointment for my customers. Not to mention that I've got quite a bit of cash wrapped up in this deal. I'd like to at least make my investment back."

"I think you've already managed that," I said. "The crowds at the Slab have been pretty good for the past week."

"I guess," said Pete, sullenly. "I suppose I can always use the coffee mugs. But I still have about a gross of these shirts. I'll tell you one thing. If I do manage to make another VM cinnamon roll, this time I'm going to polyurethane it right away and put a lock on the case."

"Breakfast?" I suggested again.

"I'll get it," said Collette.

"I'm giving D'Artagnan a call anyway," said Noylene with a note of finality as she got to her feet.

"Who?" I asked.

"You know. My son."

"His name is D'Artagnan? D'Artagnan Fabergé?"

"He's a detective."

"By the way," said Marilyn as I walked by on my way up to the choir loft. "You missed the staff meeting this morning."

"Couldn't be helped," I said. "There were big doin's a-foot at the Slab. It's a major crime scene."

"Yes, well, I thought you should probably know that there will be a 'Puppet-Moment' during the worship service a week from Sunday."

"A Puppet-Moment?"

"Brenda's back from her Puppet Ministry Conference. I believe she purchased four fairly expensive puppets. She's very excited."

"I'll bet."

"I thought you should know. Just in case there will be some special music as well."

I could feel a shiver creeping up my spine. "Thanks."

"You're welcome," said Marilyn in her sweetest, yet somehow cruelest voice.

Chapter 11

I had heard of Jimmy Leggs. Everyone had. Jimmy was the most notorious button-man in the biz. No one I knew had ever seen him. He could blend in like a midget nun at a penguin convention.

"Why do you think it was Jimmy Leggs?" I asked Toby Taps.

"It's his bindle. He's sendin' a message."

"A message to who?"

"To Piggy."

"What's the message?"

"How should I know?" said Toby, shrugging his shoulders like Janet Reno shivering off horse-flies. "I'm not Piggy."

"This is excellent writing," said Fred, one of the St. Barnabas basses, as the tardy members of the choir made their way up to the loft for choir practice.

"I second that," said Bob Solomon. " I can just about picture Janet Reno shivering off horse-flies."

"Please stop encouraging him," said Meg.

"I second *that*," said McKenna. "I don't want to picture Janet Reno doing anything."

"Are we singing for the All Saints Service?" asked Marjorie, reaching for the flask she kept in her music rack.

"Two weeks from Monday night. November 1st. Seven o'clock," I said.

"Halloween's on Sunday then?" She took a swig.

"It is," I said. "*How Lovely is Thy Dwelling Place* on All Saint's Sunday. *Give Us the Wings of Faith* for the Monday night service. There's only one more rehearsal after this one. Next Wednesday is the vestry election so there will be no choir practice."

"Are we singing anything for the puppet show?" asked Elaine.

"How did you find out about the puppet show?"

"Brenda's telling everyone," said Georgia. "It's not a secret, you know."

"I don't have any information yet on the puppet show. We have a lot of music to learn, though, so let's get started."

"Have you shown this latest episode to your ghost?" asked Rebecca.

"Nope. He hasn't shown up." I decided to treat this latest revelation as humorously as I could. I hadn't known that my ghost story had made the St. Germaine grapevine.

"Maybe you could send it to Janet Reno," Meg said.

I was interested in the chicken. I had gotten the word about Brother Hog's second service. Apparently the chicken had chosen Romans 6:23 as the scripture of the evening. That was one good chicken. Second Corinthians 11 on the first night followed by "The wages of sin is death." Brother Hog might be good, but I suspected that he was hedging his bets. What were the chances that, out of 31,102 verses in the Bible (a number I just happen to know thanks to my religion class in college and a defect in my brain that also remembers Avogadro's Number and the value of Pi to twelve places), Binny Hen managed to pick out two of the most quoted, most preached on, and most familiar scriptures in the entire book? Slim, I thought. Chicken slim. Anorexic. Even *with* the Holy Spirit.

Chickens, I suspected, were fairly stupid. I didn't know this to be true, never having actually owned a chicken, but, like everyone else, I had my prejudices. As Americans, we like to think that we only eat dumb animals—animals that wouldn't really care if they were eaten or not. Horses, cats, dogs, parakeets, pet monkeys: these are off limits. Pigs were the exception. Pigs are reputedly the geniuses of the animal kingdom, often found working out differential equations in the mud. Unfortunately for them, they are ugly and it's our God-given right to eat ugly animals. Either dumb or ugly, that's the rule. Or if they taste really good.

I stopped by the revival tent on my way into work and found it set up exactly as I had the first time I'd visited. The table, with its sawdust-covered top and clip-on pleated fabric sides was directly in front of the pulpit. The Bible was not on the table, probably having been put away until time for the next service. It was the Bible I was looking for.

In my opinion, there was one of four explanations for the Great Chicken Revival. Number one, and the one I had to be careful of, was that it really *was* the Holy Spirit causing the chicken to choose scriptures that would allow Brother Hog's message to move the hearts of the men and women who heard him. I was doubtful, but I certainly wasn't going to discount the possibility. I had seen stranger things. Number two—Binny Hen could have been one of those chicken geniuses. A *poulet-savant*. I was prepared to dismiss this explanation. I hadn't met the Scripture Chicken, but chicken geniuses were almost unheard of north of Atlanta. The third explanation was that the readers had somehow been prompted to read a pre-selected scripture. Brother Hog had someone from the congregation read the pre-chosen passage. But Ardine was the reader last Saturday, and I knew she wouldn't have been in cahoots with the minister in any kind of deception. That left number four. The Bible was rigged.

I pulled back one of the fabric panels, looked under the table and saw a large, black fiberboard case that was the perfect size, I surmised, to hold the book in question. I opened the case, took out the huge Bible and laid it on the table in front of me. I opened it and read a bit of Isaiah. Then I turned over to Second Corinthians to see if I could spot anything on the page that would cause the chicken to choose that particular scripture. I flipped through some pages, smiled, closed the book, put it back in its case and put the case back where I'd found it. Tomorrow, I thought, would be a good night to come to the revival.

Thursday was always a good day to lunch at the Ginger Cat—this Thursday in particular. The weather was cool, breezy and overcast, foreshadowing a hard winter like a bad novelist. It wasn't cold yet, but the conditions hinted at the prompt possibility. Thursdays were good because on Thursdays the soup chef came up from Asheville. She drove up in the morning, her respite from the restaurant that was her full-time job, cooked the soups for the week and headed back to the big city. I didn't know what kind of arrangement Anne Cooke had made with her, but whatever the cost, it was worth it. Thursdays were the best. During the rest of the week, the choice of soup was limited to one. On Thursdays, the customers could sample any of the five or six kinds that were currently brewing.

The Ginger Cat was more of an up-scale gift shop than a restaurant. There were only four tables, almost always commandeered at lunchtime, and today was no exception. Due to the lack of seating, most customers chose to get their lunch "to-go." Meg had arrived early however, garnered us a table, and was going over her soup options with Cynthia when I arrived.

"What's on the menu today?" I asked Cynthia as I pulled out a chair.

Cynthia looked down at her pad. "Pumpkin, Zesty Tomato Lentil, Winter Vegetable, Garlic, Sausage Bean Chowder and Split Pea."

"Garlic Soup?" Meg asked, wrinkling up her nose.

"It smells really good. We have sourdough bread bowls today, too. Eleanor brought them up with her from Asheville."

"I'll have the Sausage Bean Chowder," I said, "in a bread bowl."

Meg pursed her lips and decided. "I guess I'll have the Tomato."

"And I'd like one of those African Yorgi-whatchamacallits. The coffee thing."

"Ah yes, our Ethiopian Yergacheffe."

"Exactly," I said. Cynthia looked over at Meg.

"Tea, please. Assam Golden Tip."

"What's that?" I asked.

"Our newest tea from India," said Cynthia, jumping in, eager to show off her tea-knowledge. "Assam is a province. Golden Tip is a flowery orange pekoe with a sweet malty taste, hints of honey, toast, and a just a bit of wood."

"You sound like a wine-snob," I said with a laugh.

"A tea-snob," said Cynthia, departing with a sniff.

"Hayden!" said a voice from front of the shop. I recognized it and took a deep breath. It was Rob Brannon and I was still miffed.

"I'm waiting for my soup order," he said, sitting down in an unoccupied chair. "Then I've got to walk the puppies."

"I'll bet they're cute," said Meg. To Meg, all puppies were cute. "What kind are they?"

"Actually, they're not puppies anymore. I just call them that as sort of a joke. Lucifer and Gabriel are guard dogs. Rottweilers to be exact."

"Are they vicious?"

"They are...well-trained," said Rob, choosing his words carefully.

"Glad to hear it," I said.

"What kind of soup did you get?" asked Megan, changing the subject.

"Pumpkin. I've never had Pumpkin Soup." He turned his attention to me. "Did you ever hear anything about the dead fellow?"

"He was murdered, but it was a long time ago. Probably

nothing we can do at this point. I doubt the culprit is still alive."

Rob seemed disappointed. "What about the condition of the body?"

"Very strange. Kent didn't know what to make of it. He's doing some more tests. It started to decompose at a normal rate as soon as it arrived at the morgue."

"Weird. By the way, Hayden, I heard about that cinnamon roll. Did you know it was being advertised on eBay?"

"What?" I was genuinely shocked.

"You might want to give it a look. The bidding is over four thousand dollars."

"Four thousand dollars? For a cinnamon roll? Who's selling it?"

"Just give it a look."

Rob's number was called, and he got up and walked over to the counter to pick up his lunch.

"You guys have a great day," he called over his shoulder.

After a delicious lunch, I went back to the station, walked into my office, closed the door, got onto the computer and went to the eBay site. I clicked on the search field and typed in "Immaculate Confection." Only one item was found. I clicked on it. There, on my computer screen, was a picture of the cinnamon roll in all its sanctified glory. It had been photographed on the altar of a church. It was an altar I recognized. I scanned the page. There had been eight bids starting at twenty-five dollars. The highest bid was now four thousand eight hundred sixty. I clicked on the bid history. Three of the eight bids were by the same person. The other five bidders were all different. I clicked back and scanned the page again. The on-line auction had a week to go, the bidding having started yesterday evening at 8:00 PM. I looked over to get the seller's information. His (or her) eBay seller name was Esterhazy. The item location was listed as North Carolina. I clicked on "seller information." There was none. This was the seller's first transaction. There was no feedback and he'd only been a member since the day the ad appeared. I clicked on "ID history." It listed the ID (Esterhazy), the effective date (yesterday) and a partially blocked out e-mail address. I clicked back, went to "ask the seller a question" and found I had to register to do so. I didn't bother. Instead, I got up, walked over to the door and opened it.

"Nancy, could you come in here a second?"

"Sure."

When Nancy came in, I pointed her to the computer monitor. She sat down in my chair and read the screen quickly.

"Esterhazy? What's up with that?"

"It's a pretty thinly veiled attempt to point the finger at Yours Truly."

"Why would it point to you?"

"Prince Esterhazy was the benefactor of Haydn in the eighteenth century. Probably the most famous patron of the arts ever. Well, after the Medicis."

"Hmmm," said Nancy. "Haydn, eh? I remember the name, now that you mention it. But how many people would know that? One in a hundred? Five hundred?"

"Probably five hundred. It's obscure enough to make it sound like something I'd come up with, but easily figured out if the right person sees it. What do you think?"

"You're right. It sounds just like you. Very droll and obtuse, but smug and just a bit too enamored of your cleverness."

"Hey..." I said, "I think I'm offended."

"I'm agreeing with you," said Nancy with a smile. "Who would know? If they saw it, that is?"

"Meg would know. Rhiza. Maybe a couple of people in the choir. I probably mentioned Esterhazy at some point when we were doing the *Little Organ Mass*."

"That's quite a few."

"Yeah, but all the people I know tend to be interested in music. Esterhazy is pretty basic music history stuff."

"Why would Pete know?"

"He was a music major in college for a couple of semesters—saxophone and jazz. Anyway, find out who posted this, will you? And let me know as quickly as you can."

"It's up to fifty-five hundred," Nancy said.

"Sheesh."

Chapter 12

"Seems to me you've written yourself into a corner," said Meg.

"How so?"

"Well, let's see. You have six main characters not counting the detective—Starr, Candy, Alice, Piggy, Toby Taps and Harry Leggs."

"Jimmy Leggs."

"Whatever. Starr is dead. That leaves five. Toby didn't do it. Toby says Piggy didn't do it. Alice is a fed. Candy is the sister of the deceased. That leaves Harry Leggs."

"Jimmy."

"Yeah, yeah. So where's the mystery? You definitely need some more characters."

"Aha! You forgot about Marilyn. Also Kit, the Girl-Friday."

"They didn't do it."

"You're probably right. I'll have to mull this one over a bit."

"Maybe Skinny could come and visit his brother Harry."

"No. No, he could not."

"What about cousin Bo?"

"Out!"

I put the word out for Jimmy Leggs--not that I had much of a chance. Hunting Jimmy was going to be about as easy as Jonah finding that white whale. My only hope was that he would find me.

I headed to the Powder Puff Room at the No-Tel Hotel where I figured Piggy Wilson was holding court. He was in his usual place, a table in the back by the men's room door. Piggy was bigger than four regular-sized men, although probably only two championship pigs, and most of his five hundred pounds hung over the edges of his steel-reinforced seat like an extra helping of mozzarella oozing over the side of the pizza pan.

"Sit," he grunted, chomping down on an ear of corn. "We needs to talk."

I sat down across from Piggy's toadies and ordered a beer.

"What was the message, Piggy?" I asked.

"What message?"

"Toby Taps says that Candy Blather's murder was a message. A message to you."

"That tap-dancin' fool talks too much," Piggy oinked. "There wasn't no message."

"I didn't take it, Pete," I said.

"Yeah. I know. I just wish I could figure out who did. Eight thousand bucks. That's a lot of money."

"Have you cooked up another one yet?"

Pete nodded, then gave a yell. "Hey Noylene! Bring that pan of cinnamon rolls out here, will you."

"I'll be out in a minute," came the response from the kitchen.

I had come in early to tell Pete about the eBay auction, but he'd already found out about it.

"This takes the charge up to grand larceny, doesn't it?" asked Pete. "I mean, if the bun's worth eight thousand dollars, maybe I can collect on my insurance policy."

"That's an interesting point. I don't think the insurance company would go for it though. They'll probably only pay out on the actual cost of the roll. That is, unless you took out an eight thousand dollar rider."

"Of course not. Who knew it was going to be worth eight thousand dollars?"

"I'm not even sure we can make grand larceny stick. Maybe breaking and entering, although there wasn't really any break-in. Maybe malicious mischief, although they didn't maliciously mess the place up. Maybe petty theft although it's probably a stretch."

"I could sue them though," said Pete, hopefully.

"You could definitely sue them. At least for what the roll sells for plus emotional distress, loss of business income...any number of things."

"Excellent."

"That is, if you can find out who's selling it. And if they still have the money."

The door of the Slab opened and Nancy walked in. "I've got some news."

"You found out who's got the BVMCR?" Pete asked.

"BVMCR?"

"Blessed Virgin Mary Cinnamon Roll."

"No clue. The techie at eBay says the only information about the seller they can tell me is his e-mail address—impossible to trace since it goes to one of those free internet mailboxes. He wouldn't give me any other information. I say 'impossible to trace.' It's not, of course, and if we had some high-powered computers and a really good hacker, we could probably trace it right down to his computer. Although, if I had stolen it," she said with a shrug, "I'd just use a computer in the library. We can get some more information from eBay, but we're going to need all kinds of warrants. Federal, too. Not just state. They're going to make us jump through all the hoops. Even then, the information is probably false. We may never find out who it is."

"I'm not sure it's going to be worth the trouble, Pete." I said.

"The one thing I did do," said Nancy, "was put a stop on the auction. I faxed eBay a police report stating that the item in question was indeed stolen. They cancelled the auction until further notice."

"If it's not worth anything to the thief, he might bring it back," I suggested.

"I doubt it," said Nancy. "He probably won't get any more money than what's already been offered, but he has the e-mail addresses of the people that have already bid on it. He could contact those bidders directly. Even move to another on-line auction. We'd never know."

"Here's the first batch," said Noylene, appearing at the table with a cookie sheet on which rested eight misshapen buns.

"Hmmm," I said, studying the cookie sheet carefully. "Not so good. This one here sort of looks like a car accident victim."

"Oh, man," said Nancy. "That's disturbing. They don't even look like cinnamon rolls. I sure wouldn't eat one."

"I sort of tried to form her face in the dough before I cooked it. It didn't work though," said Pete.

I nodded and took the car accident roll. "I see that. Maybe she was a miracle after all."

"Told you," said Noylene.

I met Meg and her mother, Ruby, at the police station at six o'clock. It was a short walk over to Brother Hog's tent and the service wasn't until six-thirty, but we wanted to get a good seat. Other folks had the same idea and we ended up sitting about halfway back. The tent held about three hundred chairs and it looked as though Brother Hog would need every one of them.

The musical entertainment for the evening was the choir from the Sinking Pond Baptist Church. It was made up of three basses, one seventy-two year old tenor who was introduced by their director as Edith, six altos and five sopranos. The electronic organ was an addition I hadn't seen yesterday. The choir began with *Come to the Church in the Wildwood,* moved on to *There is a Mansion,* and finished their pre-game show with *Rescue the Perishing*.

"They aren't bad," said Meg.

"Nope. That banjo really spices things up."

"I like a banjo," said Ruby. "It makes me smile."

"Me too," I said.

Brother Hog had taken the stage.

"Brothers and sisters," he began, "welcome to Brother Hogmanay McTavish's Gospel Tent Revival."

As the service unfolded, prayers were humbly offered, the Holy Spirit was invoked, an offering was taken, and then, finally, the moment had come that I, as well as the rest of the congregation, had been waiting for. Brother Hog reached behind the table and picked up the biggest chicken I had ever seen.

"I'll bet that chicken weighs every bit of twenty pounds," Meg said in a hushed voice.

"I don't think so. Probably closer to twelve. It's a Jersey Giant," whispered Ruby. "We had them when I was growing up. They get real big and they're very smart. For a chicken, that is. It looks a lot bigger because its feathers are all ruffled up."

The rest of the crowd was murmuring in anticipation. When the chicken was placed on the table, I noticed that the folks still in their chairs—that is, the folks in the first ten rows or so—had, by craning their necks, added an extra three inches to their collective height. The ones in the back were standing, and the ones in the very back stood on their chairs.

"This is Binny Hen, the Scripture Chicken," Brother Hog said into his microphone. "Binny will choose the scripture that I will preach on this evening, but always remember, the Holy Ghost works through any instrument of faith and it's God's Word that will be proclaimed this night."

With those words, Brother Hog placed Binny on the table just behind the massive Bible. The crowd grew quiet and watched in amazement as the preacher opened the Bible about half way and stepped back from the table. Binny Hen jumped up onto the pages. As large as she was, the huge Bible dwarfed her. Binny looked around with her quick, chicken-like movements and then started scratching at the leaves. She kicked back page after page—sometimes turning only one, sometimes more than one. As she stood on each newly turned page, she looked down on it, tilted her head left and right, as if considering each verse before offering an occasional cluck and resuming her quest. The crowd was silent in anticipation. Binny certainly took her time in the spotlight. She continued her search for six or seven minutes and gave every indication that she was studying the scriptures, looking diligently for just the right text. Finally she stopped scratching, cocked her head twice, looked at the page she stood on with first one golden eye and then the other, opened her wings and gave a great clucking noise. Then she put her head down and started pecking.

"Binny Hen has chosen the scripture," Brother Hog cried. "Let the Word of God be read!"

I didn't know the reader that Brother Hog had chosen for this evening, but he stood up and walked over to the Bible. He was a tall, thin man wearing a green sport coat, an orange tie and a pair of checkered trousers. Brother Hog picked up the chicken and held her aloft. The man looked hard at the text where Binny had been pecking.

"If it were me, I'd want to preach on the scripture that says 'He that believeth and is baptized shall be saved,'" I whispered to Megan. "Mark 16. You know, the one with the snakes."

"I'm sure you would," Meg said sarcastically. "Now hush."

"Mark 16" the reader announced in a clear baritone. "Hear the word of the Lord."

"Afterward he appeared unto the eleven as they sat at meat, and upbraided them with their unbelief and hardness of heart, because they believed not them which had seen him after he was risen. And he said unto them, Go ye into all the world, and preach the gospel to every creature. He that believeth and is baptized shall be saved; but he that believeth not shall be damned. And these signs shall follow them that believe; In my name shall they cast out devils; they shall speak with new tongues; They shall take up serpents; and if they drink any deadly thing, it shall not hurt them; they shall lay hands on the sick, and they shall recover. So then after the Lord had spoken unto them, he was received up into heaven, and sat on the right hand of God. And they went forth, and preached everywhere, the Lord working with them, and confirming the word with signs following. Amen."

"That's the one I would have picked," I said under my breath, but loud enough for Meg to hear. She looked at me with incredulity, amazement evident on her face.

"How did you do that?' she whispered, suddenly suspicious.

"Shhh. Later. I want to hear the sermon. There may be some snakes involved."

The sermon was forty minutes of old-time religion and unfortunately didn't include any snakes. The invitation that followed was given as the choir from Sinking Pond Baptist sang that old favorite, *Softly and Tenderly*. The banjo player had another commitment down at the Copper Kettle, so the choir was accompanied by the Hammond organ that Brother Hog had finagled in Charlotte for the price of an advertisement: a sign on the back of the organ proclaiming in large letters "Courtesy of Brodt Music Company." The tremolo kicked in as the congregation joined in on the chorus.

"Come home, Come home,
Ye who are weary come home..."

There were a number of people moving forward with public decisions and Brother Hog waited for them at the front with open arms. Meg, Ruby and I snuck out the side of the tent. You're not supposed to leave during an invitation—it's considered bad form. But I had been to enough church for one night.

We stopped at the Slab for a cup of coffee and a piece of pie, beating the crowd that Pete was expecting. Ever since the Scripture Chicken had made her appearance at the revival, Pete had been packed on Friday and Saturday nights after the service. There had been so many people that the Ginger Cat had been staying open as well.

"I'll have a slice of Boston Cream Pie and a cup of coffee," I said to Noylene, taking off my coat and helping Ruby off with hers. Meg had her coat and scarf off before I could get around the table. Still, I managed to pull out both of their chairs, getting a few manner-points back.

"Same for me," said Ruby.

"Just coffee," said Meg. "Decaf." She turned to me. "Now, squeal, detective!"

"What?" asked Ruby.

"He knew what scripture the chicken was going to pick. In advance."

"Now how could he know that?"

"Yes, how indeed?" I asked innocently.

"I don't know, but we're about to find out."

"It was just a lucky guess," I said. "I can honestly say that it's what I would have chosen if I were a chicken."

"I suspect so. The question is 'why would you have chosen it?'"

"Maybe we'll know tomorrow night."

"We're going back?"

"Oh, yes. I wouldn't miss it."

Chapter 13

It was ingenious, when I thought about it. The chicken had been trained to scratch at the pages until it saw something that it wanted. Food. When I had first looked at the Bible, it had fallen open to the sixteenth chapter of Mark, mostly due to the kernel of corn, smashed almost flat, in the center of the page, acting like an edible bookmark. Binny Hen was after the corn. The other thing that I noticed was that, although this wasn't a red-letter edition—that is, the words of Jesus in red type—the reading that was delivered by Brother Hog's chosen assistant *was* in red. It was a brilliant psychological ploy. Once the chicken had picked the page, the reader's eye would go inevitably to the passage in red. Not only that, but the reader would, ninety-nine times out of a hundred, read the entire highlighted section rather than a specific scripture verse. I know I would have. I had confirmed my suspicions by flipping quickly through the New Testament checking for red highlighted passages. I found them. Mark 16, John 3, Acts 2, Romans 3, 6 and 8, II Corinthians 11, Ephesians 2. I didn't check everything, but I found enough to appreciate the genius of it. I surmised that Brother Hog must have had this Bible made, or altered, just for his revivals.

I also figured that, like most evangelists, Brother Hog tended to favor the New Testament, at least for evangelistic purposes. I wondered what he might do with a passage that wasn't quite so familiar. The text wouldn't be highlighted in red, but it might be worth a try.

Ruby, Meg and I got to the tent a little earlier than the night before, but we didn't get better seats. The music for the evening was being provided by the Melody Mountain Singers—a family gospel group consisting of a grandmother singing lead, her three daughters backing her up, the husband of one playing a keyboard, and a couple of grandsons playing guitar and string bass. When we walked in, they were in the middle of their signature tune, *I Wanna Be A Jesus Cowboy in the Holy Ghost Corral.*

The Indians of Satan were comin' at us fast,
To spiritually scalp us, don't you see;
Well, we just stood there prayin'
and we were saved at last
By the cavalry from Calvary!

"Nice lyrics," I said to Meg. "Not exactly politically correct. The 'Indians of Satan?'"

"Would you please keep your voice down? At least they didn't try to rhyme 'Jesus' with 'cheeses,'" said Meg, referring to one of my more colorful choral compositions. The Melody Mountain Singers launched into the chorus.

I wanna be a Jesus cowboy in the Holy Ghost Corral,
I wanna rope them little doggies, by and by,
I'm gonna brand them wayward cattle,
if you'll only show me how,
I wanna be there for that round-up in the sky!

The gospel group performed four more songs before Brother Hog took the stage. I had to hand it to him. He had it down to an art form. We began with prayers, a couple of choruses led by the Gospel group, before finally coming to the moment that the crowd had gathered to see.

Brother Hog lifted Binny Hen into the air and held her aloft for all to see. "This is Binny Hen the Scripture Chicken," said Brother Hog, repeating, almost exactly, the introduction we had heard the night before. "Binny will choose the scripture that I will preach on this evening, but remember, the Holy Ghost can work through any instrument of faith, and it's God's Holy Word that will be proclaimed this night."

Again, Brother Hog placed Binny on the table behind the Bible. I looked around the tent. Everyone was studying the chicken intently. The people that were in the back were standing on their chairs. Brother Hog opened the Bible and stepped back to let Binny Hen perform her consecrated task.

The chicken jumped up onto the pages of the enormous book and began her scratching. Page after page flipped while the congregation looked on in wonder. Five minutes passed. Then six. Then seven. I looked at Brother Hog. He wasn't anxious. This was just part of the show. He stood back, a smile spreading across his ample face. His spray-tamed hair swooped majestically around his head like a salt-and-pepper halo. His bright white suit was luminescent in the spotlights and he almost seemed to glow like a great, round Chinese lantern. Eight minutes. Nine. The crowd was starting to murmur and, for the first time, Brother Hog was starting to look uncomfortable. Then it happened. Binny Hen stopped scratching, cocked her head first one way and then the other, flapped her wings mightily and made a huge clucking sound. Then she started pecking furiously.

"Binny Hen has chosen the scripture," Brother Hog cried with obvious relief. "Let the Word of God be read!"

I wondered if Brother Hog might choose a woman to read the scripture, since the night before it had been a man. He didn't. The reader was Nelson Kendrick. I knew Nelson. Nelson was the minister of education at Martin Street Baptist Church and the organizer of the Iron Mike Men's Retreat. I thought that he might have a seminary degree. I also thought he might need one.

"What's the scripture this evening?" whispered Meg. "I know that you know." I just shrugged and tried to look pious.

"He might be expecting John 3:16."

"He might?"

Nelson moved confidently to the table. Brother Hog walked beside him, lifted Binny Hen off the table, stepped back, and bowed his head for the reading of God's word. We all waited expectantly as Nelson scanned the page. He looked confused and shot a glance over to Brother Hog.

"Read it brother," said Brother Hog softly, but loud enough for us to hear him.

"I don't know where to start," said Nelson under his breath and near panic.

"Just start reading. The Holy Ghost will direct you."

"But where?" Nelson's voice was starting to rise.

"Start at the beginning of the chapter." Brother Hog's voice was still calm and quiet, but I suspected that he was regretting his choice scripture readers. Nelson was over-thinking the whole thing. "Go ahead, brother. Don't be ashamed of God's word."

"I'm not ashamed of God's word," Nelson said, his anger rising.

"Of course you're not. Just read it," said Brother Hog, his impatience now evident and his voice rising in pitch as well as volume. "And don't stop till you're finished," he bellowed. "Just keep reading the word!"

"Fine. I will." Nelson raised his voice as well. "Genesis 14," he called out. "Hear the word of the Lord."

I flashed a quick look over to Brother Hog. He was still holding the chicken, but all the blood had drained from his face. His eyes had narrowed and his lips were moving as if trying to remember the passage from Genesis.

"And it came to pass," Nelson read, looking over toward Brother Hog with raised eyebrows and a you-asked-for-it look on his face, "in the days of Amraphel king of Shinar, Arioch king of Ellasar, Chedorlaomer king of Elam, and Tidal king of nations; that these made war with Bera king of Sodom, and with Birsha king of Gomorrah, Shinab king of Admah, and Shemeber king of Zeboiim, and the king of Bela, which is Zoar."

I felt a smile creeping into the corners of my mouth. Nelson didn't stumble over any of the kings. I looked around. The crowd was still listening intently.

"All these were joined together in the vale of Siddim, which is the salt sea. Twelve years they served Chedorlaomer, and in the thirteenth year they rebelled. And in the fourteenth year came Chedorlaomer, and the kings that were with him, and smote the Rephaims in Ashteroth Karnaim, and the Zuzims in Ham, and the Emins in Shaveh Kiriathaim, and the Horites in their mount Seir, unto Elparan, which is by the wilderness."

"Zuzims?" said Meg. "Zuzims?"

"In Ham," I added. "Zuzims in Ham. Throw in the Chedor and it sounds like a lunch special at the Ginger Cat."

"What the hell is that stupid son-of-a-bitch talking about?" The outburst came from the row in front of us. It was Skeeter and Skeeter Donalson wasn't known for his gentility and quiet manner. He was, as everyone in town knew, a few limpets short of a chowder and although he was harmless, when he got upset, he got pretty vocal. However, the question that Skeeter had posed had the effect of causing the people within hearing distance of his off-color query to snap out of their scripturally-induced daze. They reacted as if they had just awakened from trance.

"And they returned, and came to Enmishpat, which is Kadesh, and smote all the country of the Amalekites, and also the Amorites, that dwelt in..." Nelson paused. "Haz-ez-on-ta-mar," he sounded out. It was the first time that Nelson had stumbled. But I couldn't blame him. Hazezontamar was a heck of a name to have to pronounce, even for a bunch of Amorites.

"What the hell are you readin' anyway?" hollered Skeeter, standing up. "You'd better shut up!" An audible buzz started going through the crowd. Nelson might have been tempted to stop, but with Brother Hog's admonition still ringing in his ears, he decided to kick it up a notch.

"And there went out the king of Sodom, and the king of Gomorrah, and the king of Admah, and the king of Zeboiim, and the king of Bela, the same is Zoar; and they joined battle with them in the vale of Siddim; with Chedorlaomer the king of Elam, and with Tidal king of nations, and Amraphel king of Shinar, and Arioch king of Ellasar; four kings with five."

The congregation was loud and getting louder. Some folks were on their feet. I'd never seen the reading of scripture have such an effect although the crowd was probably reacting to Skeeter who was, for his own unfathomable reason, incensed. In any case, I hoped they would calm down. I definitely wasn't prepared for a riot. Nelson raised his voice to a yell. Even with his microphone, he was having trouble being heard above the rising din.

"And the vale of Siddim was full of slime-pits," he bellowed. "And the kings of Sodom and Gomorrah fled, and fell there; and they that remained fled to the mountain."

"Slime-pits?" asked Meg. "There are slime-pits in the Bible?"

"It was *full* of slime-pits," I said nodding toward Nelson. "You heard him."

Brother Hogmanay McTavish walked slowly to the pulpit and raised his arms for quiet. The crowd hushed and took their seats although many of them were still visibly upset.

"The Holy Ghost has given us this scripture, and it is my delight to preach upon it. I think we can all agree that it is a difficult passage, but it surely has a message for us tonight."

"That's a good start," I whispered, looking over at Skeeter. He seemed to have calmed down.

"We've heard about kings. Kings in trouble with the Lord," sang out Brother Hog, his comb-over all a-quiver. "The kings of *Sodom* and *Gemorrah!*" He spat out the names of the cities like he was expelling a wayward fly out of his mouth. It was a nice effect.

"Amen!" came the choral response. The Melody Mountain Singers were apparently well-versed in sermon punctuation. The crowd had settled down and many people were nodding appreciably. They had heard of Sodom and Gemorrah.

"They were in sin. They did not know the Lord Jesus! And because of their sin, God destroyed their cities and all were cast into the eternal slime-pit."

"Amen! Yes! The slime-pit! Halleluia!" sang the choir.

"For all have sinned and fallen short of the glory of God."

"Nice transition," I said. "Well done. Almost there." Meg glared at me.

"We have fallen short of his glory the same as these heathen kings." Brother Hog was on a roll. "But we don't need to fear the slime-pit! There is redemption!"

"Redemption! Yes, Lord!" answered the choir.

"For God so loved the world that he gave his only begotten Son..."

"Halleluia!"

"...that whosoever believeth in Him should not perish, but have everlasting life!" Brother Hog pulled out a big white handkerchief and wiped his face. He'd been perspiring pretty heavily, but he now had the sermon under control.

"And there we are," I said, smiling at Meg. "John 3:16. He did a pretty good job. Once he had Sodom and Gemorrah, it was a cakewalk. The slime-pit helped, too. It might have been trickier if he'd been stuck with the Zuzims."

"You are an evil man," said Meg. "And I'm glad he got out of your little trap."

"What trap? I'm innocent. You saw it. The chicken picked the scripture."

"I don't believe you. You know too much."

The rest of the service went as Brother Hog expected. He was a pretty fair evangelist. Once he got to his chosen scripture, the sermon moved right along. There were no more surprises and the crowd that moved forward during the invitation included Skeeter and Ruby. Since Ruby was heading to the front, Megan and I stayed till the end.

"Mom always likes to rededicate herself during these revivals," Meg said.

"Nothing wrong with that," I said. "We don't have anywhere else to go. And I'm beginning to appreciate the charms of the family gospel quartet."

"Where *did* you find that scripture?" Meg asked innocently.

I shrugged modestly, but I was always happy to show off in front of my gal. "It's pretty famous among Old Testament scholars. If Nelson had read another few verses, he'd have gotten to the part where Melchizedek the priest brings the first offering of bread and wine. That's the reason it's still in the lectionary. It's the first time the elements of communion are mentioned in the Bible."

"Aha! I knew that you did it!" Meg crowed. "You are hoisted on your own petard."

"Oh, man..."

Chapter 14

"Okay, Piggy. On your feet." I grabbed Piggy by his lapels and gave a heave. My lapel-yank could get most men up out of their chairs quicker than a floozy carrying loaded mousetraps in her undies, but yanking on Piggy left me with nothing but two fistfuls of lapel-shaped seersucker and a stupid look on my face.

"You ruined my suit," he managed to oink while stuffing an entire apple into his mouth. "I'm gonna fix you good!"

"Hang on, Piggy. It'll take you twenty minutes to peel yourself out of that chair and by then I'll be long gone. Besides, your suit looks pretty good like that. Very contemporary. Nehru-like."

"Yeah? You think?"

"Absolutely." I looked across the table. "Right, boys?" Piggy's henchmen nodded agreeably and put their faces back into their troughs.

"Now listen, Piggy," I said, wiping his mouth with one of his lapels. "I need to find Jimmy Leggs. It's pretty clear that Candy Blather's murder was a warning to you to lay off the hymnal-fix."

"Maybe it was, maybe it wasn't." Piggy hoofed a slab of limburger up to his snout. "I generally don't take no warnings."

"But you'll take it if it was from Jimmy Leggs?"

Piggy grunted in the affirmative and flapped his jowls up and down. "It ain't a good career move to go against Jimmy Leggs."

"Where can I find him, Piggy?"

"You don't find him. He finds you."

"How were you and Candy cooking the hymnal?" I waved a protein-bar under his snout, and he was on it like a piranha on a corndog.

"It was easy money. All we had to do was make sure that people's favorites appeared in the new hymnal. One grand a pop. Candy had the connections. I provided the muscle."

"So, if I wanted to include 'Jesus, Friend Of Thronging Pilgrims?'"

"Cost you a grand."

"'Love Grew Where The Blood Fell?'"

"A grand."

"'Onward Christian Soldiers?'"

"Heh, heh. That one would probably cost you two grand," giggled Piggy. "There's a lot of hostility goin' around about that one." He snorked up a handful of jellybeans. "We could also rig some 'inclusive' language if you wanted," he said in-between chomps. "You know, like 'All Creatures of our God and Pal' and 'Sponge of Ages'".

"'Sponge of Ages?'"

"Yeah. Candy said that some minister thought that 'Rock' was too masculine and aggressive. It sent the wrong message. 'Sponge' is nurturing and more in keeping with today's theology."

"So you changed it?"

Piggy grunted gleefully. "We been doing it for years! Not bad, eh? Any hymn you wanted. Cost you a grand. Me and Candy could work it in."

"What're you going to do now?"

"Guess I'll go back to hustling green grocers."

"There much slop in that?"

"Beats workin'."

"Not bad. I like Piggy. He's a good character."

"Yeah, thanks."

"And you seem to actually have a plot."

"I think so," I answered. "Although it's hard to tell sometimes."

"Yeah. I used to feel that way, too." He pulled his fedora down over his eyes, adjusted his glasses and lit his pipe. I watched the smoke curl up around his head. "I'd work for two weeks straight on what I thought was a pretty good story and end up tossing the whole lot. How's your murder case coming?"

"Murder case?" I asked.

"The body you found in the church."

"It's not really a case," I said, as I clicked off the light and stacked the one-page chapters to my serial mystery neatly beside the typewriter. "He's been dead for years. The killer's dead by now, too."

"It has been said that nobody cares about the corpse. This is nonsense, of course. You're a writer, aren't you? Writers don't throw away a valuable element to their story. It's like saying that this man means no more to you than the murder of an unknown man in a city you never heard of."

"Hmmm. You're right."

"I could help you with your story. I've got a lot of plots left over. Poodle Springs. I never finished that one."

"I think someone finished it for you," I said.

"Really? Any good?"

"Yeah. Yeah, it was."

"Hayden," said Father George, taking off his cassock in the sacristy, "that was quite a nice service. Do you have just a second to chat?"

"Absolutely. What's up?"

"Remember when I told you that we were going to be looking for a parish administrator?"

"Sure. Have you found someone? I didn't even know we had advertised the position."

"I was talking with Rob Brannon...have you two met?"

"Yep."

"And he indicated that since he doesn't really have his law practice up and running, he'd be happy to do it until we found a full-time person."

"Uh huh. And when would that full-time person start?"

"Maybe sometime next summer."

"Well, George, I think that would be an extremely bad idea."

Father George bristled. "And why is that?"

I shrugged and decided to hold my peace. "Just a gut reaction, I guess."

"Well, it's my decision and I think that Rob would be fine in the position. He's available, he's helpful, and he really wants to get involved in the life of the church."

"As you said, George, it's your decision," I said.

"Also, have you spoken with Brenda about her 'puppet-moment?' I suggested to her that some music might be nice. She didn't seem too keen on the idea, but I think it might get the Puppet-Moment off to a good start."

"Is this puppet thing something that we're going to do on a regular basis?" I asked, dreading the answer.

"Maybe once a month or so. It depends on how it goes."

"I hear your son's in town," said Nancy to Noylene as she made her way to our table. Sundays were usually Noylene's day off, but she was filling in for one of the other waitresses. I was sitting glumly at the "after church" table with Meg, Beverly Greene and Georgia Wester. Nancy, dressed in her new black motorcycle leathers, joined us, but apart from our little group, the place was empty.

Noylene was beaming. "He got in last night. He'll be stopping by in a little bit."

"Why so gloomy?" Nancy asked. "I thought I'd come in and

show off my new duds, but you guys look pretty much down in the dumps."

"Church business," Bev said. "I do like your outfit, though."

"Rob Brannon has been made 'parish administrator,'" Georgia added.

"I don't trust that guy as far as I could throw him," said Nancy, joining our circle of dejection.

"And you've got a pretty good arm," I said. "I know what you mean. I've got a bad feeling about him, too. Can't put my finger on it though."

"Well, we've been through worse," Meg said. "Just remember back to this time last year."

We all looked at her, trying hard to remember last year's sacramental angst.

"The Wimmyn's Conference?"

We all silently nodded and took a unison sip of our coffees.

"Mother Ryan? And the sex dolls?" *

We sipped again.

"So, this too will pass," said Meg, hopefully.

We nodded once more, all of us staring down at the table in a picture of dejection.

"And he might not be bad at all." Meg wasn't convincing any of us.

"Nothing we can do anyway," said Bev. "So let's look on the bright side. Maybe he'll get everything running smoothly."

"Maybe," said Georgia.

"Maybe," said Meg.

"In a pig's eye," I snarled.

"This here's my son, D'Artagnan," said Noylene, interrupting our melancholy with a happy chirp. "He's studyin' to be a detective."

* see *The Alto Wore Tweed*

We all looked up at Noylene who had come up unnoticed. On her arm was one of the strangest looking men I ever hoped to meet. D'Artagnan Fabergé was about six foot, six inches tall and as big around as a medium-sized pencil. His hair style might once have been called a "mullet," but he'd taken it to another level. The top and sides of his coif were cut short, the notable exception being the thick lime-green strip of hair that ran right down the middle of his head and was just long enough to fold over on itself like the comb of a giant Martian rooster. In the back, his hair flowed in pink locks down to his shoulders. He was wearing black horn-rimmed glasses of the sort favored by Buddy Holly and he sported a wispy blonde mustache, a bad complexion and an earring made from a Pepsi bottle cap and a paperclip.

It wasn't terribly cold out, but mid-October generally meant sweater weather in St. Germaine and this Sunday was no exception. D'Artagnan, in contrast with the rest of us, was wearing a thin white t-shirt, faded jeans and orange high-top Converse tennis shoes. The arms sticking out of his t-shirt looked like long, animated twigs.

I heard a gasp, but it wasn't me, although I thought at first that it might have been. It was Bev. I just smiled and gulped, "Hi there."

"Would you like something to eat?" asked Georgia, the first at our table to regain her wits. She pushed a plate of Pete's rejected cinnamon Madonnas across the table. "You look starved. I mean...you look famished. I mean...you must be very hungry."

"Georgia!" Bev whispered through clenched teeth and unmoving lips. "Shhh."

"Nah. He just ate," said Noylene. "I made him a big lunch before I came in."

"I wouldn't mind having one for dessert," said D'Artagnan in a bass voice an octave lower than my own and accentuated with a prominent North Carolina drawl. He took the largest roll, the one that I thought looked a little like a genetic accident involving Yitzhak Rabin and a lobster, pushed the entire bun into his mouth and finished it in two quick bites as we all watched in amazed silence.

"I..." started Megan. I looked over at her. Her mouth was moving, but no sound was coming out. Finally she managed, "I hear you're a detective."

"Well, ma'am, I just now got my certifyables, but I'm not really a detective, per se," said D'Artagnan, with special emphasis on the *per se*. "I'm a bounty hunter."

"A bounty hunter," said Georgia. "Fascinating. And whom do you hunt?"

"Criminals mostly." D'Artagnan sniffed with an air of authority that Barney Fife would envy. "Bail jumpers." He nodded his head and flipped his mullet off his shoulder with a wave of his skeletal hand.

"And are there many criminals in St. Germaine?" asked Beverly.

"I wouldn't know 'bout that, ma'am. I come to find the missin' artifac'."

"I don't like his hair like this," said Noylene, flipping the bottle cap hanging from the paper-clip with a long red fingernail. "Or that earring. He was such a handsome boy."

"I *tol'* you, Mama," D'Artagnan said as he pushed her hand away and stopped the miniature pendulum banging him in the neck. "I need to blend in with the unsavories. That's my job."

"Do you carry a gun?" I asked, knowing I didn't want to hear the answer. Everyone at the table stopped breathing.

"Not yet," he admitted. The table relaxed. "I applied for my permit though. It'll take three weeks." He brightened. "You know, I'm allowed to shoot folks. If they don't comply, that is."

"Yes. I remember reading that somewhere."

"But you're going to be working in Asheville, right?" asked Georgia.

"Yeah. Mostly. Now tell me about this artifac' I'm supposed to be lookin' for."

"Let me get Pete," Noylene said. "He can give you the particulars."

Pete and D'Artagnan took a booth over in the corner while the rest of us finished commiserating.

"Hey, Nancy," I said. "Before I forget, what do you think about following up on the Lester Gifford case?"

"I thought we'd sort of put that one to bed. Whoever did it is most likely dead by now anyway."

"True. But it's a remarkable case: body that didn't decompose, a seventy-year-old murder in the church. If you could solve it, it'd be worth some state and maybe national recognition in the journals."

Nancy nodded thoughtfully. "Yeah... it would."

"You could hit the law-enforcement convention circuit. Maybe do a couple of forensic papers. Kent said he'd be happy to help you out. Who knows? It might work out really well."

"Yeah. It might."

"Of course, you'd have to solve it."

"Oh, I'll solve it."

"We haven't heard anything for a while," said Georgia. "Can you fill us in?"

"Sure," said Nancy, pulling her pad out of an inside pocket of her black leather jacket.

"You carry that thing with you all the time?" I asked.

"All the time. Here's what I've got.

"Lester Gifford was found in the church on October 6th. He was probably murdered sometime between January 15th and February 8th, 1937. He was thirty-two and worked as an assistant manager at Watauga County Bank. He left a wife, Mavis. No kids that I could find."

"How did you come up with the dates that he might have been killed?" asked Bev.

"He was mentioned in a newspaper article on January 15th. There was a bank merger that happened at the end of February. There was a fire in the records room of St. Barnabas on February 8th. I don't think the fire is a coincidence, but it might be."

"No, I think you're probably right about that," I said. "I'd put his murder closer to the 8th."

"Me too," said Nancy. "So we'll assume he was killed on or around February 8th, 1937."

Everyone nodded their assent.

"Did his wife report him missing?" asked Bev.

"We don't know for sure, but I assume she did. The police records about that sort of thing don't go back that far," said Nancy. "Kent says that Lester was hit in the back of the head by a blunt object. That's what killed him. His body, strangely, didn't decompose in the normal manner. As a result, no one found the body until Billy and his crew dropped the altar and the back popped off."

Nancy turned a page and continued. "Neither Lester nor his wife ever had any connection with St. Barnabas as far as we could tell, but the president of the bank, Harold Lynn, was also the Senior Warden of St. Barnabas. And there was a Sunday School teacher named Jacob Winston who was arrested, but never tried for the murder of Lester Gifford."

"How do you know?" asked Meg.

"The arrest record was in the paper in March. I did another search for Jacob Winston to see if there was any kind of trial. There wasn't. He is mentioned in an article about St. Barnabas and the war effort in 1945, so I've got to assume that nothing ever came of his arrest."

"We still have those papers back at the office," I said. "They're in the folder that we found with Lester's body. Maybe there's something in there."

"You haven't even looked through them?" Georgia asked.

"Rob has," I answered. "It's not a high priority. There's nothing we can do. There's no murderer left. No family we can find. It's a non-case."

"I think you owe it to Lester to find his murderer," said Bev.

"Which is what Nancy plans to do. Right, Nance?" I said.

"Yeah. I'll find out who did it."

"What are they going to do with the body?" Meg asked.

"Kent did an autopsy," I said. "It was the strangest thing. As soon as the body got to the morgue, it started to decompose at a normal rate. So Kent embalmed him and he's lying in the cooler. We can bury him whenever we're ready."

"How about Friday?" said Georgia. "I'm out of town until Friday, but I want to be there. We really should give him a decent burial."

"It's all right with me," I said, looking around the table. The others nodded. "I'll ask George to do the service. Two o'clock okay?"

Pete came up to the table and sat down with a heavy sigh. D'Artagnan had disappeared from sight.

"Well, he's on the case."

"You're a nice man, Pete," said Meg. "How much did you offer him to find the bun?"

"He wanted a thousand dollar finder's fee."

"And what was your counter offer?" I asked with a laugh.

"Let's just say we settled on fifty."

"Fifty dollars?" said Georgia. "That's not much."

"Plus breakfast for a week while he's looking." Pete shrugged and smiled. "How much can he eat? He's skin and bones."

"Speaking of favors, you owe me, Pete—" I said.

"Excuse me? I don't think we were speaking of any favors I owe you."

"Be that as it may, remember when I got you out of that speeding ticket in Hickory?"

"Yeah."

"And Asheville? And the one in Lenoir, and that other one in Hendersonville?"

"Yeah." Pete was getting worried. This was a lot of payback.

"I need you to go with me tomorrow."

"Where?" Pete was wary.

"I have to go on this overnight event. And you have to go with me." I looked over at Meg. She was smiling demurely and sipping her coffee.

"And then we're even?"

"As even as we can be."

"Okay," said Pete. "I'll do it. But then we're square."

"We're square," I said.

"Where are we going?"

"The Iron Mike Men's Retreat," I said with a grin.

It's a good thing that the place was almost empty because Pete's cry of anguish would have put most of his patrons off their feed.

Chapter 15

Pete and I threw our stuff into the back of the pick-up late on Monday afternoon. I figured it would take us no more than an hour to find a campsite and get set up before the first activity of the Iron Mike Men's Retreat began. We brought a couple of sleeping bags, a good-sized tent, some snacks, and enough dry wood for a campfire. The stuff at the campsite was bound to be wet, and I wanted to be able to start a fire if we wanted one. Pete was all for bringing a case of beer, but I vetoed it. There was no beer allowed on the premises, and I didn't want to get kicked out before the fulfillment of my wager was complete. Meg had made her stipulations quite clear. And, after all, there was still Seattle to look forward to.

"What do you think of D'Artagnan?" Pete asked.

"I don't know. He's an odd fellow."

"I can tell you this much. I hope he finds that bun before too long. He ate about thirty bucks worth of stuff for breakfast this morning."

"He's thin as a rail. I thought you said he wouldn't eat much."

"Guess he's got a tapeworm or something. I've never seen anyone eat like him."

"What about Haystacks Hornby?" I asked, referring to our local four hundred pound pie-eating champion.

"This guy'd eat Haystacks under the table. I'm not kiddin'. Oh, Haystacks is good—there's no denying that. But D'Artagnan had four plates of eggs down his neck as quick as Noylene could bring them to the table."

"Well, eggs..."

"Plus about fourteen pancakes, a pound of bacon, some country ham, two baskets of biscuits, molasses, grits and about a gallon of orange juice." Pete sighed. "That's just while I was watching. I don't even know what else he ate."

"Wow!"

"Yeah, wow. I told him he had to find that stupid bun within a week, but I don't know if I can afford him that long. He indicated that tomorrow he'd like some waffles."

"Waffles are cheap. Just try to keep him away from the meat," I suggested.

"That's a good plan. I'll try it," said Pete. "Now, tell me again why we're going to get in touch with our inner man."

"Because Meg said so."

"Oh. Right."

I sat in my office, looking out the window, watching the sun disappear behind the city skyline like a giant orange-yellow yolk being slowly consumed by a determined egg-sucking weasel. I had put out the word for Jimmy Leggs, but I hadn't heard anything. I might never hear anything. Jimmy showed up when he wanted and where he wanted. I was pretty sure that he was the one who capped Candy Blather né Latte Espresso. It was his M.O. The question was, who had hired him?

I needed a suspect and I needed one bad. Toby Taps? Piggy? But who was behind it? I was thinking. Thinking hard. So hard it made my hair hurt. So hard that I didn't hear the voice at the door.

"Excuse me."

I spun around in my chair with my .38 in my hand, leveled it at the squeaky voice and let two shots go, just for meanness, right above his head. He hit the floor like a burlap sack filled with 120 pounds of tuna casserole.

"Didn't anyone ever tell you not to sneak up on a P.I.?" I growled.

"Yes, yes they did. They told me, but I forgot," stammered the mouse in front of me, brushing himself off and getting to his feet. He was a diminutive man--bald, with a mustache that looked like a wooly caterpillar without all those little pink feet.

"Whaddya want?" I was still sounding mean.

"I heard you were looking for a suspect. In the Candy Blather case."

"Maybe. What's it to you?" I waved him into the client chair with the barrel of my roscoe.

"I was her friend."

"Her friend?" I asked, menacingly.

"Well, her boyfriend, actually. Her lover."

"Her lover?" I lowered the gun in astonishment. Candy was about five foot ten. This guy might make it up to her belly-button. If he was wearing lifts.

"I know who did it," he squeaked. "I know who set her up."

Pete and I turned into the Baptist Conference Center at about 4:30. There were cardboard signs directing us past the main building and down a dirt road toward the campground. We drove up and pulled in behind several cars that had already arrived.

"Y'all are going to want to go on and pick out a campsite," said a genial man clad in hunting fatigues as he came up to my open window. "Just head down this road until you find one that's not taken. You guys already registered?" He lifted his clipboard up to the window.

"I believe we are," I said. "Hayden Konig and Peter Moss. We're here to get in touch with our inner men."

"Yep. Here you are." He checked us off his list. "All squared away. Y'all go get yourselves a site. Pitch your tent if you want. We won't get started till it gets dark."

"Great," I said. "We can't wait."

The beauty of a pop-up tent is that you can pitch it in about a minute and a half. It takes slightly longer to take down, but not much. What took us the most time was filling our air mattresses from the electric pump that I had plugged into the cigarette lighter.

"This isn't too bad," said Pete as he tried out his mattress. "Remember that time in college when we went squirrel hunting? Three days in the rain, sleeping bags lying soaked on the ground and nothing to eat but that one mangy squirrel that wandered up to the campfire."

"That squirrel wasn't right," I said. "A squirrel just doesn't walk up to a campfire, sit down and stare down the barrel of a .22 rifle."

"I remember that I was praying for him to," said Pete. "It was the one truly religious experience of my life."

"Well, get ready then 'cause you're about to have another one."

Our first meeting—our orientation—was just after a pretty good supper of steaks and baked potatoes. A "he-man" supper, Pete called it. No salad. No broccoli. No quiche. No key lime pie. Just a big t-bone steak and a one-pound baked potato. A beer would have been nice—and appropriate to the character of the manly repast—but rules were rules. We had iced tea. Unsweetened.

There were eighteen of us, plus the staff—Nelson Kendrick, the organizer of the IMMR, Bernie Majors, the fellow in camouflage gear who had checked us in, and our guest facilitator, Dr. Renquist Sampson, PhD. "Dr. Ren" for short. We were all sitting around the fire in plastic lounge chairs with more than a few extras piled up by one of the trucks. I was getting pretty comfortable and was thinking I could probably doze off for a few minutes and no one would notice.

"We are gathered around this bonfire," Dr. Ren began, "because we are men. We created this fire. The earth was given to man in Genesis; on that we can all be clear. Women came after."

I looked around the circle and across the flames at the heads nodding in agreement. Dr. Ren was a big man, about sixty, with a flowing white mane and a large round belly. He was wearing what looked to be a beaded deerskin shirt open to his navel and pants with fringe hanging from every possible seam.

"Did you all bring your stones?" Dr. Ren asked. Again, nods of ascent.

"I didn't know I was supposed to bring one," said Pete, raising his hand. "What's it for?"

"Tomorrow we will build a monument to Yahweh," said Dr. Ren. "You can find a large stone somewhere in the woods. Didn't you read your information sheet?"

"Alas, no," said Pete, trying his best to look chagrined.

Suddenly, Nelson and Bernie began beating on drums. I hadn't noticed the drums before.

"We no longer have images of real men," Dr. Ren said, as the drumbeat continued. "The tom-toms honor the body as opposed to the mind. God wants us to honor the body. One of the things we will do is go back to the very old stories, the stories of the Old Testament, five thousand years ago, where the view of a man, what a man is, is healthier. It is time to take back our manhood."

I heard some grunting coming from around the fire, but I couldn't tell if it was from the participants or being supplied by the drummers.

"God wants us to be real men. Wild men. God wants you to hooooooowl!"

A howl went up from around the fire. It started—this time I

was sure—with the drummers, Nelson and Bernie, but the other men took it up with a vengeance. I looked over at Pete. He was grinning at me and howling for all he was worth. I shrugged and gave a half-hearted yelp.

"It is time to bring the Old Testament warrior back to life!" Dr. Ren shrieked. "You have to take back the power you have given to your mother. You must direct your energy away from pleasing Mommy."

He spread his arms and gave the command, "Reach under your chair and take up your Mommy-Stick!"

We all looked under our chairs and there they were—right on cue—our Mommy-Sticks. They were bamboo, about two feet long and painted different pastel colors. Mine, unfortunately, was pink.

Dr. Ren's was yellow and he held it out over the fire. "I shall begin," he said in a huge voice. "This Mommy-Stick is *I can relate to that!"* He snapped it in two and threw it into the flames amidst cheers from the men.

"Who's next," he bellowed. "Who will break their Mommy-Stick?"

I jumped forward. I had once been caught at this game when I was a camp counselor, the object being to take all the good quotations early and leave the last person struggling for something to say. I didn't want any part of that. Besides, I didn't want to have this pink Mommy-Stick in my hand any longer than I had to.

"This Mommy-Stick," I yelled, breaking it in half and throwing it into the fire, "is *I just want you to open up!"*

"Yes!" The other men yelled. *"I just want you to open up!"*

The floodgate was broken. Calls of *"I feel your pain!"* and *"Let me share your space!"* echoed around the campfire as the men jumped toward the fire and back again, the drums beating a rhythmic thrum and lending—yes, I had to admit it—a primordial atmosphere to the gathering.

"Why can't we discuss our feelings!" bawled a short, rotund, accountant-like man in a high-pitched wail.

Finally, the only person left was Pete. He was looking dazed and holding a lime-green Mommy-Stick. I knew he was desperately trying to come up with something to say without repeating one of the others. It's the very reason I went first.

All eyes were on Pete and the last Mommy-Stick. The drums were starting to get louder and the other men had taken up the chant "Mommy-Stick, Mommy-Stick, Mommy-Stick..." It was now obvious that it was Pete that had to bring a close to this ritual and he was close to panic.

"This Mommy-Stick..." he finally screamed over the din. The immediate silence was almost deafening. The drums stopped. The men became deathly quiet. The only sound we could hear was the faint crackling of the now diminishing campfire. I looked at Pete. He was shaking. I could understand it. The atmosphere was electric.

"This Mommy-Stick," he screamed again, "is *Why can't you put the damn toilet seat down!"*

"Hoooooooowwwwwwl!" went the men. The drums started up again, even faster than before and about half of the men started dancing around the campfire like the Wild Men they had become.

"The Great Mother's authority has become too great." Dr. Ren called over the howls. "Men's societies are disappearing, partly under pressure from women with hurt feelings. Too many women are raising boys with no man in the house. It is now time for you to reclaim your birthright. It is time for you to build your lair."

At this, the men who had obviously read their information sheets, or those that had come to the IMMR before, ran over to the pile of extra lounge chairs and grabbed as many as they could carry. Pete and I, along with one other confused soul, stood by and watched our cohorts shape the lounge chairs into small forts, which they then crawled into.

"That was a good one," I whispered to Pete, trying not to move my lips. "Why can't you put the damn toilet seat down! Outstanding!" I looked around for my chair, but it had been purloined by another fellow who was exercising his God-given, animal right to take whatever he could get away with.

"It's all I could think of," he whispered back.

"After three marriages, that's all you could think of?"

"What can I say?" Pete shrugged. "I froze."

"Come out of your lairs," called Dr. Renquist Sampson, Motivator Extraordinaire, as the drums began anew. "As you came out of the water at your baptism, now come out of your lairs and be transformed into the men God wants you to be."

The men who had hidden under their chairs now crawled out and stood in the circle around the fire. Dr. Ren slowly dropped to his knees.

"Some of you may want to temporarily leave the world of the two-legged, and join me in the world of the four-legged," he said.

One by one, all of us dropped to our hands and knees, following his example. I don't remember if I was the last to do so, but I caught sight of Pete dropping to the ground like a sack of doorknobs. I knew what he was thinking. He wasn't about to be caught again.

"You may find yourself behaving like these four-leggeds; you may be scratching the earth, getting in contact with the dirt and the world around you," Dr. Ren said. As he spoke, some of the men began pawing at the ground. "You may find yourself behaving like the most masculine of all animals—the ram," Dr. Ren said in a coaxing voice. "You may find unfamiliar noises emerging from your throats!"

There were gurgles, bleats, and a few more wolf calls. Out of the corner of my eye, I saw the accountant coming toward me, head down, tufts of white hair ringing a bald spot. I shuffled myself around on all fours and looked at Pete.

"You look ridiculous," I said.

"Ditto," said Pete with a grin. "How did we get into this?"

I felt a slight presence at my rear, and turned to see the accountant beginning to sniff my buttocks.

"Woof!" he said.

"That was some night," said Pete as we collapsed onto the mattresses. "I'm really getting in touch with you-know-who."

"Yeah. My inner man is just itching to get out. I'm hoping this face-paint comes off with soap and water. Otherwise, we have to drive into town wearing this stuff. Do you think it's a sign of alcoholism that I *really* want a beer just about now?"

"Yep. You're an alcoholic for sure and I'm right behind you."

"I'm glad you were there for the trust-spin. That accountant was being *way* too friendly. I'm not sure he could have caught me anyway."

"What's on for tomorrow?" asked Pete.

"I stole somebody's information sheet," I said, pulling it out of my pocket.

"You stole it? You? A cop?"

"It's my right as a wild-man," I said. "I take what I need. Woof!" I held the paper up to the lantern that was lighting our tent. "Right after breakfast we build the altar to Yahweh. Then the Mud-Dance and the Naked Piglet Chase."

"The WHAT?"

"Just kidding," I said with a laugh. "No piglets. It ends with lunch and a big group hug."

"Thank God."

"See? You're getting religion after all."

The troop was awakened the next morning by the call of the ram's horn. We knew it was a ram's horn because it was printed quite clearly on our information sheet. I'm pretty sure it was a recording though. A ram's horn is a difficult instrument to play. I had a go at it once when I was playing the organ at a Jewish temple years ago. I'm not a proficient brass player by any means, but I had a brass methods class in college and I can still play a few tunes on a tuba. Yet the sound that came out of the ram's horn when I gave it my best honk might only have been appropriate to call together a convocation of flatulent band directors. Still, maybe Nelson or Bernie had been practicing. We exited our tent and saw that they hadn't. The ram's horn was still sounding and the two of them were standing at attention in front of the tents wearing nothing but loincloths and war paint and shivering like newborn pups.

"Aren't you guys cold?" asked Pete. Pete and I both had on our parkas. "The weather report said twenty-five degrees this morning."

"Breakfast is in a half-hour," managed Nelson, through chattering teeth. "You g-g-g-guys can use the facilities up at the main b-b-building."

"Can't we just go in the woods?" asked the accountant hopefully. We'd found out during the course of the previous evening that his name was Vernon Speck and that he wasn't really an accountant. He was a dentist. This was his fourth time to attend the Iron Mike Men's Retreat.

"No you c-c-c-can't," said Nelson. "There's a girl-scout troop in here this afternoon. They d-d-don't want any surprises like last time."

By the time breakfast was over, it had warmed up to a comfortable thirty degrees. Comfortable for Pete and I and one other man, that is. Our information sheet had informed us that loincloths were optional for the second day and since neither Pete nor I had remembered to pack our loincloths, we were in jeans and sweatshirts. The loin-clothed crew was still shivering and jockeying for position around the campfire.

"I packed mine, but decided I didn't want to wear it this morning," said a man named Jim, sidling up to us.

"A wise choice," I replied.

"My wife made it for me after she read the information sheet. This whole thing is the marriage counselor's idea. I think it's just weird, but I agreed to come."

Pete and I nodded compassionately.

"It's time to build our altar," called Dr. Ren. "Collect your stones and let us begin."

"Collect our stones," said Pete. "Now there's a Freudian observation if ever I heard one."

I had found what I thought were a couple of good-sized rocks behind our tent. They were maybe seven or eight pounds and as big around as grapefruits. They certainly were manageable enough that mindlessly tossing them a couple of inches into the air and catching them as we made our way from our tents back to the campfire wasn't a problem. We were astonished, therefore, to see the rest of the men, hunched over and lugging stones the size of microwave ovens. One stout fellow with the physique of a lumberjack had a stone on each shoulder—each one weighing at least eighty to a hundred pounds.

"I feel emasculated," whispered Pete. "Just look at the size of our stones compared to those other guys."

"We may be emasculated, but at least we're not herniated," I whispered back. "Pebble envy seems to be the point of this exercise. Anyway, mine's definitely bigger than yours."

"You wish! What did the information sheet say?"

"That we should bring the largest stone we could carry for the glory of Yahweh."

"Oh, man..."

We followed Dr. Ren, in procession, carrying our stones down a wide path into the woods for about three hundred yards until we came to the altar. It was more of a cairn, I thought, consisting of a six foot by six foot collection of stones rising in a pyramid, the top of which stood about five feet high above the forest floor. It had been built and added on to through the years by the past conference attendees.

"Let us begin," said Dr. Ren. "The smallest stones first."

Everyone looked at Pete and me. I gave him a nudge.

"That's you," I said as Nelson and Bernie began thumping on their tom-toms. "Yours is the smallest."

Pete sullenly made his way to the altar and placed his stone about a foot from the top.

"We build this altar to you, O Yahweh!" called Dr. Ren.

"We build this altar to you," the men replied.

I was next and the rest of the group followed in order of manliness. There were a few disagreements when the sizes were fairly close, but Dr. Ren was the final arbiter. He pointed to one or the other and they came forward as they were chosen. The chant followed the placing of each stone. Pete and I were actually glad that we had been first, not that it really mattered. Our stones were pretty light. The rest of the men were valiantly trying to keep their stones aloft for the entire ceremony. Most of them, the ones carrying the larger stones, finally had to drop them on the ground, picking them up again when it was their turn to approach the altar. A few stalwart souls held them the whole time.

The last one to place his stones was Lumberjack. He stood stoically and waited, never forsaking his burden, and by the end, sweat was pouring off him despite his loincloth, the fairly cold temperature and the wind that had begun to pick up. The rest of the loincloths were shivering shamelessly. Only Dr. Ren seemed to be immune from the cold. As Lumberjack's stones crunched into the side of the altar, a cheer went up from the men and they dashed back toward the campfire.

"Wait," yelled Dr. Ren. "We build this altar to you, O Yahweh." But it was too late. Most of his audience had turned tail and run for the fire. It was left for Pete, Lumberjack, Jim and me to finish up.

"We build this altar to you," we replied, half-heartedly. With that, the drums stopped, and Nelson and Bernie followed the others in quick pursuit as fast as their naked legs could carry them. Lumberjack just grunted. He was doubled over, still trying to catch his breath.

"Are you okay?" I asked.

"I...I..." wheezed Lumberjack.

"Everything all right here?" It was Dr. Ren.

"Don't know yet," I said, turning back to Lumberjack. "Talk to me, big guy." His answer was to pitch forward on his face and lay unmoving in the pine straw.

"Get the truck," I said to Pete, but he was already running full speed for the campsite.

"Be back in a minute," he yelled over his shoulder.

"Help me turn him over." Jim and Dr. Ren complied.

"He's not breathing," said Jim.

"You know CPR?" asked Dr. Ren, near panic.

"Yeah," I said. "Step back."

I was about three minutes into the CPR when Lumberjack started breathing on his own. Pete drove up just moments later.

"Let's get him into the truck and we'll get him to the hospital pretty quickly," I said, slapping the blue police light onto the roof of the cab.

"You're a cop?" asked Dr. Ren.

"Yeah. Let's get him in."

Four pairs of willing hands lifted Lumberjack into the cab. He was conscious now, but still too groggy to speak. Pete slid in beside him on the passenger side as I jumped behind the wheel.

"We'll be back for lunch," Pete called out the window as I gunned the old truck down the path and out of the woods.

"The doctor says you'll be okay," I said to Lumberjack as he "rested comfortably" in the emergency room bed. "I'm Hayden Konig, by the way. Pete Moss and I brought you in."

"My name's Jack Rutledge. And thanks. The doc said that he thinks I had a heart attack."

"I'm not surprised. Those rocks were pretty heavy."

"Ah," he shrugged. "They weren't that bad, but I may have overdone it. They think I might have a blockage and they're going to keep me in for some tests. Sorry you had to miss the rest of the retreat."

Just then, Pete came through the privacy curtain.

"How you doin'?"

"I'll be okay. I really want to thank you guys."

"No problem," said Pete magnanimously. "All in a day's work. Not only did we save your life, but we didn't have to do the Mud-Dance or the Naked Piglet Chase."

"Naked Piglet Chase? Oh man! Did I miss that?" Jack sounded despondent.

"I'm sure they'll let you go again next year," I said, "if you promise to bring smaller stones."

Pete and I got back to the retreat just in time for lunch. We had used the facilities at the hospital to take the opportunity to clean the paint off our faces. We drove up as the men were putting their bratwursts on sticks for grilling over the coals of what was left of their campfire.

"How is he?" asked Dr. Ren, the first one up to our truck.

"He'll be fine," I said, getting out. "The doctor thinks he had a heart attack."

"Thank God he's all right," said Nelson. "Nothing like that has ever happened before."

"It's a shame you missed the Mud-Dance," said Vernon Speck. I almost couldn't tell who he was. He was covered in dark brown mud from his white hair to his feet. His loincloth wasn't nearly as muddy as the rest of him. I suspected that he had removed it to perform his plastering job, but I didn't dare ask.

"Aren't you cold?" asked Pete.

"Nah. Once the mud starts to dry, it sort of heats up on you."

"Well, we're sorry to have missed it," I said with what I hoped was a tinge of regret in my voice.

"You can come back next year," said Nelson. "No charge for either of you."

"That's great!" said Pete.

"We'll be here with bells on our loincloths," I added. "Now how about some of that bratwurst?"

Chapter 16

"Come on over here where I can get a good look at you," I said, still brandishing my heater. He walked up to the desk.

"Now, spill," I said.

"I know who killed Candy. What's it worth to you?"

"Why, you little weasel..." I put a stogy in my mouth with my free hand and lit it with another blast from my shooter. He jumped like a freshman cheerleader at homecoming.

"Jeez! Don't do that."

"Don't do what?" I asked. Kapow! I fired off another round, this one aimed at the radio in the corner. It was a lucky shot, but the radio came on full blast, and the sounds of The All American Polka Band filled the room. Kablam! I hated to waste another bullet, but I hated polka music more.

"Okay, okay. I'll talk," stammered the little pipsqueak.

"You bet you will." I took my time and reloaded, letting him watch each bullet as it wriggled into the chamber. "Now, how do you know who killed Candy?"

"I saw it! I saw the whole thing. I was hiding in the kitchen." He squirmed like a salted slug. "But I want something in return."

"You see this?" I put the gun on the desk. "This is like a game of spin-the-bottle. I ask you a question and then I spin the gun. If it points to you, I shoot off one of your thumbs. Got it?" I spun the gun.

"Wait! Wait! What's the question?" The gun was slowing.

"Who did it?"

The gun stopped and pointed right at him, but then, I've always been lucky at spin-the-bottle. Just ask any of the clarinet players in fourth period band at Redbug Junior

High School. I was responsible for more gum swapping than Mickey Mantle's rookie baseball card.

"Don't shoot me! I'll tell you what you want to know." He was as scared as a college fund in a room full of stockbrokers.

I shrugged and reached for my gun. "You'd better be fast."

I hadn't even finished my sentence when a bullet smashed through the window and whinnied over my shoulder. The glass shattered and I jumped over the desk and down onto the floor quicker than a secretary on the boss's birthday.

"Get down," I yelled. I looked over at my visitor. He was already down. And a hole was in his chest.

"Wow." Meg said. "Action. Veiled threats, vague yet intriguing character development, brilliant use of the shameless simile, sexual innuendo, gun violence and finally, another murder."

"Not bad, eh?" I said proudly.

"There's just one problem."

"What?" I asked. "What's the problem?"

"Well you managed to introduce another character. You know...another suspect."

"Yeah. Just in time, too. I was running out of ideas."

"And then," Meg said slowly, as if explaining to a small child, "you killed him."

"Um...wait! Wait just one second. He's not dead yet!"

"Oh, brother..."

I crawled over to the body and looked down at him. He was hurt. Hurt bad.

"I'm not dead yet," he managed to gurgle.

"Told you," I said to Meg.

"Oh, please. Why don't you just give it up? You're not fooling anyone but yourself."

"Who did it? Who killed Candy Blather?" I was insistent now. As insistent as last night's burritos.

"It was..."

I leaned close to his face. He could barely speak.

"Who? Who was it?" I asked again.

A bubble was forming on his lips--an expanding pink globule, reminiscent of the championship performance of Parker "Bubbles" Ramsay in the '62 Tri-state Bazooka Challenge, growing ever larger as the poor sap tried to force his last words through the darkening blackness; finally exploding in a frothy fountain of foam and releasing a single word, carried aloft in a gossamer web of scarlet saliva.

"Rosebud."

"Rosebud? That's the dumbest thing I've ever read!"

"No. It's a clue," I said. "Really."

It was around four o'clock when I got back to the Slab. Pete, like myself, had managed a shower and was behind the counter, making a pot of coffee.

"Hey there," I called as I came in. "You recovered yet?"

"Yeah. It wasn't too bad. I'm glad we missed that mud-dance though. Those guys are never going to get that mud out of their mmm...crevices."

"Want to go back next year?"

"Not only am I never going back, but those speeding tickets you took care of? I figure you owe me three more."

"Fair enough," I said. "That Mommy-Stick ceremony was enough to..."

"Did I say three?" Pete interrupted. "I meant five. And if you say another word, it'll be seven."

"This Mommy-Stick is *'Why can't you put the damn toilet seat down!'* That was great!"

"Seven!" said Pete. "And if you tell anyone, it'll be ten! And besides, *you're* the one who got sniffed."

"Okay, okay," I said with a chuckle. "I appreciate you going with me. Anyway, all I told Meg was that we weren't allowed to speak a word of what went on at the conference. We all took a man-oath."

"That's good. A man-oath." Pete thought about it and nodded in agreement. "A *moath,* if you will."

"Yeah, a moath. Could I get a Reuben sandwich?" I asked, changing the subject. "I'm supposed to meet Billy here in a couple of minutes."

"Yep. I'll get it working."

"And a cup of coffee."

"It'll be up in a jiffy."

I took a seat at a table in the back. Billy and my Reuben arrived at almost the same time.

"What's that?" Billy asked as he sat down across the table from me. "Looks good."

"Reuben sandwich. "

Billy looked puzzled.

"Corned beef, sauerkraut, Swiss cheese and Russian dressing on rye. Best sandwich ever invented."

"I'll take your word for it." He looked over his shoulder for Pete. "Can I get a burger and some fries?" he called.

"Got it," said Pete from behind the counter.

"And a Coke," added Billy.

"So what's up?" I asked between bites.

"I'm withdrawing my name from consideration for Senior Warden."

"You are? Why?"

"Well, you know I do a lot of work over at the church. I keep the graveyard looking nice, mow the grass, plant shrubs and flowers in the spring."

"Yeah. So?"

"I guess there's a problem," said Billy. "If I'm Senior Warden, there's a big conflict of interest. I really need the graveyard contract and the work I do for the church isn't peanuts either. If I was Senior Warden, I'd have to give up the contract for St. Barnabas."

"Who says?"

"Well, it was Rob Brannon who pointed it out. It makes sense, you know. I can't really hire myself."

"But you're Junior Warden now."

"I know, but I'm giving that up, too."

I was incredulous. "But why? No one's ever complained before."

"I know, but things are changing."

"Billy, that's just plain stupid. Everyone knows you do a great job for a fair price."

"Rob says that if I'm Senior Warden, or even Junior Warden, the job would have to be put up for bid. I might get the contract, but I might not. I just can't afford it."

"There's something fishy going on, Billy. I don't know what it is yet, but I mean to find out. You should go ahead and run."

"Sorry, Hayden. I can't."

Pete came over with a burger, fries and a Coke and put it down in front of Billy.

"Everything okay?" he asked, seeing our faces.

"Yeah," said Billy glumly. "Everything's okay."

"Harumph," I said, my mouth full of sauerkraut.

Wednesday morning found me practicing in the choir loft. I had forgotten about the "Puppet-Moment" scheduled for

Sunday and was only reminded when I got to the organ console and found a note from Brenda—Princess Foo-Foo—taped to the music rack. The Children's Moment in the service had lost momentum after our last interim priest, Father Barna, had not enjoyed all the success he might have wished for. It had been shelved indefinitely, but the powers-that-be had decided to give it another try—this time with puppets and fair warning to Father George. Moosey, Bernadette, Ashley and Robert were all still attending services and now they had another friend—Christopher. There might even be one or two others.

JJ came up at around noon just as I was finishing up on my Handel concerto for Sunday.

"Cool," she said. "What's that?"

"*The Cuckoo and the Nightingale*. Like it? I thought I'd do it for the postlude since Brenda's doing a Puppet-Moment."

"Sounds good to me. Care for a bite of lunch?"

"Sure. What's cooking?"

"I'm fixing some soup for tonight's church meeting. You can come down and give it a taste. I've also got some pimento cheese sandwiches in the fridge."

"I'll be right down," I said. "Any rats I need to bring my gun for?"

"I don't think so."

"See you in a minute then."

I found JJ in the kitchen, stirring her pot. Rob Brannon was standing over the counter, finishing a bowl of soup. It smelled delicious.

"Hayden!" he said as I came through the swinging door. "I was just going to come up and see you. Soon as I tasted this soup."

"Hi, Rob," I answered, picking up a bowl of my own. I turned my attention to the pot. JJ was a good cook, but I had found, over the years, that it was always a good idea to find out what was in the pot. She was stirring the soup with the lower half of a wooden canoe paddle

"This smells excellent," I said. "What kind is it?"

"Gumbo," said JJ with a smile and a genteel drawl reminiscent of her Louisiana heritage.

"Gumbo. That sounds great." I was still wary and holding my bowl close. "What kind of gumbo?

"Squirrel-head gumbo."

Rob spit his last spoonful of soup back into his bowl and wiped his tongue on a paper napkin as unobtrusively as he could— a gesture that didn't go unnoticed by either of us. I didn't mind squirrel-head gumbo. It actually didn't matter what kind of meat was in the gumbo—after a few hours it all tasted the same anyway. The alarming part of the meal was the title and, of course, the surprise at the bottom of the pot. Rob, however, looked rather startled. I didn't mind playing along.

"Well, fill it up," I said, holding my bowl out.

"You want a head or not?"

I could feel Rob looking at JJ in alarm. He was suspicious, but I didn't think he was a true believer. Not yet.

"Sure. I'll take a head."

JJ reached her ladle deep into the twenty-gallon pot and clanged it around the bottom. It only took her a few moments to find what she was looking for. She pulled her prize to the top and dropped it into my bowl where it floated nicely on the roux, vegetables, and other savory ingredients. I deliberately set it down next to Rob and a picked up a big soupspoon. Rob went from startled to green quicker than a chameleon. There, looking up at him, looking very much like a skinned rat, was a squirrel head. There wasn't much meat left on the skull, but the eyes were a nice opaque bluish-creamy color and the teeth, stained brown from thc roux, and looked like something out of a horror film. It was what the kids in the congregation loved to see, even though the moms all dreaded the moment. I knew there were two or three heads in the pot and that the kids would take great delight in carrying them from table to table after supper, showing everyone who would look. I ate a big spoonful.

"It tastes great, JJ," I said with a smack of my lips. "Top-notch squirrel-head gumbo." I could feel Rob shudder from three feet away.

"Is that what you're serving for the church meeting?" he asked quietly.

"One of the things," said JJ. "It's a St. Barnabas tradition. There's also some roasted chicken and other stuff."

"Thank God," said Rob.

"Did you want to talk to me?" I asked, this time following my question with an audible slurp.

"Yes," he said. "As you know, I'm the new Parish Administrator."

"Interim," I added.

"Yes, whatever. Anyway, it's my opinion, and Father George agrees, that we need to keep track of expenses in a much more business-like fashion. Therefore, I'm instigating a policy of purchase orders and vouchers."

"Really," I commented in my snidest fashion, not bothering to inflect the one word observation into the form of a question.

"If you need to order something—let's say choir music, for example—you'll have to fill out a voucher with the vendor, the description of goods or services, and the cost, get it approved by the worship committee and Father George. Then it will come to me for approval. If it's consistent with your budget line item, I'll approve it and you may fill out a purchase order, then send or fax it to the vendor. The purchase order number and voucher approval number must be on all incoming invoices or they won't be paid."

"How long do you expect this process to take?" I asked. "Start to finish?"

"Two or three weeks. I know it seems like a long time, but you just have to plan ahead."

"Hmmm," I slurped again. "Seems like a lot of work just to order some music. How about if I just pay for it myself?"

"No, I'm afraid not. We need to find out exactly how much money we're spending. It doesn't do us any good if you're undermining the system."

"You realize, of course, that I donate all of my salary back into the music discretionary fund," I said.

"We're stopping that as well. It's not a good policy for parishioners to be able to allocate where they want their money to go. It sends a bad message. Gifts and tithes should be made without designation. Otherwise popular programs would flourish and programs that we need, but aren't as noticeable, would fall by the wayside. Janitorial services, for instance. Or AA meetings."

"Good point, and I agree with you. But I tithe as well. My tithe may certainly go wherever the church deems fit. But my gift is my gift. It goes where I want it to go."

"We think it's a bad idea," said Rob.

"The music discretionary fund has over ten thousand dollars in it. What happens to that?"

"I think it should be turned over to the vestry, but Father George disagrees. So it will remain in the music fund and be used for music only, but there won't be any more added to it. Next year, when it runs out, you'll have to submit a budget request like every other department."

"I don't think I will," I said, feeling my anger emerging. "And you understand that I'll be taking my salary in full from this point on."

"It's better this way. We'll finally understand how much money it takes to keep St. Barnabas going. People don't realize it because the numbers have been so skewed. What we lose in your salary will more than be made up once the parishioners realize the situation."

"Maybe." I slurped again. "But I'm not going to fill out any stupid vouchers."

"You will or you'll leave," he said smugly, spinning on his heel and marching out of the kitchen.

"My," I said to JJ. "That went well."

"Hayden, I think you'd better come out," said Nancy's crackling voice on my cell phone. Nancy and Meg were the only two people with my cell number. I had resisted getting one to the bitter end, my excuse being that reception up in the mountains made them practically useless. But then, of course, technology caught up with us mountain folks and the towers started springing up. Nancy finally convinced me that cell phones were the easiest way to keep in touch, and since I rarely answered the phone at my house, I decided to acquiesce.

"There's been an incident. At Gwen Jackson's house."

Gwen Jackson, a faithful member of St. Barnabas, was the veterinarian in St. Germaine. She was unmarried, fiftyish and had been practicing in the town for over twenty years.

"I've got to be at a meeting over at the church."

"It'll have to wait. Someone shot out her front windows. Her neighbor called it in. I'm on my way out there now."

"Okay. I'm out on Forsyth Road anyway. I'll turn around and head back to her house."

Gwen Jackson lived about twelve miles out of town in the opposite direction from my farm. It was close to six o'clock and already dark by the time I got out to her house. Nancy was in the driveway with a man I took to be the neighbor. Some lights in Gwen's house were on, but her car wasn't in the driveway. She wasn't home.

"Did you try and call her to tell her what happened?" I asked Nancy.

"There was no answer at the office. I called at about five-thirty."

"She's probably at the church. There's a parish meeting tonight. Supper, then the parish meeting, followed by the vestry election. I called St. Barnabas to leave a message for her, but there wasn't any answer. Not surprising really. The phone only rings in the offices."

"What time's the meeting?"

"It should be starting right now," I said as we walked over to the neighbor.

"Hi, Len," I said, shaking his hand. "You know Nancy?

Len nodded toward her. "Len Purvis. Pleased to meet you."

"Can you tell us what happened?" I asked.

"We were eating supper when we heard these shots coming from outside."

"We?" asked Nancy, writing all the information in her pad.

"Me and my wife. We was having pork chops. She's still in the kitchen if you need to talk to her."

"We'll talk with her directly," I said. "Did you hear a car?"

"Heard one leave after the shots and the glass breaking. There were three or four shots, I guess. Shotgun. Twelve gauge."

"How do you know it was a shotgun?" asked Nancy.

"I know a shotgun when I hear one."

"So you heard the shots and the glass breaking, and you came out?" I asked.

"Not right away. I ain't stupid."

"Of course not," I said.

"When we heard the car drive off. That's when we came out."

Nancy had left the driveway and walked the twenty feet over to the front of the house. "Were the lights on when you came out?"

He nodded. "They're usually not on till Dr. Jackson gets home. But I guess they're programmed for burglars or something. They were on when we came out."

"Does she have an alarm system?" I wondered.

"I've never seen one. I think they're just motion lights. Some of them come on when you walk up to the door."

Nancy walked back over to us. "The picture window in front is gone. There's glass everywhere. The two side windows are gone, too. I don't know what else yet."

"Did you see the car?" I asked.

"Nope. It was dark."

"Not that dark when it happened," said Nancy.

"I looked out the window," Len said. "But I couldn't see anything. I wasn't about to come outside."

"What did the car sound like?" Nancy asked.

"Well, it needed a muffler. Or it might have been a truck, I guess. An older truck. You know, it had that rumble. That's all I noticed. I wasn't coming outside. Not till I was sure they were gone."

I turned to Nancy. She nodded and jotted the information in her pad.

"Let's walk around the house, make sure it's secure. Then we'll go talk to Mrs. Purvis..."

"Roweena," interrupted Len.

"Roweena. Then I'll go into town, tell Gwen and come back out with her and get an inventory of the damage. You want to stay here till we get back?"

"Yeah. I'll stay and clean up what I can," said Nancy.

"She'll appreciate it, I'm sure. I don't think we can get any repair people here until tomorrow so she'll probably have to stay in town tonight."

"Her name's Roweena," Len said to Nancy, "but everyone calls her Weenie."

"I'm sure they do," Nancy replied.

"Can I go back to my pork chops?" asked Len.

"Yes sir, you certainly may," said Nancy with just a twinge of sarcasm in her voice. "Thanks for your help."

I pulled up to St. Barnabas at five till eight, just as people were beginning to come out of the Parish Hall. I presumed that the parish meeting had just concluded. I parked the truck and went into the church to find Gwen Jackson. I found her talking to Davis Boothe and Father George by the kitchen door. Meg spotted me coming in and came over to join us.

"Hello, Hayden," said Gwen. "We missed you at the meeting."

"It couldn't be helped. Can I talk to you for a second?" I indicated we should go outside onto the patio.

"Sure." Gwen slipped on her coat and headed for the door.

"I'll be back in a second," I whispered to Meg as I turned to follow Gwen. Meg gave me a wink and fell into a conversation with Father George and Davis.

"How was the election?" I asked Gwen as I hurried to catch up with her.

"Well, I'm on the vestry again."

"Really? That's great. Who else was elected?"

"Davis and Russ Stafford. That's what we were talking about when you came in. Rob Brannon was elected Junior Warden. That was a surprise."

"Yeah. How about Senior Warden?"

"Jed Pierce."

"He'll do a good job," I said, as we exited the double doors and made our way onto the patio. It was a nice night. Cool, but not too chilly. "Listen, Gwen. There's been some vandalism out at your house."

"What kind of vandalism?" She was shocked.

"Someone shot out the windows of your living room. A shotgun we think. I'd like to take you out there and walk through the house. Nancy's out there now."

"Okay. Sure. I'm not staying out there tonight, though. I'll get a room in town."

"I thought you would. Do you mind if Meg comes out with us?"

"No, I'd like that. May she ride with me?"

"Of course. I'll go get her. Then I'll follow you two to your house. Do you know anyone who might have any reason to do this?"

"Of course not."

"No teenager's favorite pet that might have had to be put down? Nothing like that?"

She shook her head. "I don't think so. I'll go back and look through the files, but I think I would remember."

"Go back a ways, will you?"

"Sure. I'll do it first thing tomorrow."

Chapter 17

It was around nine in the morning when Kent Murphee, Ace Coroner, came into the police station.

"I thought you guys would be over at the Slab," he said to Nancy, who was working the desk.

"Not this morning," said Nancy. "We sent Dave for some donuts though. He should be back in a couple of minutes."

"Excellent. I'll be happy to wait. If you offered me some coffee, I wouldn't refuse it."

"I'll put on a fresh pot."

"Hi Kent. Anything new on our friend?" I said as I came out of my office.

"As a matter of fact, that's why I'm here. I need to look at the altar if you don't mind."

"Okay with me. I'll go let you into the church."

"Let's wait for Dave first," Kent said. "I haven't had any breakfast."

"Do you have a theory?" Nancy asked.

Kent smiled. "I just might. I heard you guys had a shooting last night."

"Yeah. Over at Gwen Jackson's place," I said. Then for Nancy's and my sake, as well as Kent's curiosity, I went over the details.

We didn't have any leads on who shot the windows out of Gwen Jackson's house. When Gwen, Meg and I arrived, Nancy had the lights in the house on and most of the glass swept up. Roweena Purvis didn't have anything to add to her husband's account. She didn't even come outside. Len had told her to stay in the kitchen and call the police. The road was paved, so there weren't any tire tracks. As near as we could tell, the windows were shot from the front yard. Maybe twenty feet away. There were shotgun pellets in the house, but most of the damage was done to the glass. Whoever pulled the trigger blew out the eight-foot plate glass window in the living room, two full-length windows on either side of the front door, the bathroom window in the front of the house and one of the small windows on the garage door. Gwen had called the insurance company and they were meeting her this morning. We, the long arm of the law, had nothing. No clues except a witness hearing a twelve-gauge shotgun—a suspicion borne out by empty twelve-gauge shells on the lawn—and what might be an old car or truck in need of a muffler. Nancy had collected the spent shells, but there were no fingerprints to be found on any of them. She thought that this pointed to an adult rather than a kid bent on mischief. Not many kids bothered to wipe the shells clean before loading them or to put on gloves before handling the ammo. Gloves were clumsy when handling a twelve gauge.

"You catch the guy?" asked Kent, after I had reviewed the evidence.

"Nope. And no leads either. I think that whoever did it knew she wasn't home. It wasn't as though they were looking to break in or do her any harm. They just wanted to make a mess. Maybe scare her a little."

"Is she scared?"

"They obviously don't know Dr. Jackson," Nancy said. "If she finds out who did it, she'll turn them every way but loose."

"Did you guys find out anything about Lester Gifford? Or have you been too busy?"

"As a matter of fact," Nancy said, "I've found out a few interesting things."

The door opened and Dave came in with a box of donuts.

"Set them over here, Dave," said Kent. "I'm the guest."

Nancy had pulled out her pad and was flipping through a few pages while we all made ourselves comfortable.

"I did some background on the church first. Did you know that Robert Brannon, Sr. (Rob's great-grandfather) was a major contributor to St. Barnabas in the early years?"

"We knew that," I said. "Rob has pointed it out to anyone who will listen on more than one occasion. There are several stained-glass windows with a Brannon family dedication inscribed at the bottom."

"Right. Robert Brannon, Sr. made his fortune in the Civil War. He was originally from Maryland and received one of many contracts from the government to supply rations to the Army of the Potomac. By the time the war was over, he had amassed several million dollars and bought eight hundred acres just outside of St. Germaine. By 1899, he had sold most of it and had moved into town."

"Okay," I asked, "what happened in 1899?"

"In 1899, St. Barnabas burned down. January to be exact. Rob, Sr. was sixty-two years old. In March of that year, the rector of St. Barnabas named Caleb Mortenson, Rob Sr., and two parishioners were killed in a flash flood. According to the newspaper, they were picnicking by the New River. All four of the bodies were found downstream."

"Quite a tragedy for the church," said Dave.

"Yep. The church was rebuilt in 1904. It took them that long to raise the money. I found a couple of letters—Marilyn gave me access to the archives—mentioning that if Rob, Sr. was still alive, the church might have been completed sooner. Rob's son, Rob, Jr., was not enamored of St. Barnabas and didn't see rebuilding as a priority.

"I'm jumping ahead now. It's 1937 and Lester Gifford, our deceased, is an assistant manager at the Watauga County Bank in Boone. There's a merger in the works and, according to the bank records, an extensive audit is underway prior to the merger. Part of this audit, the part that Lester is in charge of, is the identification of the owners of accounts that have not been accessed for several years. Remember, all these records were on paper. There weren't any computers or electronic files. Ledgers, notes, bankbooks, bonds, and certificates were the order of the day. On February 8th, 1937, Lester Gifford was murdered and placed in the altar of St. Barnabas."

"How did you come up with the date?" asked Kent.

"He was mentioned in an article in the *Watauga Democrat* on January 15th. The bank merger happened on February 25th. There was a fire in the records room of St. Barnabas on February 8th. Most, but not all, of the records were lost. The fire went out on its own and didn't spread to the rest of the church. The newspaper said that arson was suspected, but it was just a blurb. No real details, but I don't think the fire was an accident.

"Got it," said Kent.

"Neither Lester, nor his wife Mavis, had any connection with the church that I could find; however, the Senior Warden of St. Barnabas, a Mr. Harold Lynn, was also the owner and president of Watauga County Bank. His father, Wesley Lynn, was the president of the bank in 1899. "

"Coincidence?" asked Kent.

"I doubt it. But if you think so, here's another one. There was a Sunday School teacher named Jacob Winston who was also the church historian. His day job was as a teller at Watauga County Bank. Jacob was arrested on March 4th on the charge of murder. There was no trial and the charges were dismissed—lack of evidence and no body—but Jacob wasn't hired by Northwestern Bank after the merger. Jacob died in 1942. Harold Lynn died in 1958."

"So you think that Jacob did it?" asked Dave.

"No. Actually, I think that Harold Lynn did it."

Kent and I nodded in unison.

"I think that Lester found something in the audit—something

that would have impeded the sale of the bank that was about to go through. I also think that it had something to do with the church. That's why the record room was set on fire. Whatever Lester found was also probably in the record room."

"So, if Harold Lynn killed him, it was probably over a financial document," I added.

Nancy nodded. "Yep. And it would have stopped the merger from going through. It's not a big leap to make. Lester found out something, brought it to Harold Lynn. Harold killed him and set Jacob up to take the rap."

"How about this?" I said. "What if Lester went to Jacob, since he was the historian, and enlisted his help to find whatever document might have been in the church records room?"

"And Harold Lynn didn't know if Jacob knew anything or not," Nancy added with a smile. "So he framed him to make sure he wouldn't talk. I'd buy that."

"So," I said, "the only question is, what kind of financial document, that the church would have in its possession, would Harold Lynn think was worth committing murder to keep under wraps?"

Nancy shrugged. "I don't know. Something to stop the sale of the bank. That much is obvious."

"And why didn't Lester's body decompose?" asked Dave.

"That's what I'm about to find out," said Kent.

It was Thursday—Soup Thursday—and Meg was saving me a table at the Ginger Cat. It was, as usual on any Thursday, packed for lunch.

"Hi there," I said. "Did you order for me?"

"I did indeed. It feels like a clam chowder sort of day."

"I agree," I said, taking my seat. "That sounds great. Anything else happening?"

"Well...there's some scuttlebutt around town."

"Care to fill me in?" I asked.

"It's about you."

"Me?"

"Uh huh. It seems that you've been channeling Raymond Chandler's ghost."

"Well, sure. But you knew about that article."

"Yes, I knew. But it was reprinted in the *Democrat* this morning so now everyone in town's read it."

"Maybe they'll see the humor in it."

"Maybe, but I don't think so," Meg said. "Some people are also saying that you tampered with Brother Hog's chicken and tried to sabotage the service."

"Hmmm," I said, chewing on my bottom lip.

"They're saying that you were the one who stole the Blessed Virgin Mary Cinnamon Roll and put it up for auction on eBay. Whoever tried to sell it went by the name Esterhazy. As you know..."

"Yes," I interrupted, "I know."

"Some folks are saying that it might have been you who shot the windows out of Gwen Jackson's house."

"That's absurd. Why would I do that?"

"Heavens, Hayden! I don't know and no one else does either. The prevailing view is that you've been working too hard and that you're about to have a breakdown."

"Okay," I said, taking a deep breath. "First, I'd like to know who is saying these things."

"I heard it from Georgia. She doesn't believe it, of course, but she thought I should be aware of the gossip."

"Did she say where she heard it?"

"She was at the library and heard some ladies talking. So tell me, do you have an alibi for last night? About the time when Gwen's windows were shot?"

"No. I was driving back to town from Ardine's."

"So you were in the neighborhood. Ardine's trailer is only a couple miles from Gwen's house, isn't it?"

"Yes."

"And you have a twelvc-gauge shotgun in your truck?"

"You know I do. Right behind the seat. I'm a police officer," I argued.

"I'm just saying..." said Megan.

"I get your point."

Chapter 18

Marilyn sauntered in to the office, looking like half a million bucks. I could tell something was up. I'm a detective.

"What's up?"

Marilyn gave her girdle a suggestive tug and flapped her eyelashes like a couple of black spiders doing push-ups.

"I was just over for a job interview at Kelly's Detective Agency and Automat."

"You going to be making sandwiches?"

"No, smart guy. I'm going to be working in the front office. Kelly's talking two bucks an hour."

"I'm sure he is. How about if I give you a twenty-cent bump?" We went through this every year. Marilyn would get all dolled up and schedule an interview with Kelly's. I couldn't afford a raise, but I couldn't afford to lose her. She knew it and I knew it and she knew I knew--it was one of the things she knew.

"How about thirty?"

"Sheesh, Marilyn, I can't even afford twenty. How about twenty-two?"

"OK, but Kelly says he'll give me lunch every day."

"I'll tell you what. I'll give you lunch at Kelly's every day, too." Kelly's Automat was a dump. When the health inspector showed up, the roaches disguised themselves as raisins and hid in the bran muffins.

"Never mind," said Marilyn, lighting up a cigar. "Now in honor of my new raise, I'll give you some information."

I perked up like Juan Valdez's cappuccino machine.

"When I was waiting in the office, I heard some talk behind the office door. Toby Taps was reporting to Kelly."

"What did you hear?"

"It has to do with a hymn. That's why Candy was killed. She wouldn't put it in the new hymnal. She said it wasn't worth any amount of money."

"So Toby is in on it?"

"Yeah. Him and Kelly and Piggy--although Piggy was just the hoofer. You'd better be careful. Toby isn't anyone to mess with."

"Neither am I."

"I need to talk to you," said Jed Pierce as I picked up the phone at the cabin. I hadn't showered yet. It wasn't even six o'clock. I'd gotten up early though, fed Baxter, let him out and put a couple of mice on the sill for Archimedes.

"Sure," I said, "What can I do for you?"

"Have you seen *The Tattler* this morning?"

"No. I don't get a paper out here. I usually pick one up in town." *The Tattler* was the St. Germaine weekly equivalent of the small town papers all across America that listed the comings and goings of its residents, recipes, relatives who were visiting, quilting-bee schedules and the like.

"Well, it seems that I'm on page four."

"Is this a good thing?"

"It is not," answered Jed in an angry voice. Jed was a pharmacist. He worked in Boone, but lived in St. Germaine. "It's a short article about St. Barnabas and the new vestry."

"It must be a slow news week."

"Yes it must be. The only reason that I can fathom that the newspaper included it is the mention of me being elected Senior Warden."

"Why is that newsworthy?" I asked.

"Don't play innocent with me Hayden. You're the only one in St. Germaine I ever told about that accident."

I remembered. Jed had been involved in a fatal car accident in South Carolina about twelve years ago. I found out about it when I was running a background check on him for a pharmaceutical company. There was an elderly woman killed, and Jed, the driver of the other car, had originally been charged with a DWI. The charges were subsequently dropped when there was no evidence other than the arresting officer's testimony. The Breathalyzer test had been administered, but lost. I had asked Jed about it at the time, and he had told me the entire story—including denying being drunk at the time. All this, including the denial, was in the public record, but would be tough to find unless you knew where to look.

"The accident report is in the paper?"

"Not all of it. Here's what it says. 'Newly elected Senior Warden of St. Barnabas is pharmacist Jed Pierce of St. Germaine. Mr. Pierce may seem a strange choice to head the Episcopal congregation given the fact that he escaped a felony indictment for vehicular manslaughter in 1982 when evidence of intoxication was misplaced by the police.'"

"Why would they print such a thing?"

"You tell me."

"I didn't have anything to do with it," I said. "You have my word."

"I don't believe you. You're the only one that knew about the accident. You stole the cinnamon roll. You're talking to a ghost. You probably shot out the windows of Gwen Jackson's house..."

"I certainly did not," I said calmly. "Why don't you call the paper and ask them who called?"

"I did. It was an 'anonymous tip.' They said they checked it out and it turned out to be true."

"It wasn't me."

"Yeah, sure. Anyway, I thought you should know that I'm resigning from the vestry," he said, slamming down the phone.

Nancy and I met Kent Murphee in the nave of the church. He came walking down the aisle, carrying a black case the size of a shoebox. We were waiting for him, as he requested, by the altar.

"Good morning," said Kent. "Bring your flashlights?"

"You certainly seem to be in a good mood this morning," said Nancy, still nursing a hot cup of coffee she'd brought with her from the office. I held a couple of Maglites aloft in answer to Kent's inquiry.

"I have some good news," said Kent. "I may have solved the riddle."

Nancy and I watched as Kent put his case on the floor, opened it and pulled out a handheld black electronic device about the same size as a large calculator.

"What is it?" asked Nancy.

Kent just smiled and clicked a button on the side, making the dials jump momentarily with the power surge. "I borrowed it from the geology department at the university. It's a Geiger counter."

He walked around the nave, playing with the knobs until we could all hear a steady click coming from the box. Then he made his way toward us. The clicks gradually increased in speed until the box was rattling like hail on a tin roof.

"We're radioactive?" asked Nancy.

"Not you," said Kent, pointing the Geiger counter towards the altar. "This. Specifically, the top."

"Marble isn't radioactive," I said.

Kent turned the machine off and set it down. "Help me take the back off of this thing."

We removed the back, and Kent turned the Geiger counter on and held it inside the altar. The speed of the clicks increased to machine gun status.

"That's roughly 1400 CPM—clicks per minute—which is how

these counters measure radiation. It's a pretty basic instrument, consisting of the Geiger-Mueller tube, a visual readout in milliroentgens per hour and an audio click. Each radioactive particle makes a click as it travels through the tube. I took the readings yesterday and then had the lab at the university analyze them."

"And the verdict?" I asked.

"Thorite."

"Never heard of it," said Nancy. "I've heard of uranium. Cobalt." She paused. "Radium. That's about it."

"Thorite is about three times as abundant as uranium and about as plentiful as lead," explained Kent. "The principal use is for something called the Welsbach mantle—you know, the part of a gas lantern that glows when it's heated by the flame. The Welsbach mantle is particularly efficient. Thorite is also used in making glass, specifically for high quality camera lenses. As far as being a useful mineral, it's estimated that there's more energy available from thorite than in both uranium and fossil fuels combined. We just haven't explored the technology yet."

"Interesting," I said, "but how does this pertain to us?"

Kent pointed at the marble top of the altar.

"See these brownish-black streaks in the marble? That's the thorite."

"I thought that was marble as well," I said. "Just a different color."

"It's polished, but you can tell the difference in the crystals if you look closely." Kent had a magnifying glass out now and was pointing to the two different minerals. "On the top of the altar, you can't feel the difference because of the finish. It feels like wax to me, but I don't know. Underneath, though, you can run your fingers across the black streaks and feel the dissimilarity. Also, look at the streaks compared to the marble. There are crystals present. They're almost opaque."

Nancy and I were under the altar, flashlights in hand,

following Kent's explanation as best we could.

"Okay," I said. "So it's thorite. It's radioactive. What else?"

"It's *highly* radioactive. And if you look here," Kent shone his flashlight onto the bottom of the slab, "you'll see that the black streaks are much more prevalent than they are on the top. So much so, that the inside of the altar is getting quite a dose of radiation."

"And that means...?" asked Nancy.

"That our friend, Lester Gifford, was pretty well irradiated as soon as he was put in there. Remember when I told you about accidental preservation after death?"

"Yeah," I said. "A body can be buried in a hot, dry area and not decompose at a normal rate."

"Or in a frigid area, or even in a peat bog if the conditions are right. But there's one other way," said Kent.

"Radiation," said Nancy.

"Exactly," said Kent. "And as soon as we took him out, he began to decay."

"How much radiation is this slab giving off?" I asked.

"Quite a bit—and more off the bottom than the top. Much more. As I said before, the top has been sealed with something, so that inhibits the particles even further. The techies at the lab say the radiation is probably nothing to worry about since exposure to parishioners is limited to a couple of hours a week and, even then, mainly just the priests, but you guys might want to think seriously about replacing the top."

"I'll let them know," I said.

"This will look great in my report," said Nancy with a grin. "A body kept incorruptible by accidental radiation. Just great!"

It was almost three o'clock, the appointed hour, when I drove up to the Mountainview Cemetery for the long-delayed interment of Lester Gifford. He had died, by our reckoning, in 1937, and now, sixty-seven years later, he'd finally be laid to rest. It was a beautiful afternoon—the air was perfectly still, highlighting that rare autumn mixture of coolness and warmth. The perceived temperature depended chiefly on whether you happened to be standing in the shade of one of the pine trees hovering over the graves on the outskirts of the cemetery, or whether you had chosen to bask in the last vestiges of St. Germain's Indian Summer.

The crowd, and it turned out to be a sizable one, was gathering. Although the funeral hadn't been officially advertised, word had spread through the St. Barnabas congregation and many of the parishioners had come to pay their respects to someone who, however unwillingly, had been a part of their fellowship for so many years. Nancy and Meg were standing, one row back, on the sunny side of the grave as were most, but not all, of the attendees. The few that had chosen to watch from the shadows of the pines were huddled in their coats and stuffing their hands deep into their pockets. They had a better view, but, in my opinion, the vantage point wasn't worth the chill. Kent obviously disagreed. He was there, next to the graveside, clad only in a tweed jacket and shivering like a leaf. Next to him was JJ, who, unlike Kent, had bundled up in her winter togs and was obviously quite comfortable. Pete and Noylene, both of whom had taken the designated hour off work, were beside JJ, but were currently rethinking their position and shimmying toward the sunlight. On the sunny side, nearest the grave, stood Bev, Elaine and Billy Hixon and Georgia. Behind them were about fifty other folks, all of whom I recognized from St. Barnabas. Malcolm and Rhiza Walker were there, as well as most of the choir and the vestry. Rob Brannon was not. As I walked up to join Meg, she nodded toward the back of the crowd, and when I turned to look, I was surprised to see Brother Hog standing by himself, behind the other congregants.

Father George opened his prayer book and took a step

toward the head of the coffin. A stiff breeze suddenly came up, sending a shiver through the entire crowd—even those on the sunlit side—carrying with it the unmistakable scent of North Carolina pines mixed with approaching rain.

"I am Resurrection and I am Life, says the Lord," recited Father George. "Whoever has faith in me shall have life, even though he die. And everyone who has life, and has committed himself to me in faith, shall not die forever."

The prayer book service unfolded as usual, but was strangely unsettling. As soon as the opening sentences were read by Father George, the sun, which had begun the service as a beacon of warmth, moved behind a dark cloud; a cloud that had been unnoticed until its presence caused a premature twilight to cover the cemetery and the temperature to drop ten degrees in a matter of moments. An unexpected thunderstorm, coming out of nowhere, was common in the mountains—especially in October—but arriving at the exact moment of Lester's burial was unnerving to everyone present. Having no reason to expect any bad weather and, I suspected, in an effort to save a few bucks, Swallow's Mortuary had dispensed with the tent that should have covered the grave and the coffin. Mr. Swallow, a tall, thin man that I had never seen unless he was dressed in his black suit, was shifting from one foot to the other in obvious anticipation of the impending storm.

"The Holy Gospel of our Lord Jesus Christ according to John," said Father George, now hurrying his words and cutting to the chase.

The rumble of thunder that began miles away, rolled slowly across the mountain, taking a full minute to reach us before dying away in the distance. We all exchanged uneasy glances. If this was the thunderstorm we had every right to expect, it was best to get away from the pine trees and under shelter fairly soon. The wind had picked up as well and with it came the distinct whiff of ozone that is the portent of imminent lightning.

Father George was moving at a good clip and leaving out what he could.

"Father of all, we pray to you for Lester, and for all those whom we love but see no longer. Grant to them eternal rest. Let light perpetual shine upon them. May his soul and the souls of all the departed, through the mercy of God, rest in peace."

"Amen," said the crowd, quickly.

Mr. Swallow and one of his men moved to the coffin and lowered it into the grave.

"In sure and certain hope of the resurrection to eternal life through our Lord Jesus Christ, we commend to Almighty God our Lester, and we commit his body to the ground," said Father George. Bev, Elaine and Georgia each stepped forward in turn, bent down, took a handful of dirt, and tossed it on the coffin.

"Our Father..." began Father George.

"Who art in heaven..." continued the crowd.

As soon as the Lord's Prayer had begun, the impending storm subsided. For how long was anyone's guess, but for the moment, at least, the wind stopped, and the sun, a moment ago covered by the massive black clouds billowing above us, managed to find a hole in the canopy and force its way through.

Father George sounded relieved as he gave his benediction. "The God of peace, who brought again from the dead our Lord Jesus Christ, the great Shepherd of the sheep, through the blood of the everlasting covenant, make you perfect in every good work to do His will, working in you that which is well-pleasing in His sight; through Jesus Christ, to whom be glory for ever and ever."

"Amen," said the crowd just as the sun disappeared again and the heavens opened in an October gusher. Instinctively, at the last "Amen," we all ran for our cars, leaving Mr. Swallow and his helper to the mercy of the weather. A few moments later, as I looked back at the grave through my windshield, I could see them both, barely visible in the torrential downpour and semi-darkness, standing beside the mound of what must now be mud—Mr. Swallow in an awkward position, holding an umbrella over his helper as the man struggled with a shovel, trying his best to fill the hole. I sighed, pulled on the all-weather jacket, gloves and boots I kept in the truck, put on my old fedora, got a shovel out of the back, and went to help.

An hour later, I slogged into the Slab, feeling and looking like a drowned rat. I was covered in mud from my boots to my waist, but my shirt was relatively clean. I'd left my jacket in the back of the truck, hoping the rain would wash some of the mud off of it on my way home.

"Stay to fill in the hole?" asked Pete.

"Yeah. I felt bad leaving it."

Pete nodded and pulled a dishtowel from behind the counter. "Sit on this, will you? I'll get you a cup of coffee."

"He don't need any more coffee," said Noylene. "It ain't good for you to drink all that coffee. I'll get you a cup of hot chocolate."

"That'd be great."

"You guys get it filled in?" Pete put the towel on the chair and I sat down on it.

"Mostly," I said. "It was pretty muddy. They'll have to clean it up when it dries out a little."

Noylene put a big mug of hot chocolate on the table in front of me. "Here you go."

"Thanks, Noylene."

"Did Meg know you were staying out there?" asked Pete.

"I called her from my cell. She told me to be sure and take some vitamin C and a hot shower, but she declined to come back and help."

"You going to the revival tonight?" interrupted Noylene. "I'm going to get revirginated."

"Excuse me?" said Pete and I in unison.

"You're getting *what?"* said Pete, recovering before I did. In my defense though, I was cold and wet and unprepared for this new religious wrinkle.

"I'm getting revirginated," said Noylene with a smile. "God has forgiven me all my transgressions and He wants me to be a new creation in Him."

"That's fine, Noylene," I said. "He certainly has and certainly does, but what's this about revirgination?"

"If I'm a new creature and all my sins are washed away, why shouldn't I be a virgin again? A new creature is a virgin, right?""

Pete looked at me as if I could answer this theological question.

"It's like this, Noylene. Once you've done something, it can't be undone. You can certainly be forgiven for it and that's what God does for us and what we do for each other. But you can't un-ring the bell."

"You mean that if I murder Pete here..."

"Hey, wait just a minute," said Pete.

"...it can't be wiped clean?" finished Noylene without missing a beat.

"You certainly can be forgiven for the sin..."

"Not by me," said Pete. He reached for a menu, turned it over and started writing.

"But, he's still dead," I said. "It doesn't mean you didn't do it. "

"Brother Hog says it does. He says that in God's eyes, it's like we never did it."

"I think he meant that you've been absolved of the transgression—that Jesus has paid for your sins. Look at it this way," I explained. "I come into the Slab and order breakfast. Then Nancy comes in later and pays for it. You still have the receipt. Just because Nancy paid the bill doesn't mean I never ate breakfast.

"You never *do* pay for breakfast," said Pete.

"That's right," said Noylene, thoughtfully. "And I never even write you up a ticket. So it's like you never even had breakfast."

"Yeah," grinned Pete.

"Okay. Sorry. That was a bad example."

"And if you never had breakfast, it's like you were a breakfast virgin," said Pete.

"No," I said, putting up my hands. "Wait a minute. That's not it at all."

"That's what Brother Hog said. He said we could be forgiven our sexual indiscretions and...and... armadillos..."

"Peccadillos," I corrected.

"Yeah, that. And we could all be pure," continued Noylene. "Brother Hog says that if the Pope can say you've never been married, even after ten years and fifteen kids, then there's no reason that we can't all be virgins again."

"Well now, that's a good point," interjected Pete, still writing. "The Catholic Church has been granting annulments for years. Just depends on who you know and how much money you have."

"That's not exactly true," I said. "Hey, wait a minute. Who's *all?"*

"Just a few of the girls. I'm not namin' any names. It's a private ceremony after the regular service."

"Anyone I know?"

"None of your business."

"But, Noylene," I said in exasperation. "You have a thirty-year-old son."

"Yeah, but the way he was conceived ain't nothin' to write to Billy Graham about. I ain't proud of it."

"Besides," Pete said. "If Noylene is a virgin again, then D'Artagnan is an immaculate conception. If that's the situation, I can put *him* in a pie case and not worry about the BVMCR."

"I suppose so," I said as I saw Noylene try to puzzle her

way out of this new observation on her trip back to the kitchen. "How's the search for the roll going, by the way?"

"Well, that skinny sucker is eating me out of business little by little even though I only give him breakfast. He's taken up with Moosey, too. I saw them walking down the street together this morning."

"Oh no."

"I'm sure it's fine. Moosey was just showing him around town."

"He's supposed to be in school."

"Oh yeah. I forgot about that," said Pete, putting his pencil down and turning his attention back to Noylene.

"Hey Noylene," he called, "are they singing any revirgination hymns during the service? I've got one for you."

"Let me get a better pencil," said Noylene, making her way back to the table. "I'll write it down and give it to Brother Hog tonight."

I rolled my eyes. I knew that the minute Pete had heard about the Ceremony of Revirgination, his brain had clicked into "irreverent mode."

"How about this?" he said. "Here's the first verse. You can sing it to the tune of *Amazing Grace,* but you have to throw in an extra note to make it fit."

O Lord who doth make all things new.
We pray with faith emerging.
Just tell us what we ought to do
And grant us thy re-virging.

"That's pretty good," said Noylene, scribbling away.

"That's *not* good," I said. "It's awful. I put it right up there with *Crown Him You Many Clowns."*

"Another masterpiece," said Pete, "even though I didn't write that one. Here's the second verse."

When in temptation's path we're found,
And feel our lust upsurging,
Give us the strength to turn around,
And grant us thy re-virging.

I laughed out loud. Noylene bit her lip and tried to keep up, her pencil flying over the paper.

"Okay, genius. I've got one," I said. "I think this says it all."

When we have drunken far too much
And find ourselves regurging,
Just tell us when we've had enough,
And grant us thy re-virging.

Pete and I laughed like we were back in college again, and I felt much better even though I was still wet and muddy. I hoped, only halfheartedly, that Noylene would lose the hymn before the service.

Chapter 19

I had questions--questions with no answers, answers with no questions and a few queries with a lot of other posers thrown in.

First on my list was "Who killed Candy Blather?" I had no answer, but if I could come up with one, I'd make my monthly nut with room to spare.

Every other question was just oatmeal on the carpet. Who was Rosebud? What was the hymn that Candy wouldn't include? What would Piggy be eating next? Where or who was Jimmy Leggs? Why was Kelly trying to hire Marilyn? What kind of underwear did Starrbuck Espresso wear and why was Alice calling me at all hours?

"Kit," I called. "I got questions."

"Well, answer them," she yelled back. "That's why you're the detective."

"Yes. Sound advice from a professional Girl-Friday."

"Why don't you work backwards? Last question first."

"Okay," I said. "Why is Alice calling me at all hours?"

"Because she wants to know what you know. It's certainly not your good looks and charm," Kit said.

"OK, next question. What kind of underwear does Starr Espresso wear?"

"Sounds like you need to do a little research, boss," grinned Kit.

I drove slowly down Main Street on Saturday morning, looking for Megan, following her mother's inclination that she had headed into town. I didn't find Meg, but I did happen upon a most unusual pair walking through Sterling Park. D'Artagnan Faberge and Moosey looked less like Mutt and Jeff and more like a giant alien parrot creature with his chickadee sidekick. I rolled down my window and gave them a yell.

"Hey you guys! Come here a second will you?"

Moosey recognized my truck right away and scampered over. D'Artagnan took his time, walking with as much cool as he could muster, his hands pushed deep into his pockets.

"Hayden!" Moosey said. "Me and D'Artagnan are searching for the Blessed Virgin Mary Cinnamon Roll. He's gonna pay me two bucks when we find it."

"A princely sum," I said, "but why weren't you in school yesterday?"

"Aw, who told?"

"Never mind. You do it again and I'll tell your mother. Then you *know* what'll happen."

"Yessir," said Moosey. "I won't do it no more." Then he brightened as D'Artagnan strolled up. "Look at our shoes! They're exactly the same!" Moosey held his foot up as high as he could manage without falling over. He was wearing his bright orange high-top tennis shoes—the ones I had bought for him when he had played the Penguin of Bethlehem. I looked at D'Artagnan's shoes. They were the same, though a size fifteen.

"Did you know that D'Artagnan was named after a famous Mouseketeer?" said Moosey.

"Musketeer," muttered D'Artagnan through the strands of his wispy mustache.

"I remember reading that," I said. "Have you guys had any luck in finding the Immaculate Confection?

"Most folks think that *you* stole it," said D'Artagnan, matter-of-factly.

"I assure you I did not."

"We already know that," exclaimed Moosey. "We almost know who did it."

"Hush up, Moosey," said D'Artagnan.

"Care to let me in on it?" I asked.

"Not yet," said D'Artagnan. "All ya'll will know soon enough."

"Fair enough. Good luck, then. By the way, have you seen Meg?"

"She's over at the post office," said Moosey.

"Thanks," I said. "And no more skipping school."

"No sir. I won't."

Meg had decided to accompany her mother to Saturday night's tent meeting. She had invited me as well, but I declined. I did acquiesce to meet them both for the potluck supper following the service, a potluck featuring peach pies courtesy of Ruby and sautéed portabello mushrooms in garlic from the kitchen of Megan Farthing. Brother Hog had tables ready to set up in the tent as soon as the chairs were cleared away, so Meg told me to meet them at the tent at 7:30 for supper. They'd do their best to save me a place.

I appeared promptly at the designated time and looked around the tent for Meg and Ruby. I spotted them near the back at a table with Noylene, D'Artagnan, Ardine, Moosey and Pauli Girl. The eighth seat was saved for me.

"Hi there," I said. "Did you get me a plate of food?"

"Right here," said Meg, gesturing to the extra plate in front of her place. "Come and sit down."

I sat down in between Noylene and Meg and put the plate that Meg had garnered for me in front of my place. "How did the service go last night, Noylene? Did you get...you know?"

"I certainly did," said Noylene, "and I feel just awesome."

"Awesome, eh? Did you guys sing Pete's hymn?"

"I wanted to, but we didn't have time."

"That's a shame."

"What are you two talking about?" asked Meg.

"I'll tell you later," whispered Noylene.

"And how was the service tonight?" I asked of no one in particular.

"It was fine," said Meg.

"Great!" said Moosey. "Binny Hen was just great."

"It was a good service," said Pearl. "This dinner is good, too."

"I didn't go to the service," said D'Artagnan. "I was busy cookin'."

"I didn't know you could cook, boy," said Noylene. "When did you learn how to do that?"

"Ain't nothin' to it," said D'Artagnan. "Just gotta have something to cook and a big skillet full of hog lard."

"What did you bring, Noylene?" asked Meg, taking a bite of fried chicken.

"I brought my three-bean salad," said Noylene. "A potluck isn't a potluck without some three-bean salad. How about you D'Artagnan?"

"I brought that fried chicken," he said, pointing to the big plate in the middle of our table.

"Aren't you supposed to put the plate of food on the big table so everyone can have a taste?" I asked.

"Sorry," said D'Artagnan. "I got here late.

"Well, it sure is good," said Meg.

"I agree," I said. "Maybe the best I've ever had."

"It should be," said D'Artagnan through a mouthful of mashed potatoes. "It's the freshest fried chicken you're ever likely to eat."

The whole table froze. Even Moosey and Pauli Girl stopped in mid-forkful. Only D'Artagnan kept eating.

"What do you mean, son?" said Noylene.

"I mean that chicken was poultry on the hoof about an hour ago."

We all looked at him in horror.

"What?" he said, putting down his fork. "That chicken didn't belong to nobody. She was just out scratchin' behind the tent. Free range, you know? And, I might add, she was the biggest chicken I ever saw."

"Oh my God," said Ardine, putting the chicken leg back on the plate. "Oh my God."

"What?" said D'Artagnan.

"You cooked Binny Hen! That's what!" hissed Noylene. "Now what're you gonna do?"

"Who's Binny Hen?" asked D'Artagnan.

"Brother Hog's Scripture Chicken. You cooked her! She was ordained!"

"Didn't know he had a Scripture Chicken," said D'Artagnan with a shrug. "Nothin' we can do about it now anyway." He reached over to the plate of chicken and took another piece.

"He has a point," I said, reaching across the table with my fork. "And this is really good fried chicken."

"I just can't eat it," said Ardine.

"Can I have your piece?" asked Moosey, passing his plate across the table to his mother.

"Someone's going to have to tell Brother Hog," Meg said.

"I'll tell him. I'm the one who did it," said D'Artagnan. "Anyone want any more?"

"Well, I think I'd like a piece," said Ruby, ignoring the glare that Meg gave her—a look that would melt the congealed salad sitting uneaten on her plate.

"I mean, if it's *that* good."

Chapter 20

I walked around the corner, heading for my favorite pub--the Possum 'n Peasel-- the rain bouncing off my hat with a plink-plink like someone playing a Bach invention on a three-note piano gone flat. Starr was waiting for me in a lime-green and black number that looked like she'd been spray-painted by a couple of graffiti artists and rolled in a dumpster full of sequins. If I was here to discern what kind of underwear Starr was wearing, I didn't have to discern very long. If there was any room for underwear between her skin and what passed for evening wear, it would have to be as thin as my list of suspects.

"Starr, baby," I said, lighting up a stogy. "Lovely to see you again. Nice outfit."

"Like it? I had it sprayed on this afternoon. It's the latest thing."

"So, those really are your...?"

"You bet they are mister," she said proudly. "These sequins are sort of prickly, though."

"Let's take a seat, Starr."

"Sorry. I can't sit down. It'd kill me."

"Ah, right," I said. "Let's get a drink at the bar then."

We walked up to the bar--me, shamelessly checking out her paint-job and she, doing her best to scuttle as gracefully as she could, mildly hampered by the fact that every time her thighs rubbed together, her sequins harmonized like a chorus of crickets singing the Duruflé Requiem, then popped off like it was molting season at a majorette convention.

"I'll have a beer and a bump," I said to Stumpy.

"I'll have a Chocolate Martini with just a jiggle of Kahlua," cooed Starr.

"This here's a pub," said Stumpy, banging on the floor with his wooden peg-leg. "Not one of your Nancy-bars. Order a real drink."

"A Kiwi Daiquiri?"

"No."

"A Purple Hooter?"

"No."

"An Apricot Squirt?"

"No."

"Give her a beer," I said. "And put it in a dirty glass."

"I like this installment," said Rebecca Watts on Sunday morning as we gathered for the service. "I used to be a majorette, you know."

"Really? And did you twirl fire-batons as well as regular ones? I ask because Pentecost is only seven months away, and I'd like to start planning ahead."

"Yes, fire-batons are no problem. Just tell me when to be here."

"There will be no fire-batons," said Meg. "And I hope this literary exercise is almost over because it's starting to give me hives. Really! I mean it! Look here." She extended her arm.

"I think that's just a mosquito bite," said Rebecca.

The service, on that particular Sunday, included readings from II Timothy and the Gospel of Luke as well as words of gloom and doom from Jeremiah and Psalm 84. The Gospel lesson was the story of the Pharisee and the tax collector, and the choir was going to highlight the reading of the gospel with Heinrich Schütz's dialogue and chorus. Randy Hatteberg and Bob

Solomon were in the title roles and the choir was well prepared to end the argument with the words of Our Savior. The puppets, however, were going to be illustrating the Epistle Lesson—the second letter from Paul to Timothy in which he (Paul) proclaims, "I have fought the good fight, I have finished the race, I have kept the faith." At least, that was the current plan.

The Puppet-Moment had been scheduled right after the Psalm, so the kids hadn't even heard the Epistle lesson when Father George called them forth. They walked tentatively down the aisle—small and cunning creatures like those little dinosaurs that looked so cute, but then ate Wayne Knight in the first *Jurassic Park* movie.

Brenda, a.k.a. Princess Foo-Foo, had taken her place behind the puppet stage along with Lynn Askew and JJ. I knew why JJ had volunteered. She was always ready for anything that looked like it might be reasonably entertaining.

I had walked by the first through third grade Sunday School classroom on my way up to the choir loft and had heard the children getting prepped like witnesses getting ready to go before the grand jury.

"Now, children," I had heard Princess Foo-Foo say, "we're going to have you come down for a Puppet-Moment during church."

"I love puppets," said Moosey.

"Moosey, you're not to say a word. Do you understand? Not one word, or I'll call your mother and tell her about you trying to push the altar candles up Robert's nose."

"We were playing 'The Walrus of Bethlehem.'"

Foo-Foo ignored him. "And none of the rest of you had better say anything either. Do I make myself clear?"

I headed to the loft with a big grin on my face and donned an even bigger one as they were called forward; the dinosaur children now stalking the oblivious Director of Christian Ed. Leading the pack was Bernadette, followed by Moosey, Ashley,

Robert, Christopher and a girl I didn't know. They gathered around the portable puppet stage—PVC pipes pushed together into a flimsy frame strewn with some dark blue material left over from the Christmas Pageant. They sat down and waited expectantly for the show to begin. Father George had moved beside the stage, possibly to facilitate the interaction, but more probably to exercise damage control if things got out of hand.

Up popped a puppet. It was one of those Sesame Street type puppets dressed as an old man with gray hair and a mustache, half a body with a big head and one arm worked by a supporting rod. Old Man Puppet was followed by a lady puppet, if one could believe the red wig, and a younger female in golden Wagnerian pigtails. The children clapped politely.

Princess Foo-Foo, obviously playing the part of the old man, spoke in a gravelly voice.

"Good morning children. This morning we'd like to talk to you about working with diligence for the Lord in preparation for our final reward in heaven." The children nodded politely.

Pigtails spoke next. It was JJ and she was reading from the script.

"I'm going to describe something and I want you to raise your hand when you know what it is."

The children nodded politely.

"They're ready," said Father George in complete control. The members of the choir were leaning forward in their chairs with anticipation.

"This thing," said Pigtails, "lives in trees and eats nuts."

Silence.

"Anyone know?"

"Here's another hint," said Red Hair, alias Lynn. "It's gray and has a long bushy tail."

Silence.

"Raise your hands, children, when you know the answer," said Father George, a worried timbre creeping into his voice. Still nothing. They were perfect angels following previous orders.

"Here's another hint," said Old Man Puppet. "He jumps from branch to branch."

Silence.

Old Man Puppet was running out of clues and was now deviating from the script. The entire congregation could all sense it and the anticipation was almost palpable.

"He chatters when he's excited," said Old Man Puppet.

"He flips his tail and has big teeth," interrupted Pigtails, trying to help.

Silence.

Followed by more silence.

"Bernadette" said Father George. "Do you know?" She shook her head side to side very slowly.

It was obvious that the puppets couldn't continue without an answer. Their script depended on it and the cast was out of clues.

"It's gray," summed up Father George, "has a long, bushy tail and big teeth...jumps from branch to branch and chatters when he's excited..."

Finally, a tentative hand went up. It was Christopher. Everyone in the congregation breathed an audible sigh of relief. Father George pointed to him.

"Well," said Christopher, as the congregation leaned forward to hear him, "I know the answer must be Jesus, but it sure sounds like a squirrel to me!"

A roar went up from the church. JJ was the first to fall, literally howling with laughter. She had one hand inside Pigtails and the other working a rod with the puppet arm attached and hence, couldn't catch herself when her guffawing threw her totally off balance and into the PVC puppet stage. The stage came down over the children in a cascade of blue velveteen and plastic piping. Lynn tried to catch it, but overbalanced as well and collapsed—now as hysterical as JJ—on top of the pile, her hands still entangled in her own puppet. Neither one of them could manage to get up, or even get a breath, because every time they looked at each other, rolling in that velveteen ocean surrounded by diminutive arms, legs, and heads poking through the waves of material looking for all the world like the aftermath of Noah's flood, another roar went up from the two of them. The congregation was in convulsions as well. Even Father George had to sit down for a moment, fighting in vain the smile trying to cross his visage. Only Brenda, with a stern look on her face, remained upright, the last bastion of all things well-rehearsed.

The congregation was still laughing as a couple of folks in the front two pews managed to get everyone untangled from the remains of the jumbled stage. Two of the ushers finally made it to the front and collected the conglomeration of plastic pipes, material and two lifeless puppets and carried the wreckage out the side door and into the chapel for restoration. The children, still on their best behavior, however rumpled from the experience, strolled in pairs back down the center aisle.

"Was it a squirrel?" asked Christopher, walking hand-in-hand with Ashley.

"No, I think you were right," said Ashley. "It was Jesus."

"Hayden, may I speak with you for a moment?"

I looked up from my postlude following the uneventful remainder of the service to see Davis Boothe standing in the choir loft. Davis wasn't in the choir, although I had tried to recruit him many times. He had a very good singing voice and had told me, when he first moved to St. Germaine, that he had done some stage work in community theaters around the Asheville area. Davis was new to the vestry and worked at Don's—the clothing store on the square. He was unmarried, in his thirties, genteel and fairly obviously gay, although I had never seen him with a significant other. If he wasn't, said Nancy, he was missing a heck of a chance.

"Sure, Davis. What's up?"

"My car was spray painted last night. I didn't call downtown because I knew I'd see you this morning."

"I'm really sorry. You think it was kids?"

"I don't think so, but I don't know. I went to bed around eleven. When I came out to get in my car this morning, I was greeted with this." He handed me a picture printed from a digital camera. His dark blue Volvo was covered in yellow graffiti. "Queer," "homo," and "fag" were the largest and most visible of the epithets.

"Aw, jeeze," I groaned. We hadn't seen this sort of thing for a long time.

"I drove my old VW in this morning. The Volvo's still at the house. Can you come and look at it? I need a police report for the insurance company."

"Yeah," I sighed. "I need to go to this vestry meeting. Then Nancy or I will come out, take some pictures and file a report."

"I have to stay for the meeting, too."

"Okay, then. I'll see you in the Parish Hall."

The first meeting of the new vestry always began with a lunch. Usually it was a catered lunch, and this year was no exception. I attended because I was on the staff. I didn't have a vote. I was just there as a courtesy. Brenda was there; Father George, old and new vestry members, Marilyn, and Carol Sterling. Jed Pierce was noticeably absent. After a delicious lunch, Father George walked up to the podium and addressed the twelve vestry members and Rob Brannon, our new Junior Warden.

"First of all, I'd like to welcome our new members—Davis Boothe, Gwen Jackson, Russ Stafford and Megan Farthing. Although Meg has just rotated off, she was elected again and has agreed to serve another three years."

"As most of you know," he continued, "Jed Pierce has

resigned from the position of Senior Warden. According to our by-laws, in the case of a resignation, I am charged, with the approval of the rest of the vestry, to appoint a successor until the next election comes up. That being the case, I'd like to offer the name of Rob Brannon as Senior Warden. He's already assumed responsibility as our Parish Administrator, and he has a good handle on what we need to do to accomplish our goals.

"I second the motion," said Rhiza. I glared at her.

"If I'm appointed Senior Warden," Rob said graciously, "I think we should get Billy Hixon to remain as Junior Warden. I think he'd be more than happy to continue in that position."

"Wait a minute," I said, "what about the conflict of interest? I thought that he couldn't have the lawn service contract if he's in the position of Junior Warden."

"Hayden," said Father George, "I'm surprised at you. That's never been a problem for us in the past, and I don't see why it would be a problem now."

I was dumbfounded. Flummoxed. Flabbergasted.

"I don't think this is a good idea," I sputtered. "Rob has been here less than three months and the election only took place last week. It's not like we're halfway through the year. There's plenty of time... "

"I think we all know your position, Hayden," said Logan Askew. "You've made it pretty clear."

"Excuse me?"

"I think we should call the question," said Father George. "All in favor?"

"Aye," was the majority declaration.

"Opposed?"

"Nay," said Meg and Mark Wells, a long-time member of St. B's.

"Motion carried. I'll ask Billy if he would be willing to serve as Junior Warden as well. As Senior Warden, Mr. Brannon, will you take the chair?"

"Gladly. Thanks, George." Rob had a folder with his agenda already intact. I understood at last.

"All of you have already received a copy of the agenda in the mail with a couple of items of interest," Rob said. "The first is a system of vouchers and purchase orders I'd like to implement that will make the financial position much clearer for the congregation to understand. This will help immeasurably when we begin our stewardship drive next week."

"Did you mention losing the twenty-five thousand that goes into the music fund each year?" I said. "Because I'm not supporting this."

"I certainly did, Hayden. Thanks for bringing that to everyone's attention. It's on page three everyone, if you'd please turn to it and read it over again."

He paused while everyone read.

"It certainly seems reasonable to me," said Logan. "It makes sense."

"Me, too," said Davis to nods by the rest of the group. I didn't have the letter and one wasn't being offered to me. Even Meg was studying her paper and conspicuously avoiding my gaze.

"I think we can go ahead and approve this," said Gwen.

"All in favor?" asked Rob.

"Aye," was the almost unanimous verdict.

"Opposed?"

"Nay," said Meg, suddenly looking up. "You may put me down as a 'nay.' This is foolishness."

"Thank you, Meg," said Rob in his oiliest voice. "Motion carried. Next on the agenda..." He paused and consulted his notebook. "Father George?"

Father George got up and brought a sheaf of papers to the podium.

"We have received quite a blessing this week. As many of you know, St. Barnabas is in need of a new furnace. We've kept it repaired, but it's now close to twenty years old. The cost for this will be close to nine thousand dollars. That's quite a hefty sum. We could put the word out and probably raise the money, but with our stewardship campaign coming up, it might undermine our efforts. Still, we're going to need the furnace this winter."

"On Monday, I received the following letter from *The Sons of Richmond*, a non-profit group from Richmond, Virginia. They are starting a museum and one of their members, when he was vacationing in St. Germaine a couple of years ago, saw the two Civil War stock certificates that we have framed and hanging in the parlor. The face value of the shares is three hundred confederate dollars. Quite worthless, I think, except to a collector. This group has offered to purchase the certificates and any interest we might have in any pre-existing financial institution for $4500. Half of the cost of our new heating system."

Father George sat down.

"It sounds like quite a deal," said Gwen Jackson, "But what if it turns out that the shares are worth much more?"

"I thought the same thing," said Rob. "So I called Randall and had him check on them. Randall?"

Randall Stamps stood up in the back of the room. He was St. Barnabas' accountant and had been for forty years. He was in his seventies and as crusty as he was shrewd.

"I called a couple of Civil War buffs, then took the stock certificates into Asheville for three appraisals. The bank that sold those shares was burned in 1864. It doesn't exist any more. It wasn't sold and there are no assets. As for the certificates themselves, they might be worth $500 a piece to a collector. Not much more than that. I brought the appraisals with me if anyone want to see them."

"Thank you, Randall," said Rob. "Would you please put that in a report and send it to me? I'll be happy to forward it to the rest of the vestry. I think it would be a good idea to go ahead and investigate selling the certificates to *The Sons of Richmond*."

"So moved," said Annette Passaglio.

"Wait just one second!" I said, jumping to my feet. "You can't just sell off the church's property! It's illegal!"

"It certainly isn't illegal," said Rob, calmly reciting what I heard as a prepared speech. "You should read your charter. The vestry is in charge of the finances of the church and if these certificates are actionable, which apparently they are, it's our job to decide if we should cash them or not. Stocks and bonds, whether or not they are worthless, whether they have an indeterminate value as collectibles, or whether they are current securities, are still considered to be financial instruments."

"This is insanity!" I bellowed, finally losing my temper.

"You're out of order, Hayden," said Father George. "You're only here as a courtesy, and I think we all know that you've been under quite a strain lately."

"You people are crazy! What are you thinking?"

"Hayden, I think you should leave," said Father George.

"Yeah," I yelled, slamming my chair against the wall and heading for the door. "I'll leave. You have my resignation. Effective immediately."

I stomped out onto the patio.

"We have a motion," said Rob calmly. "Do I hear a second?"

I walked out of the church and into the brisk October air. I had a temper. It didn't surface often, but when it did, it was best that I took some time to cool off. I headed across the street and made my way into the park, stopping by my truck to get out a couple of cigars. I was lighting one as I passed the first bench on my random excursion. Sitting on the wooden park bench, feeding a fat pigeon, was Brother Hogmanay McTavish.

"Hayden," he said, flashing me a big smile, "it's great to see you."

"Hello, Hog," I muttered, still mad, but chagrined enough

to be embarrassed about eating Binny Hen. "Listen, I'm sorry that D'Artagnan killed your chicken. I certainly never meant...I mean..."

"Don't worry about it, brother," said Hog. "These things happen. A chicken that size is bound to get mistaken for dinner sooner or later. You got another one of those cigars?"

I gave a half smile and pulled my second cigar out of my pocket.

"*Romeo y Julietta,*" he said in perfect Spanish. "And Cubans to boot! My own personal favorite. I get mine from a missionary in Costa Rica. He ships me a box once a month. Highly illegal, of course."

"Of course."

"You having some trouble, son? You look weary and pissed off all at the same time."

His language caught me by surprise and I glanced over at him, but he was still inspecting the cigar. "I am and I am," I answered.

"Your lady friend part of that problem?"

"No sir," I said, taking a puff on my cigar and slowly letting a circle of blue smoke rise heavenward. "She's not."

"Glad to hear it." Brother Hog took the cigar out of the tube, rolled it between his thumb and forefinger, slowly breathed in its aroma and, after these time-honored cigar traditions had been carried out, finally accepted my offering of a cutter and lighter.

"My, that's good. It's probably a sin, you know. Anything this good is probably a sin. Happily, we are saved by grace, so I'm not going to worry about it."

"That's a fine philosophy, Brother Hog."

"You going to marry that woman? She's a fine gal. I talked to her a few times over at the Ginger Kitten, or whatever the name of that place is."

"Thinkin' about it," I said, feeling the tension drain from my shoulders. Amazing thing, thinking about the one you love.

"You love her?"

"Yeah, I really do." I was amazed at my own words. And that I was telling this to Brother Hog. "I *really* do."

"Don't think about it too long then. Anyway, I'm leaving town tomorrow. No sense really in staying another weekend if I don't have a Scripture Chicken. That's where the money is. I'm going down to my brother's farm in Greenville and get another one."

"Get another one?"

"Sure," he said. "Chickens are not long-lived creatures. Two years about does it for them. Binny Hen was my sixth chicken."

"Does it take long to train one?" I asked.

"'Bout a month. By the way, I know it was you that fixed that scripture a couple of weeks ago."

"Oh, man. I apologize. It was a nasty thing to do and I'm sorry for it."

"Nonsense!" he laughed. "It was hilarious! That was the best joke on Brother Hog in many a year! Not to mention that I really had to scramble to get myself out of that one. Who'd have thought? All those kings! That was priceless! I'm puttin' it in my memoirs."

My rage was gone and I had to laugh with him.

"Don't leave your lady friend hangin' too long." He patted me on the back and headed off toward his tent.

Chapter 21

Toby Taps tinkled tidily into the Possum 'n Peasel and danced deftly up to the busy bar.

"Nice alliteration," he said with a smirk. "Although 'tinkled tidily' is a stretch."

"I do what I can," I said with all the false modesty of a really good writer. "What are you doing here, Toby?"

"Starr gave me the heads up. She said youse was askin' questions."

"Yes, but she's the one who hired me."

"Yep," said Toby, turning his attention to Starr and giving her a big smooch. "How youse doin', Rosebud?"

Suddenly, everything became as clear as one of those windows in a Windex commercial--although Starr, who might have played the housewife, singing and dancing her way to a spotless shine, neither sang nor danced, but instead produced a small hand-gun from a crevice I hadn't counted on and leveled it directly at yours truly.

"Rosebud?"

"Toby's nickname for me. Isn't that right, Snookums?"

Toby nodded and executed a flap-ball-change. Then he smiled and snapped open his blade.

I shuddered. But not from the cold.

After the vestry meeting on Sunday afternoon, I sent Nancy over to Davis Boothe's house to take his statement, get some pictures of the damage to his Volvo and file a police report. I didn't hear anything from her until later that evening when my home phone rang.

"Hi, Nancy," I answered. "You know that life was much easier when we didn't have phones."

"I'd just have to come out and get you," she said.

"What's up? Can't that police report wait until tomorrow morning?"

"Sure it can. This is something else. Beverly Greene just called. She heard some dogs barking and growling in the front yard. She turned on her front lights and there, lying in the grass, she saw a dead sheep."

"A what?" I asked, not sure I had heard correctly.

"A dead sheep. I'm out here now. What a mess! Whoever threw it out must have cut it open right before they tossed it. Anyway, the neighborhood dogs have been at it, and it's all over the front yard."

"I'm on my way."

"I think I'm going to be sick," said Bev. "I can't look at it."

JJ had come out along with Billy. Bev had called them both after Nancy had given her okay.

"We'll clean it up," said JJ. "Don't worry about it." She and Billy pulled on their rubber gloves and picked up a couple of contractor trash bags that Billy had brought with him.

I viewed the carnage from the porch, having already walked through it. It was one of the Harwood's Suffolk ewes, easily distinguished by their white coats, black faces and legs. The Harwoods were the only ones around here that raised Suffolks. I imagined that Frank Harwood would be even less pleased than Bev.

"Hey, JJ," I heard Billy say. "What's black and white and red all over?"

"Shhh. That's not funny."

I walked into the house and found Bev standing with Nancy in the dining room.

"Did you hear anything?" I asked.

"No. I just came out when I heard the dogs barking. There was nothing here when I got home just after dark, so it must have happened between seven and when I came out—around nine, I guess. I'm just sick. Who would do such a thing?"

"Someone's been causing trouble all over town for the past couple of days," said Nancy. "First Gwen, then Davis, and now you."

"Small comfort," said Bev. "I don't like being part of a pattern." She turned to me. "Where did you go after the vestry meeting, Hayden?"

"A walk in the park, then home."

"And you've been there the whole time?" Bev's tone had become accusatory.

"The whole time."

"Did Meg come over?"

"No. I haven't seen her since church."

Bev crossed her arms in front of her, turned her back on me and directed her next question to Nancy.

"Will you be able to catch whoever did this?"

"Listen, Bev," said Nancy, "whatever you're thinking, stop it." She lowered her voice, took Bev by the shoulder and walked her out of almost everyone's earshot—everyone except me—and I pretended not to hear their conversation.

"This has nothing to do with Hayden and you know it," Nancy began.

"But I *don't* know it," said Bev. "This whole thing has me unnerved. Everyone's talking about him, you know."

"I know. We'll figure it out."

"Better do it soon."

I had just arrived home when my home phone started ringing.

"Yeah?" I answered.

"Hayden, it's Nancy."

"I know," I said, unable to keep the weariness out of my voice.

"Bad news. You know Joe Perry?"

"Sure. He's a member of St. Barnabas although he doesn't really attend except Christmas, Easter and his children's baptisms. Black guy—works over at the college in Banner Elk. He's an English professor, I think."

"That's him. About an hour ago, someone burned a cross on his lawn. Eight feet tall and four feet wide wrapped in burlap soaked with diesel fuel. He didn't know it till a neighbor called the fire department. He's really furious. His wife and two daughters are scared to death."

"My God. What's going on?" I wondered aloud.

"Hayden...I hate to ask this...but where have you been for the past hour? I've been trying to get hold of you."

"I've been driving around listening to Beethoven's Sixth, trying to figure this out. I haven't had my cell phone since this morning. I thought I left it in the truck.

Silence.

"Nancy, I didn't do this."

"I know, boss. I was just thinking."

"I'll go out to Joe's."

"Don't worry about it. I took his statement and the family is staying with friends tonight."

"Do me a favor, will you? Call Joe before he leaves and ask him if he was ever in the military. Then give me a call back."

"Will do. I'll call you in a few."

I walked to the kitchen, opened the fridge and took out a much-needed beer and set it on the kitchen counter. Then I laid out a couple of mice for Archimedes and gave Baxter his nightly treat of dog biscuits that purported to freshen his breath, but unfortunately did little to squelch the terminal case of canine halitosis that cursed him—or me, since he didn't seem to mind it.

Then I opened the last of my Malheur Black Chocolates, walked into the den, and fell into my chair. The phone rang ten seconds later.

"Hayden?"

"Yeah."

"Joe Perry was in the Marines for two years. He served in Desert Storm. How did you know? You have this figured out?"

"Part of it. I'll tell you tomorrow."

I called Meg as soon as I hung up with Nancy.

"How did the rest of the vestry meeting go?" I asked after I filled her in on the latest rash of crimes.

"Nothing much after you left. A few people voiced concern that you might have been serious when you resigned. I said that you'd probably get over it, but Father George said that it might be for the best. So, I think your resignation has, most likely, been accepted."

"Fine with me," I snapped. "I've had just about as much church politics as I can stand."

"Don't get angry with *me*. I'm on your side."

"I know. Sorry."

"You're forgiven. We're meeting on Tuesday afternoon at Rob's office to review the accountant's report on the stock certificates and decide whether or not to sell them. My inclination is that most of the vestry will vote to do so."

"That's just stupid! There's something very wrong about the whole deal."

"I agree."

"Anyway," I said, "the real reason I called was to ask you out on a date."

"A real date? With flowers and dinner and such?"

"Absolutely."

"Wonderful! When?"

"Tomorrow night?"

"You men are all alike. Calling a girl with one day's notice. I don't even have time to get a new dress."

"Hmmm. I guess...maybe...Friday then?"

"No, tomorrow's fine. There was a dress in the window at Merle's that I wanted anyway. I just didn't want you to take me for granted."

"Never."

I had never ordered flowers before, but it seemed a good time to start. I walked down to the florist behind the church.

"Hi, Sandy," I said, banging the door and ringing the little bell as I went in. "I need to order some flowers."

"You've never been in here before. What's the occasion?"

"Well, um..." I hemmed. "You know..."

"I know exactly! Now, what would you like?"

"Well," I said, looking around. "How about some daisies?" It was a flower I knew and I figured I'd be safe with it.

"We don't have any," she said, sweeping some cut flowers that looked awfully familiar off her counter and onto the floor out of sight. "You mean roses?"

"Um...what about those?" I asked pointing to some bright purple carnations.

"Those are for the high school homecoming dance. They're all sold. How about some roses?"

I spotted some large flowers in the glassed refrigerator. The sign said "zinnias." They were orange and, I thought, quite fetching. "What about some of those?"

"Unfortunately, they are infected with a rare botanical disease. I have to send them back. How about some *roses,* Hayden?" She glared at me.

"Roses, eh?"

"Yes. Red roses. Two dozen."

"What about pink? Or yellow?"

"Pink roses are given to represent admiration or sympathy. Yellow roses are for friendship. You'll want the red. Two dozen."

"Two dozen?"

"Yep," she said, writing the order on her pad.

"I'll need them..."

"Pick them up tomorrow," she said, still writing. "Four o'clock."

Chapter 22

On Monday morning, the door to the office opened and D'Artagnan strode in, his green Mohawk flopping as he walked.

"I need a search warrant," he announced.

"A search warrant?" asked Dave. "For what?"

"I know where the Virgin Mary Cinnamon Roll is."

"Where?" asked Dave. I merely watched in amusement.

"I can't tell you. I just need a search warrant."

"First of all," explained Dave, "you have to have a name on the warrant. They're very specific. Second, you have to have probable cause for a search, and third, you can only get one from a judge and you can't do that unless you have the first two."

"So, I can get one from a judge?"

"Sure you can," I said. "I suggest Judge Jim Adams in Boone. There are none in St. Germaine. Please tell him I sent you."

"Thanks, I will," said D'Artagnan, exiting the office. Coming in, as he was leaving, was Georgia.

"Hayden," she said, "you need to come over to the Slab right away. Father Tony is there. Wes has been killed in a car accident!"

"Oh, no!" I said, following her out the door with Nancy on my heels. Father Tony Brown was the priest at St. Barnabas before he retired and Wesley was his son. "I didn't think about Tony."

We ran across the street and down to the Slab, banging the door open and spotting Tony, sitting with Pete at one of the back booths. He looked terrible—pale and unshaven and smoking a cigarette, a habit he had given up ten years ago.

"What happened?" I asked as I slid in across from Tony.

He looked at me with a puzzled look on his face. "Wes was killed in a car accident. There was a message on my answering machine at about three o'clock in the morning. It was from you."

"It certainly was not."

"It sounded like you. It had your number on the caller ID..."

"Did you call him?"

"No. There was no reason..."

"What's Wes' number?" I asked, holding my hand out for Nancy's cell phone. Tony pulled out his pocket calendar and read me the number. I dialed it as he called it out. Wes lived in Boulder. It was still early in Colorado.

The phone rang once. Then twice. On the third ring, a groggy voice answered.

"Hello?"

"Wes? Hayden Konig in St. Germaine. You doing okay? You sure? You're not dead or anything? Hang on. Your father wants to talk to you."

Father Tony had tears running down his cheeks as he took Nancy's phone.

"We need that answering machine," I said as I slid out of the booth. "And bring Nancy's phone back, will you?" Tony only nodded and Nancy and I left him to talk with Wes.

"What did you mean when you said 'I didn't think about Tony,'" Nancy asked as we walked back to the office.

"I thought it would be Father George. Not Tony. And frankly, I'm still mad at George, so I may have dragged my heels," I admitted.

"I don't understand," said Nancy.

"Come back to my office. I'll fill you in."

Nancy followed me into my sanctum, closed the door behind her and sat in the chair across from my desk.

"What's the story?" she asked.

"I think I'm being framed," I said. "This last thing with Tony tears it. I suspected that a priest would be next on the list. But I didn't think of Tony."

"Explain."

"The victims of all the crimes in the last week are following the text of a hymn."

"Which hymn?"

"An All Saint's Day hymn. *I Sing A Song of the Saints of God.* The hymn is by Lesbia Scott."

"Lesbia? Who would name their child Lesbia?"

"Mr. and Mrs. Scott, I guess. Seriously, though, it's a children's hymn that lists different saints. The first stanza goes like this."

I sing a song of the saints of God,
Patient and brave and true,
Who toiled and fought, and lived and died
For the Lord they loved and knew.
And one was a doctor and one was a queen,
And one was a shepherdess on the green:
They were all of them saints of God and I mean
God helping, to be one too.

"Okay," said Nancy. "So..."

"The first victim was Gwen Jackson. A veterinarian."

"The doctor?"

"Yeah," I said. "Then Davis Boothe."

"The queen. Cute. And the sheep?"

"That's what tipped me off," I said. "Why a sheep?"

"Ahhh. Shepherdess on the green. Beverly Greene."

I nodded. "The next verse lists three more," I said. "One was a soldier, and one was a priest..."

"Joe Perry was a Marine."

"And then Father Tony," I said.

"Who's left?" asked Nancy.

"And one was killed by a fierce, wild beast," I added.

"That doesn't sound good."

"No. No it doesn't."

"I'm thinking," I said to Nancy after she had gotten us a couple of cups of coffee, "that the only way this will work as a frame-up, is if the hymn is recognized. We don't sing it at all in church. The kids learn it in Sunday School. It's not an easy connection to make, but once the words are out there, the pattern is easy to discern. And who better to blame it on?"

"True," said Nancy. "It's clever, church music related, devious, and untraceable. Plus, you're dangerously unbalanced. You're channeling the ghost of Raymond Chandler, you stole your best friend's cinnamon roll, ate the scripture chicken, screamed at the vestry, and now you're wreaking havoc on the parishioners of St. Barnabas."

"It sounds bad when you put it like that."

"Yeah."

"He has to make sure that people make the correlation. I doubt that anyone will figure it out on their own, so he'll have to start the rumor. I figure it'll hit the streets tomorrow," I said. "The story of the hymn, I mean. The only way he can get his plan to work is if people make the connection to the hymn. We've got, maybe, one day."

"He?"

"Yeah. You know," I said, "this all started..."

"With the body," finished Nancy.

We got the call at three o'clock in the afternoon. It was about Randall Stamps, the church's accountant. He was dead. The call came from his housekeeper. She had gone over to his house, used her key to unlock the door and was greeted by the growling pit-bull that chased her up onto the kitchen table where she managed to use her cell phone to call 911. When we got there, the dog was still snarling and snapping at Mrs. Kellerman, who was standing on the table, screaming and shaking like a leaf. Nancy drew her gun as I inched open the door. We could see Randall Stamps lying on his face in the hall.

"Mr. Stamps is dead," Mrs. Kellerman screamed. "You've got to help me."

"Shoot the dog," I said to Nancy without hesitation.

There was an explosion of sound and then silence. I swung the door open and went to help Mrs. Kellerman down off the table. Nancy made her way over to Randall Stamps.

"He's dead," she called. "And judging from the mess in here, that dog has been in here for a few days."

"Mr. Stamps just returned this morning," Mrs. Kellerman said. "He was spending the weekend with his lady friend in Boone. He called me yesterday on his way back there from a church meeting and asked me if I could come and clean up this afternoon."

"So, the dog could have been here since Friday night," I said, "and no one would have known."

"I suppose so. He left on Friday afternoon."

"Let's call the ambulance and let Kent know he's coming in," I said. "Then call Gwen and get a rabies kit run on this dog."

"How are you feeling this evening?" asked Megan when she opened her front door. She sounded genuinely concerned and wasn't just making small talk.

"I'm fine," I said, and handed her two dozen red roses. "Really."

"How sweet! Red roses. My favorite! Let me put them in water."

She reached beside the door and dropped the roses into a waiting vase.

"You knew I was bringing flowers?"

"Of course. Ready to go? Let me get my coat."

I helped her with her coat and offered my arm as we descended her front steps.

"It was a terrible thing about Mr. Stamps," Meg said. "Did Kent call you yet about the autopsy?"

"He did. The pit-bull killed him. Got him by the throat after he fell."

"How horrible."

"Yes, it was."

"Did you hear from Gwen?" Meg asked, as we made our way to her car. Our agreement was that we'd take her Lexus whenever we went out. My old Chevy truck was more than she could bear.

"She called as well. She didn't think the dog was rabid, but she sent it away for the test. She said it was malnourished and abused and probably used in dog fights, judging by the scars on its body."

"This is all so sad."

"It is, but let's talk about something else. At least for the evening."

"Okay. Have you really quit? I mean, you are going back, aren't you?"

"To the church? I don't think so."

"But you love it."

"I'll find something else. Maybe do some subbing for a while. My friend, Virginia, subs for organists in Asheville almost every Sunday. She really enjoys it."

"Hmmm. Well, maybe something will change. Do you have any clues about the crime spree?"

"I do, but I can't share them yet. Nancy and I are working on it."

"That's good. But solve it quickly, will you. I don't like being the significant other of a pariah."

We drove down to the Hunter's Club outside of Blowing Rock and had a lovely supper—quail as the entrée, a nice Chilean chardonnay wine suggested by our waiter, dessert followed by coffee and as we were finishing our aperitifs, I lowered my voice and cleared my throat.

"Meg, there's something I want to ask you."

"Yes?"

"Um..." I cleared my throat again. "Would you like to get married?"

"You mean, to you?"

I smiled nervously. "That would be the idea."

"Well, I wondered if you were going to get around to asking me before dinner was over."

"You knew?"

"Of course I knew. Why do you think I bought a new dress?"

"You knew yesterday?"

"Uh huh."

"Does Sandy the florist know?"

Meg smiled and nodded.

"All our friends know?"

"Yep."

"Your mother?"

"Oh, yes."

"Well..." I paused. "What's your answer?"

"I'll have to think about it," she said sweetly, lifting her glass to her lips. "But, thank you for asking."

Chapter 23

The door of the pub banged open and Alice Uberdeutchland strode in like a storm-trooper in a light drizzle.

"Freeze, you moogs!" Alice yelled, dropping into her shooting stance and brandishing a heater the size of a loaf of bread--not white bread, sliced and packaged in a see-through plastic bag and tasting vaguely like paste; but rather, one of those loaves of dark rye, or maybe pumpernickel, oblong in shape and slightly smaller, although infinitely heavier than the white, complete with caraway seeds that provided a delightful texture as well as a mélange of flavors when your teeth happened to crunch down on one by accident, or maybe on purpose, and surprised you (in the good kind of way) by their unexpected presence--and that brought me back to Alice.

"YOU freeze!" oinked Piggy Wilson, his porcine head suddenly appearing from behind a newspaper at the table by the kitchen, his hoof clutching a snub-nosed .38; small and compact, which is more than I could say for Piggy.

"You ALL freeze!" barked Kit, suddenly popping up from behind the bar like a perfectly toasted English muffin and sweeping her sawed-off shotgun across the counter like a butter knife ready to spread raspberry death across the open-faced sandwich that was the Possum 'n Peasel.

"Freeze!" commanded Kelly, leaping out of the walk-in freezer, a revolver in his shivering hand and Marilyn in tow; she, at least, obeying his command, seeing as her lips were now a bluish color and she couldn't blink.

"Everybody freeze!" shouted Stumpy, turning down the thermostat to thirty-two degrees Fahrenheit because thirty-two degrees Celsius would really have felt more like early summer in the Catskills.

"Is that everyone?" I asked, lighting a stogy and giving it a puff.

"So, you finally have everyone in the same room," said Meg. "I sense a conclusion to the festivities. And I'm interested to learn the name of the hymn that was so bad that even Candy Blather wouldn't include it."

"The world waits in expectation of the news. The worst hymn ever written."

"Will we know soon?" asked Meg.

"One more chapter," I said.

Meg called me at the office after the vestry meeting.

"Have you found your cell phone?"

"Nope," I said.

"Hmmm. Anyway, we met over at Rob's office. Nine of us plus Rob and George."

"That's a quorum, I guess."

"Yes it is. Rob had a report from Randall that he said had been mailed to him on Monday morning before the...um...accident."

"No accident," I muttered. "What did the report say?"

"Pretty much what Randall had told us at the vestry meeting. That the stock certificates were probably worth $500 apiece to a collector—maybe more to *The Sons of Richmond* since they were based in Richmond and might have some ties to the old bank they were drawn on. Seven of the vestry signed the agreement plus Rob and George. Mark Wells and I wouldn't do it."

"Good for you. Did you happen to get a copy of the agreement? And a copy of Randall's report?"

"I insisted on it. They're right here."

"Could you bring them over?"

"Sure. In about an hour?"

"That would be great. By the way..."

"Yes?"

"Have you considered my...um...proposal?"

"I'm thinking about it."

"Word's out," said Nancy, coming in from the cold. "I heard folks talking about it down at the Post Office. They stopped talking as I walked by, but I definitely caught the phrase 'I Sing a Song of the Saints of God,' and 'shepherdess on the green.'"

"That didn't take too long," I said.

"There's no proof, of course, but your name is mud all over town."

"Yeah, I know. Pete called. The town council may be asking for my resignation and they're going to be asking the feds to investigate."

Nancy nodded. "Dave off today?" I grunted in the affirmative.

"I picked up the mail," said Nancy and tossed the rubber-banded collection of letters onto the desk. I slid the rubber bands off and absently started to flip through the stack. I stopped when I got to a typed envelope with a familiar return address. It was from Randall Stamps. I opened it and read it carefully. It was a copy of the report he had sent to Rob Brannon. Then I called Meg back.

"Hi, again," I said. "Look at the report that Randall sent, will you? You have it?"

"Yes, I have it."

"The last paragraph. What does it say?"

"Just what I told you. 'It is my opinion that the two Civil War stock certificates are worth about $500 a piece to a collector although possibly more to a person or group with specific ties to the bank in question. Sincerely, Randall Stamps.

"That's all?"

"That's it."

"Nothing about the mention of another bond in a letter dated 1919 in the church's archives?"

"No..."

"Bring the letter by when you get a chance. Thanks." I hung up before the questions began in earnest. "Nancy," I said. "A clue has arrived and the game is afoot."

Meg walked into the office about four minutes later, just as I knew she would.

"Come on in," I called from my office, "and bring Dave's chair with you."

I placed the letter from Randall on my desk. Meg came in and handed me her photocopy of the letter that Rob Brannon had handed out to the vestry. They were identical except for the last paragraph, the one mentioning the letter dated 1919. There was also an enclosure note indicating that Randall had forwarded the letter to Rob as well.

"Do you think he forwarded the original or do you think he made a copy?" Nancy asked. "I sure would like to get a look at that letter."

"I'm betting it was a copy," I said. "But I'd also be willing to bet that the original is no longer in the archives."

"Yeah," said Nancy. "He is, after all, the church administrator."

"And the Senior Warden," said Meg, glumly.

"Why don't you go back to Lester Gifford's folder?" asked a voice coming from behind my chair—a voice I recognized. I looked gingerly over my shoulder and saw a tall man wearing a gray suit and tie, a pair of round spectacles and a fedora pulled down over his eyes. Smoke from the pipe that he had clenched in his teeth circled his head like gray, transparent ivy.

"You guys," I began, looking first at Meg and then at Nancy, "see anything strange?"

They both looked up at me and shook their heads.

"Let's go back to Lester Gifford's folder," I said.

"I've gone through it five times," said Nancy.

"Let's look again. Maybe we missed something."

Nancy shrugged and went out to her desk to retrieve the folder. Meg leaned across the desk.

"You okay?" she whispered.

"Fine," I whispered back.

"What's up?"

"Raymond Chandler is standing behind me."

Meg looked past me and then back again. "Can he help?"

"Maybe."

Meg nodded thoughtfully. "Good," she said.

"You see," I said, still whispering, "*this* is why I want to marry you."

"And this," she replied, "is why I said I'd think about it."

Nancy came back into the office flipping through the pages. "I don't see how this will help."

"Let's divide the pages and read through them. Check them, front and back, and look for anything out of the ordinary," I suggested. I peeked over my shoulder and saw Meg's eyes follow my quick glance. Raymond nodded and took another puff.

Nancy handed a stack to me, another to Meg, and we settled back in our chairs to go through them yet again. Ten minutes later, Meg spoke up.

"What do you think this is?"

She was holding up a piece of paper so we could read it.

"It looks like a foreclosure letter to Wilmer Griggs. Second notice," said Nancy. "I remember reading it."

"Not that," said Meg. "This."

She spread the page out on the desk with the backside up and smoothed it flat. On the back were a bunch of strange markings, smudged and indecipherable.

"I can't make anything out," said Meg. "Just squiggles. And

most of them are so light that they don't really show up."

"It's backwards," said the voice behind me.

"It's backwards," I said with a smile. "Sixty years of pressing against its neighboring document has left us with an imprint, however faint."

"How are we going to read it?" asked Nancy.

"Let's take it over to the copy machine," I said. "We can try a couple of settings. If that doesn't work, we can always send it off to the lab."

Nancy, Meg and I crowded around the copier as I punched the enlargement button and adjusted the contrast and lightness. After about ten minutes, and twenty tries, we had a copy of the back of the letter on eleven by seventeen-inch paper, mostly gray but clear enough to make out a few sentences. Nancy brought in the mirror from the bathroom, set it on the desk and leaned it against the wall. Then we held the paper in front of it.

"It's a bond," said Meg. "A certificate of deposit."

"Can you make out how much it's for?"

"No," said Meg. "But it's drawn on...what was the name of the bank Lester worked for?"

"Watauga County Bank."

"I think that's it. Look...here's the 'W' and the end of 'County.' The date is eighteen something.

"There wasn't a certificate of deposit in the folder, was there, Nancy?"

"No. There was not."

"So we may presume that someone removed it."

"We may."

"And the only person who looked through this folder, other than you or me, was Mr. Brannon."

"He was."

Raymond nodded.

While Nancy and Meg went for coffee, I made a call to the Northwestern Bank in Asheville and asked for the president. After going through his secretary and waiting for about five minutes, Mr. Forsythe came on the line.

"This is Chief Hayden Konig in St. Germaine," I said, identifying myself. "I wonder if you can answer a couple of questions."

"If I can," said the voice on the other end of the phone.

"I have a case up here involving a bond issued sometime in the late 1800's.

"Funny you should mention that. I just had a request from the corporate office asking us to review the documents that were presented with an action filed to collect a bond issued in 1899. Just a moment."

There was a rustling of papers and Mr. Forsythe came back on the line.

"This is made out to St. Barnabas Church. That the one?"

I answered in the affirmative.

"The bond was issued for $75,000 at an interest rate of six percent, compounded quarterly. That was about a half point high, but not unreasonable for the time. There's a note written in pencil at the bottom indicating that it should have been cashed out in five years when it matured."

"Can you tell me whose names are on the bond?"

"As I indicated, the bond is made out to St. Barnabas Church. It was signed by Wesley Lynn, president of the Watauga County Bank. Northwestern Bank took over Watauga County Bank in 1937. It was one of the smaller acquisitions that happened at the end of the depression. There's another signature as well. Looks like Robert Brannon."

"What would the value have been in five years?" I asked. "If the bond had been cashed in 1904?"

"Interestingly, we show that it *was* cashed. But when we

found the actual bond, it was obvious to us that the bond in our records is a forgery. It's not notarized and the signatures are different. But that wasn't your question. Hang on. Let me get my calculator," he chuckled. "It's been a while since I've had to do interest calculations."

I flipped through Nancy's notes as I waited for Mr. Forsythe to come back on the line.

"You still there?" he asked.

"Still here."

"In five years, the bond should have been cashed for a little over $100,000."

"Since the bond wasn't cashed, is Northwestern Bank responsible?"

"If the documents are authentic, then the bond will eventually have to be paid, although I think it will probably go through the courts."

"How much was the bond worth in 1937 when the merger occurred?"

"Hmmm...hang on... in the thirty-eight years from 1899 to 1937, the principal and interest had grown to $686,568."

"That's a lot of money in 1937. Do you think that the acquisition of Watauga County Bank would have taken place if a debt like that had been identified?"

"My inclination would be to say no."

"And now for the sixty-four thousand dollar question, Mr. Forsythe," I said with a smile. "How much is the action to recover the bond?

"More than a sixty-four thousand dollar question, Chief. The action is seeking the full amount. Principal and interest to total $34,054,704."

"Wow! And who filed the action?"

"An organization called *The Sons of Richmond, LLC.*"

"Would you fax me a copy?"

"Be happy to. What's the number?"

My next call was to my friend, Michelle, at the Secretary of State's office in Raleigh.

"Hi, Michelle. This is Hayden."

"Hayden! How are you?"

"I'm fine. Listen, can you do me a favor real fast? I need to know who the partners are in an LLC called *The Sons of Richmond*."

"Are they incorporated in North Carolina?"

"Either here or in Virginia," I said.

"If they're here, I'll tell you in a second. Virginia might take me a couple of hours. Nope," she said. "They're here. No partners. It's a sole proprietorship registered to Robert Brannon with a Post Office box in Charlotte."

"Thanks, Michelle. I owe you one."

As soon as Nancy and Meg returned, I filled them in on what I had discovered. We compared the faxed copy of the note and the image from the back of the letter. There was no doubt. They were a match.

"I'm a bit confused," said Meg. "Can you lay it all out for me? From the beginning?"

"From the discovery of the body?" asked Nancy, pulling out her notebook and jotting down notes from this recent discovery.

"Nope," said Meg. "Starting in 1899."

"Okay, here goes. In 1899, Robert Brannon, Sr.—presumably Rob Brannon's grandfather..."

"Great-grandfather," I corrected.

"Great-grandfather," continued Nancy, "left $75,000 in the Watauga County Bank in the form of a bond, payable to St. Barnabas Church and maturing in 1904, at which time the

Watauga County Bank would pay St. Barnabas Church $100,000. The church had been destroyed in a fire and it seems likely that the sum was set aside for the rebuilding of the church. But Robert Brannon, the priest of St. Barnabas, and two parishioners were killed in a flood in March of 1899. So, in all probability, no one except the president of the bank knew about the bond, and he forgot about it over the years. That about right so far?"

"So far, so good," said Meg. "Continue."

"The bond was never cashed and so was not used during the rebuilding of the church in 1904. However, when the Watauga County Bank was getting ready to merge with Northwestern Bank in 1937, an audit was probably performed including trying to find the owners of accounts that had not been accessed for several years. It was in this audit that Lester Gifford found the bond and brought it to the attention of his boss—the owner of the bank—Harold Lynn, who was also the Sr. Warden of St. Barnabas. There's a little conjecture, I admit, but I think it will read well at my conferences," said Nancy.

"Merely corroborative detail intended to lend artistic verisimilitude to an otherwise bald and uninteresting narrative," I said. "To quote William S. Gilbert." Meg giggled. I love it when she giggles.

"Harold Lynn was in a financial bind," continued Nancy, "which was why he was selling the bank. In addition, the note offered the interest rate...no, let me change that," said Nancy, scribbling with her pencil. "The *princely* interest rate of six percent - a half percent over what most banks were offering in 1899, but the president of the bank, Wesley Lynn—Harold's father—was a member of St. Barnabas and willing to do the church a good turn."

"Nice touch," said Meg. "You should consider writing detective novels. I know where you can get a typewriter."

"There was a bond issued and, since the money wasn't withdrawn, it had grown over the thirty-eight years to $686,568.

In 1937, Harold Lynn, now president of the bank, didn't have the money to pay the bond if it had been presented. So Harold—never having seen the actual bond—forged a duplicate showing it was paid in 1904 and wiped the loan off the books. It was not a good forgery, but with no original to compare it with, it went unnoticed. He then went to St. Barnabas and set a fire to destroy the records."

"Okay," said Meg. "But why did he kill Lester?"

"When Lester was doing the audit for the merger, trying to find the owners of accounts that hadn't been accessed for years, he found the account and brought it to the attention of Harold Lynn. Lester knew about the account. And if Lester knew, he was bound to tell someone eventually."

"Got it," said Meg.

"The original bond is what Rob Brannon found in Lester Gifford's papers. Lester had gotten it from Jacob Winston, a Sunday School teacher at St. Barnabas who was also the church historian. I'm betting that Lester had asked Jacob to see if he could find anything about the deposit in the church archives."

"That would be my assumption as well," I said, trying to put my meager stamp of approval on what was turning out to be a very good job by Nancy. She just smirked at me and continued.

"Harold Lynn didn't know that Jacob had found the bond and given it to Lester. He probably thought that, if it still existed, it was with in church archives. He murdered Lester Gifford and placed him in the altar, then started the fire in the record room hoping to burn all the documents."

"Then he planted evidence implicating Jacob Winston in Lester's murder," added Meg.

"Exactly. Sincc Jacob was the church historian, Harold probably surmised, and rightly so, that Lester had already talked to him. Harold didn't know that Jacob had already given Lester the bond. And, surprisingly, Lester's dead body was never found."

"Here's the funny thing," I said. "Harold never wondered why Lester didn't smell."

Nancy jotted a couple notes and continued. "I'm sure that Harold made it clear to Jacob that he'd better keep his mouth shut or be tried for murder. Jacob kept quiet."

"But," I said, "the altar had the unique property of being highly radioactive and served to keep Lester Gifford's body from decomposing over the years. Had they found Lester in 1937, Harold or, more probably Jacob, would have been sent to prison for murder and the bond would have been discovered."

Meg nodded. "The merger wouldn't have gone through and the Watauga County Bank would have declared insolvency and gone out of business like a hundred other post-depression institutions," she added.

"Exactly," I said.

"Hey," said Nancy. "This is *my* paper. Don't be horning in...and if you do, at least give me time to write it down."

"We don't know how Rob got hold of the bank records and found out about the forged bond, but once he discovered it, it was obvious to him what happened," I said. "Then it was only a matter of getting the vestry to sign it over to him."

"What!?" said Meg. "We did no such thing!"

"Do you have the paper that the vestry signed?" I asked.

"Sure. We just sold him the two Civil War stock certificates."

"Let me see the paper." Meg handed it to me.

"St. Barnabas Church agrees," I read, "to sell the two aforementioned stock certificates *as well as any interest it may have in any pre-existing financial institution* for the sum of $4500."

"That little sneak!" Meg exclaimed. "It wasn't the Civil War stocks he wanted at all! He wanted the interest in the financial institution!"

"Did any money change hands?" I asked.

"Yes," said Meg. "Rob had a certified check from *The Sons of Richmond*. He gave it to Father George."

"Smart," I said. "It's a done deal, then."

"Wait a minute," said Meg. "What about the cinnamon roll and all the other crimes?"

"All pointing to me," I said.

"He needed Hayden out of the church and under suspicion," said Nancy. "He engineered being appointed church administrator as well as Senior Warden. The only person standing in his way was Hayden. If Randall hadn't forwarded a copy of that letter, we wouldn't have found out for several weeks. Northwestern Bank may have contacted us eventually, but St. Barnabas already signed over their rights to the bond."

"Is there anything we can do?" Meg asked.

"Maybe," I said. "It's time for a warrant. I'll call Judge Adams."

Chapter 24

I looked around the room like a hedgehog in a room full of badgers.

"Everyone, calm down," I said, "or I'll never get paid."

I don't remember who started shooting, but when it was over, it was clear that the Possum 'n Peasel would need a redecorator. Piggy was as cold as the pork salad in the walk-in, a bullet hole squarely in his short ribs. Alice was stretched out like a guitar string on a cello, as dead as a Presbyterian Revival. Kelly had sat down where he bought it, ending up, appropriately enough, sitting on the bun warmer. Marilyn didn't appear to be hurt and had retreated back into the freezer. Kit, always perky, was now, not.

Stumpy was now Double-Stumpy and didn't look like he'd last till the ambulance arrived. Toby Taps wouldn't be dancing again. He had tripped his last Fandango and gone to that big ballroom in the sky where, if there was any justice, he'd be forced to tap in the chorus of _Riverdance_ for all eternity.

The only one left, and she wasn't in good shape, was Starr Espresso. She was draped over the bar like a bad prom date.

"Why'd you do it, Starr? Why did you kill your own sister?"

"How'd you know?"

"You were the only character I had left," I said sadly. "You had to be Jimmy Leggs. That, plus the fact that you and Toby Taps were the famous dancing duo of Leggs and Tapperton, winners of last year's International Ballroom Dancing Competition held in Fargo. I saw the finals on PBS. I recognized you both right away."

"I had to kill her. She was queering the deal. We were making a fortune, but she was getting cold feet. She thought this last hymn would give us away."

"I thought you guys were rich. What about the coffee fortune?"

"It's not all jumping beans and Cremora, you know." She coughed and closed her eyes.

"Wait a second!" I said. "What was the hymn? The hymn she wouldn't put in the hymnal?"

"It was ...(cough)... 'Whispering Hope.'"

"Whispering Hope?" Meg said. "Mom loves *Whispering Hope.*"

"No accounting for taste," I said. "I just tell the story."

"So everyone's dead but Marilyn?"

"Yep. I like to wrap everything up neatly. No characters left over to muck up the next story."

"Oh, no. You mean there's going to be another one?" groaned Meg.

"Maybe. I'm not saying."

We had a warrant in our hands early the next morning. We called Rob Brannon, but he wasn't home. When we called his office, his answering machine indicated he would be back in town on Thursday. Nancy and I took our warrant and headed over to his house. As we made our way down the sidewalk, we ran into D'Artagnan and Moosey, both of them heading toward the Slab Café.

"What's up, guys?" I asked. "You seem to be in a hurry."

"Guess what we found?" said Moosey, his excitement evident.

"You didn't!" exclaimed Nancy. "For real?"

"Yep. We've got the Blessed Virgin Mary Cinnamon Roll,"

said D'Artagnan, with noticeable pride.

"Hey," I said to Moosey. "Why aren't you in school?"

"Fall break this week," said Moosey with a grin. "You wanna see it?" He held up a brown paper bag. "D'Artagnan's letting me carry it."

"Sure," I said. "Let's see it.

Moosey unrolled the top of the grocery bag and rooted around with his hand for a few seconds. Then he pulled out the BVMCR and held it, flat in his hand, for us to inspect.

"Where did you find it?" asked Nancy.

"It was in Rob Brannon's office," said D'Artagnan. "Bottom drawer of his desk. In the back."

"How did you get in there?"

"D'Artagnan's real good at that," said Moosey. "He's got a set of picks and stuff."

"Hush up, Moosey!" hissed D'Artagnan.

"That's what you wanted the warrant for?" I asked.

"Yeah."

"How did you find out who had it?"

"Traced one of the IPs from the eBay site. The e-mail was bogus and the IP address was a Holiday Inn in Charlotte, but the IP of the download of the JPEG was still on there. Everything leaves a footprint. I got a friend who has a friend that knows a guy. The JPEG was downloaded from a computer in Rob Brannon's office."

"Excellent work D!" I said, clapping him on the back. "Rob probably won't even charge you with breaking and entering."

"Huh?" He started chewing on his bottom lip. "Um...why not?"

"I'm hoping he's going to have bigger problems shortly."

"That'd be good," said D'Artagnan.

"Hey, wait a minute," said Nancy, looking closely at the cinnamon roll. "What's wrong with this thing? There's a bite out of it."

"We was pretty hungry," Moosey chagrined. "D'Artagnan just took a little bite."

"It didn't taste good either," said D'Artagnan, making a face.

"It's over a month old," said Nancy. "Of course it didn't taste good. What's this stuff?" Nancy pointed at a cloudy film covering most of the roll.

"Moosey was licking the glazin' off," said D'Artagnan. "That didn't hurt it none. I mean, it's still the BV-watchamacalit.

"Outstanding!" I said. "I'm sure Pete will be pleased. You guys better get it down there before any more of it disappears."

"Yessir!" said Moosey, stuffing the roll back in the bag.

"Yessir!" said D'Artagnan.

We met the locksmith at Rob Brannon's house. He'd been waiting for us, but indicated that he hadn't been there long. He opened the lock in about a minute and we knocked on the door to see if Rob was actually home, but more importantly, to find out the status of the two Rottweilers that Rob owned—Lucifer and Gabriel. Hearing nothing, we went in the unlocked door and looked around. I asked the locksmith to wait in the kitchen in case we needed him again.

"What are we looking for?" asked Nancy.

"Most of the crimes are virtually untraceable. Even if we do find diesel fuel or a twelve-gauge, it wouldn't prove anything and we could only charge him with malicious mischief. We might even convict him of it and he'd probably have to pay a fine. The problem is that he'd still get the money from the bond."

"Why?"

"I called Matthew Aaron, the District Attorney in Boone, and he says that even if Rob misled the vestry, he was under no legal obligation to disclose all the information since he wasn't acting as their attorney. All he was required to do by law was to convey the opinion of the accountant, which, unfortunately, he did. He told the vestry that it was Randall Stamps' opinion that they should sell the stock certificates. And it was."

"Which brings me back to my first question," said Nancy. "What are we looking for?"

"We need to find something that points to the pit-bull. If Rob had that dog here, and we can prove it, we'd have him on a murder charge and the money would be forfeited. You can't keep ill-gotten money you acquired in the commission of a crime. The other crimes weren't directly related to getting the cash. The murder was. Rob had to shut Randall up because Randall had seen the letter about the bond."

"So...?"

"A food dish maybe. Some evidence the dog was here. That would do it. I'll take the basement."

"I'll start up here."

Rob Brannon had a small, two-bedroom, one-story, arts and crafts style bungalow with a basement built in the 1920s. It was perfect for a single guy who didn't need much room, and our search went quickly.

"Nothing," I said, blinking dust out of my eyes as I came up the basement stairs.

"There's some stuff on the porch," Nancy said. "But it probably belongs to his other two dogs. There are a couple of food bowls and some chew toys."

"Any leashes?"

"Nope. Just an old muzzle hanging on a hook by the door. He probably took the dogs with him."

"I doubt it. Two big dogs like that don't travel easily. Look around for some mention of where he might have boarded them."

I looked through the kitchen drawers while Nancy picked up Rob's Watauga County phone book.

"Got it," she called a minute later. "Under 'kennels' in the yellow pages. He has one circled. Blue Vista Kennels on Highway 105 just outside of Boone."

Nancy dialed her phone and handed it to me.

"This is Detective Konig in St. Germaine," I said to the female voice. "Can you tell me if you're boarding two Rottweilers for Robert Brannon?"

"Yes we are," came the answer. "Mr. Brannon brought them in on Tuesday morning."

"Did they happen to have their own leashes with them?"

"Oh yes," she said, "they were both on leashes. Muzzles, too. We don't mess around with these two."

I smiled. "Thanks for your help."

I turned to Nancy, still grinning. "The muzzle."

Chapter 25

"Hi, Gwen," I said, as Nancy and I walked into the veterinary office.

"Hello, Hayden," she answered coldly. "Nancy."

I didn't take the time to explain why I wasn't deserving of her scorn, but cut right to the chase.

"I need that pit-bull, Gwen."

"Sorry. I sent it off to the lab in Greensboro. They do all our work. The dog didn't have rabies, though. I got the report this morning."

"Good to know," I said, "but we're after something else. Will they be sending the dog back?"

"No. After the animal is tested, it's destroyed."

"Destroyed?" asked Nancy in horror.

"Burnt."

"Have they disposed of it yet?"

"Probably," Gwen said. "I can call if you want."

"If you would."

"Just a moment." Gwen disappeared into her office. Nancy and I waited impatiently and when she came out, we could tell it was bad news.

"They destroyed it last night."

"Oh, man," said Nancy. "That's bad."

"I still have the collar. I took it off before I sent the dog to Greensboro."

"Gwen," I said, "Your beauty is only exceeded by your genius! Where is it?"

"It's in the back. I'll get it."

"Let me go with you," said Nancy, following her through the swinging door. "So we don't lose any evidence."

Nancy had bagged the pit-bull's collar. I had the muzzle from Rob Brannon's house. When we got back to the station, Nancy checked them both for fingerprints. There was a good one on the muzzle, right on the strap that hooked over the dog's ears. There was a print on the collar, as well, but it wasn't Rob's. It was probably Gwen's.

"First things first," I said to Nancy. "Can we connect the muzzle to Rob?"

"That's not a problem. It was found in his house and the print is his. All attorneys are fingerprinted and it came back as a match in about three minutes."

"Then the problem," I said, "is connecting the same muzzle to the pit bull that killed Randall."

"What about DNA?" asked Nancy.

"Hmmm. Doggie DNA?"

"Why not? Isn't the process the same as identifying human DNA?"

"I don't know. Let's find out."

It only took three phone calls and a transfer to find out that Nancy was right and five minutes later I was walking out of the office, on my way to Durham where a friend of mine worked in one of the many laboratories at Duke University. He indicated that a DNA comparison could be done in about an hour and if I could get there by three o'clock, he'd see if he could push it through before the end of the day. I didn't know if there was enough DNA on the items to make a match, but I was willing to give it a try.

"You want me to come with you?" Nancy asked.

"Nah. I'll do it. I'll call you as soon as I know something."

"You'd better."

Gary Thorndike came out of the lab, wearing the signature white coat of a lab techie and holding a clipboard in his hand.

"I think we have good news. Or bad. Depending on what you want to hear. You didn't tell me what you wanted to find."

"It's better that way if you have to testify, Doc," I said. "What's the verdict?"

"Well, there were quite a few epithelials—skin cells—on the collar. I don't know for sure, but I would say that the dog was not in good health. The collar rubbed away some of the skin as well as the hair and there was some blood on it as well. The bottom line is, we got a good DNA sample from the collar."

"And the muzzle?"

"That was more difficult. We checked the leather, but couldn't get any clean samples. We finally did get one off the metal. A pit-bull, like most dogs bred for fighting, produces an abundance of saliva. We got a good specimen."

I waited expectantly.

"And the muzzle definitely was on the dog that killed Randall Stamps."

I called Nancy on the way home and gave her the news.

"Excellent!" said Nancy. "Should I pick him up?"

"Why don't you go ahead and get a warrant for his arrest. He'll be back into town tomorrow. You can arrest him then. Tell you what," I said. "Wait until lunchtime. Tomorrow is Thursday. He'll be eating at the Ginger Cat."

"Good plan, boss."

"Wait till I get there, will you? I'm meeting Meg around noon."

"Will do."

I walked into the Ginger Cat precisely at noon. Meg was, as usual, waiting for me and holding a table. I was gratified to see Rob Brannon standing in line, waiting for his order.

"Hayden," he called to me as I came in the door. I gave him my biggest smile.

"Afternoon, Rob."

"No hard feelings?" he asked. "About the church, I mean."

"I'll let you know. I haven't decided yet."

"There was another matter I needed to talk to you about," Rob said.

"Yes?"

"My office was broken into. Probably yesterday or the night before."

I shrugged, doing my best Andy Griffith impersonation. "It seems to be happening to everyone. We just can't seem to get a handle on these crimes. Was anything taken?"

"I don't know yet. I haven't done a complete inventory." He raised his voice just enough for the rest of the lunch crowd to hear. "You know, maybe the town council should consider hiring a real detective. Maybe he could solve some of these crimes you can't seem to 'get a handle on.'" The crowd inside the Ginger Cat had quieted to hear the exchange.

"Well, let me know," I said, cheerfully. "I'll be happy to fill out a police report for your insurance company."

"Yeah. Seems like you're real good at that," said Rob with a smirk and a wink.

I smiled at him, walked over to our table and sat down by Meg. She had already ordered, and my French Onion soup was steaming up at me from my paper placemat.

"How can you let him..." she started, angrily. I held my finger up to my lips, my smile silencing her outrage, while at the same time, directing her gaze toward the door as Nancy came in with Dave.

"Robert Brannon," announced Nancy loudly, pretending to look around the room.

"Yes," said Rob.

Nancy walked up to him, grabbed him by the back of the neck and shoved him up to the bar, holding his face down on the counter while she frisked him quickly with her free hand.

"Ouch," cringed Meg. "That had to hurt."

"Hope so," I said.

"Rob Brannon," continued Nancy, still holding his face against the counter, "you're under arrest for the murder of Randall Stamps. You have the right to remain silent. You have the right to an attorney..."

"I know my rights," said Rob, through clenched teeth. But Nancy was enjoying this. She put the cuffs on him and spun him around.

"If you cannot afford one, one will be provided for you. If you give up these rights, anything you say can, and will, be used against you in a court of law. Do you understand these rights as I've explained them to you?"

All the other patrons had become deathly silent.

"I said..." Nancy continued.

"I understand. May we leave now?"

"Sure, Rob. We're going over to Boone for arraignment. I don't think there will be any bail."

"We'll see," he said, glaring at me.

"Good soup," I replied, saluting him with a spoonful.

Postlude

"Have you talked to your ghost lately?" Meg asked.

"He came by once after that time in my office. But I haven't seen him in about a month."

It was the end of November. A cold, wet November that invited everyone to start hating winter even before it arrived. Things were almost back to normal in St. Germaine.

Pete had declined to pay D'Artagnan the fifty dollars for finding the BVMCR. He said it had been irrevocably ruined, mainly because Moosey had taken yet another bite out of it, choosing not to believe D'Artagnan when he said that it tasted awful. Pete still had several hundred coffee mugs, but he had given all of his Virgin Mary Cinnamon Roll t-shirts and sweatshirts to the local shelter for a nice tax deduction. Pete tried in vain to create another "miracle", but it was not to be.

Brother Hogmanay McTavish found another chicken and began training it. According to his website, he was planning a revival in Myrtle Beach in February. I sent him an e-mail and his reply assured me that the chicken would be ready.

Megan and I, after several lengthy discussions, had decided to table my proposal. Not that she thought I was unbalanced, or so she said, but because we were so good the way we were. To tell the truth, I was a little relieved.

I kicked back in my chair and put my feet up on my desk. I lit up a stogy.

"Marilyn," I called. "Shiver your pins in here, will you?"

Marilyn hopped in like the Easter Bunny of Golgotha, still recovering from the loss of two frostbitten toes courtesy of Mr. Fridgidaire.

"Did I pick the hymns for next week yet?"

"No sir," she said, as demurely as a piece of angel food cake at a Unitarian bake-sale.

"How about 'Whispering Hope?'"

"'Whispering Hope?' Never heard of it."

"Put it down anyway, Doll, and see if you can find a copy."

Rob Brannon, after the evidence was presented to him and his lawyer, had pled guilty to manslaughter, rather than go on trial for first-degree murder. It was his contention that the pit-bull was meant to be a practical joke—the last line of the hymn—but he was selling what no one was buying and he knew it. He was sentenced to fifteen years and would probably serve seven of those. It became clear to everyone in St. Germaine that he was also responsible (but never charged) for the other crimes that happened during those two weeks—the theft of the Immaculate Confection, Gwen's window, the dead sheep on Bev's lawn, Davis Boothe's car, the burnt cross, and the call to Father Tony—and I was offered apologies by all concerned.

Nancy had already been scheduled to speak at the North Carolina Justice Academy, her alma mater, for the upcoming seminar on Cold Case Investigations. She was also hopeful about a spot on the program at the US Law Enforcement Conference in DC, but that wasn't until late May and she hadn't heard anything yet. One of her two articles had been accepted by the *Journal of Economic Crime Management* and would be published in June. She was very excited.

St. Barnabas was contacted by the Northwestern Bank and told that, according to their attorneys, the bond was original, actionable, had never been cashed, and all the papers that Rob Brannon had submitted were in order. Rob, being guilty of criminal fraud, having changed the letter sent to the vestry by Randall Stamps, not to mention the manslaughter plea, had no further claim to the money. St. Barnabas agreed to a settlement of $16,000,000. They would be receiving four annual installments beginning in May, but the bank was kind enough to advance them the ten thousand dollars they needed to replace the furnace and buy a new marble top for the altar. Billy Hixon, the new Senior Warden, said it was the least they could do.

"That's another case you solved without getting paid," said Marilyn.

"Yeah, but we got the bad guys. Plus I've got all these pictures I can sell to the daily rags." I lit another stogy. "How about a cup of java, Marilyn? And pour one for yourself."

"The church would *really* like for you to come back," Meg said, sipping her glass of wine and reclining on my leather sofa. "The congregation misses you, the choir misses you, and Mrs. Carmody isn't exactly Virgil Fox."

"Yeah, Father George has called a couple of times. I might go back in a couple of weeks. I'm thinking about doing an arrangement of the Corelli *Christmas Concerto*."

"Opus 6, Number 8?"

"Now how did you know that?"

"I had the Pastorale played at my wedding," said Meg. "What kind of an arrangement?"

"I'm thinking that I can write choral parts to go with the strings. I'm going to spell the title with K's. *The Korelli Kristmas Kantata*. Like it?"

"Good idea. Terrible title."

Marilyn limped back in like a three-legged Chernobyl walking catfish.

"Pretty good writing, eh?" I asked her.

"I've seen better." Marilyn was getting back to her old self. "Your syntax is lousy, your metaphors are mediocre, your illustrations are juvenile, your similes are mindless, your dialogue is trite and uninteresting and your plot creaks like a broken shutter in an October wind."

"I told you you'd use it," he said, chuckling, his overcoat pulled high and tight around his chin. "Your plot creaks like a broken shutter in an October wind. Great stuff." Then he pulled down the brim of his hat, puffed once on his pipe and disappeared in a swirl of odorless smoke.

About the Author

In 1974, Mark Schweizer, a brand-new high-school graduate decided to eschew the family architectural business and becomean opera singer. Against all prevailing wisdom and despite jokes from his peers such as "What does the music major say after his first job interview?" (answer: You want fries with that?), he enrolled in the Music School at Stetson University. To his father, the rationale was obvious. No math requirement.

Everything happens for a reason, however, and he now lives and works as a musician, composer, author and publisher in Hopkinsville, Kentucky with his lovely wife, Donis.

He drives a Jeep. Not one of those sissy Jeeps either. A Wrangler.

The Liturgical Mysteries

The Alto Wore Tweed
Independent Mystery Booksellers Association
"Killer Books" selection, 2004

The Baritone Wore Chiffon

The Tenor Wore Tapshoes
IMBA 2006 Dilys Award nominee

The Soprano Wore Falsettos
Southern Independent Booksellers Alliance
2007 Book Award Nominee

The Bass Wore Scales

The Mezzo Wore Mink

Just A Note

If you've enjoyed this book—or any of the other mysteries in this series—please drop me a line. My e-mail address is mark@sjmp.com. Also, don't forget to visit the website (www.sjmpbooks.com) for lots of great stuff! You'll find recordings and "downloadable" music for many of the great works mentioned in the Liturgical Mysteries including *The Pirate Eucharist, The Weasel Cantata, The Mouldy Cheese Madrigal* and a lot more.

Cheers,
Mark